"What the [...] you're doi[...]

Dillon snapped.

"Going with you," Sydney retorted. "And don't try to pretend you don't know what I'm talking about. I heard you."

"Think again, sweetheart. I work alone."

She studied him. "You have got to be the stubbornest man I've ever met. You've got a bullet in your back that could take you out of the hunt at any time, and you still think you can go after the man who put it there—by yourself. Do you have a death wish? Is that what this is all about?"

"No, of course not!"

"Then you'd better take me with you," Sydney responded. "I can help get you to safety if your back freezes up."

She had a point. With Sydney along, it would be two against one. They would at least be able to hold their own.

But he didn't like it. He didn't like it at all.

Dear Reader,

What a lineup we have for you this month. As always, we're starting out with a bang with our Heartbreakers title, Linda Turner's *The Loner*. This tale of a burned-out ex-DEA agent and the alluring journalist who is about to uncover *all* his secrets is one you won't want to miss.

Justine Davis's *The Morning Side of Dawn* is a book readers have been asking for ever since hero Dar Cordell made his first appearance. Whether or not you've met Dar before, you'll be moved beyond words by this story of the power of love to change lives. Maura Seger's *Man Without a Memory* is a terrific amnesia book, with a hero who will enter your heart and never leave. Veteran author Marcia Evanick makes her Intimate Moments debut with *By the Light of the Moon*, a novel that proves that though things are not always what they seem, you can never doubt the truth of love. *Man of Steel* is the soul-stirring finale of Kathleen Creighton's Into the Heartland trilogy. I promise, you'll be sorry to say goodbye to the Browns. Finally, welcome new author Christa Conan, whose *All I Need* will be all *you* need to finish off another month of perfect reading.

As always, enjoy!

Yours,

Leslie Wainger
Senior Editor and Editorial Coordinator

Please address questions and book requests to:
Silhouette Reader Service
U.S.: 3010 Walden Ave., P.O. Box 1325, Buffalo, NY 14269
Canadian: P.O. Box 609, Fort Erie, Ont. L2A 5X3

Linda Turner

The Loner

Silhouette®

INTIMATE™ MOMENTS®

Published by Silhouette Books

America's Publisher of Contemporary Romance

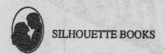 SILHOUETTE BOOKS

ISBN 0-373-07673-8

THE LONER

Copyright © 1995 by Linda Turner

Printed in U.S.A.

Books by Linda Turner

LINDA TURNER

began reading romances in high school and began writing them one night when she had nothing else to read. She's been writing ever since. Single and living in Texas, she travels every chance she gets, scouting locales for her books.

Prologue

The night was black and moonless, the air so still you could hear the insects crawling in the thick vegetation of the surrounding jungle. Sweat trickling down his neck and back, Dillon Cassidy stood as still as death at the edge of the trees, his gray eyes trained unwaveringly on the small cabin that sat in the middle of the clearing that had been hacked out of the South American wilderness. Carlos Santiago was in there, holed up like the snake that he was, just daring anyone to come in after him. Dillon was just the man to do it.

Two years, he thought coldly. He'd been tracking the bastard for two years, three months and twenty-one days. Some marriages didn't last that long. And up until tonight, he'd had nothing to show for it but missed chances and lost opportunities. And death. Wherever Carlos Santiago went, he left death in his wake. Following his trail of corpses through the U.S. and the banana republics of Central America, always a step behind him and a day late, Dillon had grown to hate the sound of the man's name.

On more than one occasion, he'd been tempted to chuck it all. He'd done his time with the agency, and no one would have blamed him for getting out while he was still in one piece. But just the thought of that coke-selling piece of trash besting him ate at his gut, and his pride had refused to let him quit. So he'd put off his retirement for two years and hung in there, promising himself that one day he would have the last laugh when it came to Santiago.

That day was finally here. He'd run the miserable excuse for a man to the ground, and there was no way in hell he was slipping through his fingers this time. A dozen DEA agents were concealed in the trees that surrounded the cabin, and between them they had enough firepower to blow the shack and Santiago off the face of the earth. If he so much as looked like he was going to run, he was a dead man.

"We know you're in there, Santiago," Dillon yelled, shattering the tense silence. "You and Angelo. And just to show you what a nice guy I am, I'm going to give you two choices. You can either throw out your weapons and come out with your hands up or we can come in after you. The choice is yours. You've got ten seconds to decide. Ten. Nine..."

His count slow and sure, his hands steady on his 9 mm semiautomatic, he motioned for his men to get ready. One way or the other, all hell was going to break loose any second now. "Four. Three..."

He never got to two. Suddenly the door of the cabin was kicked open and Santiago rushed out, yelling wildly, the automatic weapons he held in each hand spitting death as he sprayed the jungle with bullets. Swearing, Dillon fired back, the angry growl of his weapon joining those of his men. Someone cried out; Santiago grabbed at his leg and started to fall. But not before he found Dillon at the edge of the trees. Hatred burning in his black eyes, he cried, "I'll get you for this, pachuco!'' and squeezed off another round of bullets.

Dillon, in the act of ordering his men to close in, never felt the hit. Suddenly he was falling and couldn't seem to do a damn thing to help himself. His left arm hanging uselessly at his side, he hit the dirt, wincing as pain burned like a fire in his shoulder. Swearing, he rolled to his stomach, knowing he had to move damn fast or he was going to be history. Pushing himself to his knees with his right arm, he started to struggle to his feet, but he never made it. A bullet slammed into his lower back, knocking him flat on his face. This time he didn't move. He couldn't.

Chapter 1

Dillon had wanted solitude and he'd found it. The small hundred-acre spread he'd bought a couple of weeks ago was thirty miles from Lordsburg, New Mexico, and out in the middle of nowhere. The highway that ran to town was out of sight of his front porch, and his nearest neighbor, a fellow named Winslow, was ten miles down the road. He didn't bother him, and that was just the way Dillon wanted it. On most days, he had only the whisper of the wind to keep him company. It wasn't everyone's idea of retirement, but after nearly fifteen tense, dangerous years with the DEA, it damn well felt like heaven to him.

Nothing came without a price, however, not even peace of mind. The pain in his back that never seemed to go away was a constant reminder that he'd waited just a little too long to give his two weeks' notice. And then there was the silence.

He wasn't a man who was uncomfortable with his own company. In his years with the agency, he, unlike some other agents, had had no problem with the surveillance work that had required him to sit alone in a secluded spot for long hours at a time, watching some crack-peddling sleaze and waiting for him to make a mistake. But there was something about the quiet of his new surroundings that got to him. After two weeks, he still hadn't gotten used to it.

The faint, never-ending moan of the wind seemed to whisper in his ears like a temptress who wouldn't go away, haunting him until the urge to throw something just to shatter the stillness was almost more than he could bear. Muttering curses, he grabbed a hammer and a sack of nails and attacked the run-down picket fence that surrounded the white frame house that he now called home.

After more months in the hospital than he cared to remember, the physical activity felt damn good, and for a while he was able to forget that he wasn't the man he used to be. But then the muscles of his back suddenly clenched, and he froze, gasping. Pain streaked down his hips and legs like fire racing after a trail of gunpowder. His teeth clenched on an oath, he never noticed when the hammer slipped from his grasp to fall to the dirt at his feet.

"Son of a bitch!"

His hand pressed to his spine, he glared at the tool and knew there was no way in hell he was going to be able to lean down and pick it up—at least not anytime soon. Drawing in a bracing breath, he slowly, carefully, straightened until he was standing completely erect. But the task cost him. His blood was roaring in his ears, sweat popped out on his brow in spite of the coldness of the January day, and just standing there hurt like hell.

Swearing, he knew he had no one to blame but himself. The doctors had warned him not to do anything but relax and give himself a chance to heal, but the inactivity was killing him. One way or the other, he'd been working since he was sixteen. Sitting around on his duff watching the grass grow was driving him right up the wall. He needed something, anything, to do.

The sudden sound of a vehicle racing up the long gravel drive from the highway drew his attention and he looked up, squinting into the bright New Mexican sun as a patrol car from the Hidalgo County Sheriff's department dragged a trail of dust behind it as it approached. A corner of his mouth kicked up into a slow smile. He didn't have to see the driver behind the glare of the sun on the windshield to know that it was Riley Whitaker. An old friend who had worked with him at the DEA and was now the local sheriff, Riley had helped him find this place after he finally got out of the hospital and decided to move West. Every other day or so, he dropped by with the excuse that he was in the area on patrol, but Dillon wasn't fooled. Riley was worried about him.

The minute Riley stepped from his patrol car, his sharp gaze took in the hammer in the dirt and Dillon's stiff posture. "I'm not your mama or your doctor," he drawled, "but both of them would be all over you if they could see you right now. What the hell do you think you're doing?"

"Going stir-crazy sitting around listening to the wind blow," Dillon retorted. "I'm a city boy. Maybe I shouldn't have left Miami after all."

It was a thought that had crossed his mind more than once since his forced early retirement, even though there'd never been any chance of him staying in Florida after Santiago was captured the night he was shot. While he was on the operating table fighting for his life, Santiago was furiously promising revenge from jail, and no one in the DEA had doubted his ability to arrange Dillon's untimely demise. The drug lord had a long reach and powerful friends, even from behind bars, and he never made a promise he couldn't keep. Knowing Dillon would never be safe from Santiago's venom, the powers that be did the only thing they could to ensure his safety. They leaked the news that he had died on the table.

For all practical purposes, Dillon felt as if he had. Even if the decision hadn't been made for him, his days as an agent were over. The bullet that had struck him in the back had lodged near his spine and was still there. Afraid removing it would paralyze him, the doctors had left it where it was, refusing to chance touching it unless they absolutely had to.

Their intentions had been good, but when he'd regained consciousness and learned what they'd done, Dillon would have raged at them if he'd had the strength. The bullet was like a time bomb in his back that could, without warning, destroy him at any second. Night and day, he lived with the knowledge that if it shifted so much as a millimeter, he would be a paraplegic for life.

How Santiago would have laughed if he'd known. As far as revenge went, it was much better than shooting someone between the eyes.

"What's Miami got that we don't?" Riley demanded, his indignant tone ruined by a grin. "Name one thing."

"You gotta be kidding," Dillon replied, chuckling. "How about water and sandy beaches, just to name a few?"

"Hey, we've got that. Our water's just scarcer than hen's teeth and comes out of a well. And if you want sand, all you've got to do is look around."

The pain in his back forgotten, Dillon laughed. "Don't remind me. It comes right through the screens when the wind blows." Turning toward the house, he started up the steps to the porch. "Come on inside. I've got some coffee on."

Following him up onto the porch, Riley hesitated. "Actually, this isn't a social call. I've got some work for you to do if you're interested."

Arching a brow, Dillon couldn't have been more surprised if Riley had suggested he take up gymnastics. "Work? Are you kidding? What kind of work can I do? I couldn't even lean down and pick up the damn hammer a few seconds ago when I dropped it."

"Then I guess it's lucky for you that I don't want you to pick up any hammers." Reaching into the pocket of his shirt, he pulled out two wallet-size snapshots and handed them to him.

The pictures were of two boys, both teenagers with peach fuzz still on their cheeks. One was dark, the other fair, both too young to be anything but innocents. Studying them, Dillon committed their faces to memory, unable to hide the interest in his eyes when he glanced back up at Riley. "Who are they?"

"Bryan Fitzgerald and Juan Martinez. Two runaways. I want you to find them."

Even without knowing the circumstances, Dillon wanted to jump at the offer so badly he could taste it. But he was supposed to be taking it easy, dammit. "I'm not a P.I.," he began reluctantly.

"No," Riley agreed. "But you're the best damn tracker the agency ever had and you need to get up off your butt and do something before you start talking to yourself like crazy Mike Mitchell down on Eighth Street in Miami. You can do this, Dillon."

Dillon didn't doubt that he had the ability to do it, but he didn't want to start something he might not have the physical stamina to finish. His back stiff, he eased down into one of the two rocking chairs on the wide porch and stared down at the pictures again even though he could have already picked both boys out of a lineup without a second glance. "How long have they been missing?"

"It'll be a week Thursday."

"They both disappeared the same day?"

Riley nodded. That same fact had bothered him more than any other. "Their parents claim the boys don't even know each other, but I think it's damn odd that they both turn up missing on the same day. Granted, teenagers get ticked off all the time over stupid things, and occasionally, one of them will take off. But they usually turn up in a day or two. These boys have disappeared off the face of the earth."

"You think they're dead?"

His rugged face somber, he shrugged. "I don't know what to think. Every lead runs right into a brick wall, and the county doesn't have the resources for an extensive search when there's no evidence of foul play. That's where you come in. I talked to the parents about you taking over the investigation and they don't have a problem with it if you're agreeable. Neither family has a lot of money, but they're willing to pay what they can—"

Dillon dismissed that with an impatient wave of his hand. His government retirement was damn good—he didn't need the money of hardworking people who were no doubt worried sick about their sons. Sons who, regardless of how mature they were, had no business being out on their own on the streets. He knew from long years of experience just what kind of scum was out there, waiting to take advantage of innocents, and just the thought of the trouble they could find themselves in turned his stomach.

"My specialty is pushers and drug lords," he reminded Riley. "I can't make any promises I'll find them."

"It's been nearly a week, and no one's heard a word from either boy. At this point, the parents have just about given up hope of ever seeing them alive, so anything you can do will be better than nothing. Can I tell them you'll take the case?''

If he had to do much legwork, Dillon knew he was going to pay a heavy price for disobeying his doctor's orders, but what the hell did he have to lose, anyway? If the damn bullet in his back was going to shift, he'd just as soon it happened while he was doing something more constructive than sitting on his front porch cursing the skinny piece of trash who had condemned him to a life of purgatory. A muscle jumping in his jaw, he nodded. ''I'll see what I can do.''

She wasn't a woman who believed in coincidence. Happenstance just didn't exist—not in her world. A reporter for the *Hidalgo County Gazette,* Sydney O'Keefe firmly believed that everything happened for a reason. And when two boys up and disappeared from her town on the same night, there had to be a connection somewhere. She just hadn't found out what it was. But she would. She always did.

Once, long ago in another life, her editor at the *Chicago Daily News* had accused her of being as unrelenting as a bloodhound when she picked up the scent of a story—God help anyone who got in her way. He'd been irritated with her at the time for disregarding her own personal safety when tracking down the facts of a murder, but far from being insulted, she'd laughed and taken his comment as the highest compliment. In the years since then, a lot had changed, but not that. When her stomach tightened in that funny way she had come to recognize as expectation, she knew she was on the right trail.

Which was why she was headed for the abandoned rock quarry west of town a half an hour before the sun was due to set. For the past five days, she'd tried to talk to the missing boys' parents, teachers and anyone else she could find who knew them, but without much success. The kids at school had been remarkably closemouthed, and the only thing she'd been able to discover was that Juan Martinez was pretty much a loner and Bryan Fitzgerald liked to ride dirt bikes at the old quarry in the evenings. The sheriff had already checked the property and found nothing, but Sydney intended to check the place out herself. If Bryan went there often, some of the other bikers must have known him and might be persuaded to talk to her about him. She didn't doubt that Riley Whitaker had already tried questioning the same kids, but some people, especially teenagers, had a problem talking to authority figures. If she could just get them to open up...

The quarry hadn't been in operation in years and was nothing but an eyesore. The entrance had long ago been barred, and No Trespassing signs were posted everywhere, warning off intruders. Studying the faded, once-bold letters, Sydney couldn't imagine any kid worth his salt seeing the signs as anything but a joke. And a challenge. Grinning, she parked near the entrance and grabbed her purse and tape recorder.

The sun hung low in the cloudy sky, casting weak shadows that were slowly crawling across the floor of the quarry. It was a lonely spot, and cold. There was nothing to block the wind, and it felt like ice as it played with the tendrils of strawberry blond hair that had escaped the barrette at the back of her neck. Shivering, she buttoned her green corduroy jacket at her throat and approached the rusty barbed-wire fence that surrounded the property.

Her eyes on her feet and the rocky ground, she didn't see the man who approached from the opposite direction until he suddenly stepped directly in front of her and growled, "This is private property, lady. You're trespassing."

Startled, Sydney jerked to a stop, her eyes widening at the sight of the scowling stranger before her. After living in Lordsburg for the past four years, she'd thought she knew just about everyone by sight, but if she'd ever laid eyes on this man before, there was no way on earth she would have forgotten him. He blocked her path as if it were his God-given right, the fierce frown that darkened his square-cut, good-looking face just daring her to object. A tall man who towered over her own five-foot-four frame by a dozen inches or more, he was lean and gaunt and, judging from the hard glint in his gray eyes, someone she'd be wise not to tangle with.

Not easily intimidated by anyone, Sydney felt her heart thunder in her breast and resented it to no end. In her previous job, she'd tracked down stories on some of Chicago's roughest streets and interviewed more pushers, hookers and general pond scum than she cared to remember. She had a thick hide and didn't jump at shadows...or so much as blink at tall, angry men who tried to come between her and a story, she reminded herself sternly.

Drawing herself up stiffly, she returned his narrow-eyed glare with one of her own. All business, she flashed her press card at him and said coolly, "I'm Sydney O'Keefe, with the *Hidalgo County Gazette.* Are you the owner of this property?"

"No."

"The security guard?"

"No."

"Then who *are* you? And who do you think you are trying to keep me off this property? From where I'm standing, you're just as much a trespasser as I am."

Biting back a sharp retort, Dillon stared down at her in growing irritation. The lady was going to be difficult—he could see that already. Short and small boned, with delicate, old-fashioned features that could have belonged on a cameo, she was a pretty little thing. And, judging from the gleam in those large, midnight blue eyes of hers, stubborn as a bulldog with a bone between its teeth. Dammit, why hadn't Riley warned him to be on the lookout for a pushy reporter? He'd just found out this afternoon about the quarry and Bryan Fitzgerald's fascination with the place, and there was no way in hell he was letting Lois Lane here interfere with his investigation.

"Look, my name is Dillon Cassidy, not that it's any of your business. And I've got every right to keep you off this property." Nodding to the huge, rocky pit that yawned before them just beyond the barricaded entrance, he pointed out the bikers who flew over the uneven terrain like dancers performing a fast-paced ballet. "Those boys down there might know something about Bryan Fitzgerald's disappearance, and I'm not going to stand by and watch you scare them off."

It was a less-than-tactful thing to say but he was in no mood for pleasantries. It was colder than hell, his back was hurting and he just wanted to get this over with and get out of the wind. But the lady had her hackles up and wasn't going anywhere fast. Her spine as straight as a metal fence post, she glared at him, her blue eyes flashing fire. "I'm not scaring anyone off—"

"You're damn right you're not, because you're not going down there. The sheriff asked me to look into the case for the two families, so I suggest you turn your little fanny around and go back to where you came from. You won't be asking any questions around here tonight."

She gasped as if he'd struck her, hot color blooming in her cheeks. She looked as if she wanted to slug him, and he couldn't say he blamed her. He was being a jerk, but there was too much at stake for him to play nicey-nicey with a woman who made a living by sticking her cute little nose into other people's heartache. Adding insult to injury, he shooed her away like a particularly bothersome mosquito. "Go on," he growled. "Get."

A smart woman would have taken the hint and got the hell out of there, and for a second he thought she was going to do just that. Stepping back, she stared up at him consideringly and finally said huffily, "Fine. I'll go." But instead of leaving, she mockingly added, "When I'm good and ready."

She darted around him, lightning quick, catching him off guard. Swearing, Dillon instinctively grabbed for her. But just as his fingers wrapped around her slender wrist, the muscles of his back clenched tight, the sudden, searing pain sucking the breath from his lungs. His jaw rigid, a silent groan rising in his throat, he went perfectly still.

His eyes squeezed shut, all his concentration focused on just dragging slow, even breaths into his lungs, he was no more aware of his excruciatingly tight grip on the feminine wrist he still held than he was of the frowning blue eyes that were suddenly searching the harsh lines of his face in puzzlement. A few minutes more and the pain would pass, he told himself. He just had to be patient....

"Are you all right?"

The quiet question penetrated the cloying fog of agony that shrouded his senses, drawing him back to his surroundings and the woman who stood unmoving at his side. Still, it was a long moment before the pain eased enough for him to open his eyes and face her. Only then did he realize he was clutching her wrist in a fierce hold that had to be cutting off the blood supply to her fingers. Swearing softly, he released her as quickly as he'd grabbed her. "I'm sorry. That had to hurt. Are you okay?"

"I don't break that easily," she replied, not sparing a glance for the red marks on her wrist that would be bruises tomorrow. "You're the one who seems to have thrown your back out. Do you need some help getting to your car?"

His health obviously off-limits as a topic of discussion, he stiffened. "No, I—" Suddenly glancing past her shoulder to the quarry beyond, he swore. "Dammit to hell! Now look what you've done!"

Surprised, Sydney whirled, just in time to see the boys on the dirt bikes race through a downed section of the barbed-wire fence and head for town like the devil himself was after them. "Oh, no!" His words suddenly registering, she spun back to face him. "What do you mean, look what *I've* done?" she demanded indignantly. "*You* were the one who grabbed me and made a ruckus."

"Only because I was afraid you were going to do just what you did and scare them off." Irritation deepening the frown furrowing his brow, he stared after the rapidly disappearing boys and cursed in disgust. "There's no use going after them now. They're spooked. Damn!"

As far as Sydney was concerned, he had no one to blame but himself, but she had no intention of standing there and arguing with him. She'd gotten a pretty good look at two of the boys' faces and would try tracking them down tomorrow, but for now she had other work to do. "I can't say it's been a pleasure, Mr. Cassidy. Now, if you'll excuse me . . ."

"Hey, where are you going? You can't go in there!"

Already bending down to carefully ease through the barbed wire of the fence, Sydney emerged on the other side to face him, a delicately arched brow lifted in amusement. "I beg your pardon, but apparently I can. Relax, Mr. Cassidy. I'm a big girl. I know what I'm doing."

He snorted at that, not impressed. "What you're going to do is break your pretty little neck if you're not careful. In case you haven't noticed, the sun's going down. A rock quarry is no place to play in the dark.''

For an answer, she fished her car keys out of her jacket and held up the small flashlight attached to the key ring. It was hardly bigger than a penlight, but it had a surprisingly strong light that had helped her find her way out of a dark spot on more than one occasion in the past. "Then isn't it lucky I came prepared?" she said with a cocky grin that was guaranteed to set his teeth on edge. "A good reporter always does, and just for the record, I'm very good at what I do, Mr. Cassidy—"

"Dillon," he said between his teeth.

Her eyes starting to twinkle, she continued sweetly, "As I was saying, *Dillon*, I'm very good at what I do. When I smell a story, nothing gets in my way, especially a few little rocks in the dark. So if you don't mind—even if you do— Bryan Fitzgerald supposedly spent a lot of time riding his bike here and I'm going to look around. Maybe I'll be able to find something that will tell me what happened to him.''

"The sheriff's already been over every inch of this place with a magnifying glass. If there was something to find, he'd have found it. Get out of there before you hurt yourself.''

Starting toward the quarry that had been carved out of the side of a hill, Sydney waved gaily over her shoulder. "'Bye, Dillon. See you around.''

Staring after her, the circle of light cast by her flashlight bobbing over the rough terrain as she entered the quarry itself, Dillon told himself to let her go. He had it straight from the lady's mouth that she was one tough cookie who could take care of herself, so what the devil was he hanging around for? It was cold, his back was killing him and he was in no shape to play superhero to a lady reporter. If she wanted to scrounge around in the dark and chance breaking her leg on rocks the size of Pittsburgh, that was her business.

The self-directed lecture duly noted, he should have headed for his Suburban and got the hell out of there. Instead, he found himself heading for the break in the fence that the bikers had used to get in and out of the quarry, cursing himself for a fool all the way. This was all his mother's fault, he decided, swallowing a groan as his right foot landed half on a rock and pain shot up and down his back. If she hadn't raised him to be so damn solicitous of the weaker sex, he wouldn't be out here now inflicting pain on himself with these damn rocks just to watch over a woman who would probably spit in the eye of the devil himself if he dared to get between her and a stupid story.

Making his way to where she stood at the heart of the quarry, her flashlight a narrow stream of light that barely made a dent in the vast darkness that was quickly surrounding them, he surveyed her with intense dislike. "If you must do this, don't you think it would be better to come back in the daytime when you can see better? This is just a waste of time."

"Oh, I'll be back tomorrow," she assured him, her eyes and the beam of her flashlight following the bumpy, rock-strewn path the bikers had been racing over only moments before. "But right now I want to see what it looked like when Bryan Fitzgerald was here, what fascinated him about this place at night." Directing the light to a particularly rough track that left the others and disappeared into the gathering shadows, she frowned. "I wonder where that goes."

The words were hardly out of her mouth before she was following the narrow path, heading up a steep incline that led to the top of the weathered limestone cliff that had been carved out of the hill. Just like a nosy cat looking for trouble, Dillon thought irritably. One slip in the dark and she could come tumbling all the way to the bottom of the quarry. "Dammit, just wait a second, will you? You don't know how safe that cliff is. What if it starts to crumble? You could break your neck."

She didn't listen, of course, and kept right on going, which irritated him to no end. Wondering what any man saw in a stubborn, headstrong woman, he started after her, determined to shake some sense into her the second he caught up with her. But the climb was sharp and one he had no business making. Every step cost him. By the time he reached the top, he was sweating in spite of the cold bitch of a wind that swirled around him.

Furious with his own weakness, he had to take a second to drag in a bracing breath before he could continue, and even then he might not have caught her if she hadn't stopped so abruptly that he almost tripped over her. "What the hell—"

"Oh, God!"

Her gasp was ripped away by the wind that raced unchecked over the cliff path, but not before Dillon heard the horror that nearly strangled her faint words. "What?" he demanded. "What is it?"

Her eyes on the body lying at her feet in a pool of light from the suddenly less-than-steady beam of her flashlight, Sydney stared down at the reddish curls and pale, freckled face of one of the two boys she'd spent the past few days looking for. "Bryan Fitzgerald," she said quietly. "He's dead."

Dillon swore and stepped around her, blocking her view of the boy as he took the flashlight from her, then handed her the cellular phone he pulled from the inside pocket of his jacket. "Go back down the path and call Riley Whitaker. I'll join you in just a minute."

Surprised and touched by his attempt to shield her from the horror of the situation, Sydney could have told him that she'd seen death before, in more ways than she cared to remember. She hadn't been much more than a kid herself when she'd covered her first homicide in Chicago and suddenly found herself staring down at the bloody remains of a woman who had been slashed to death by her live-in boyfriend. She'd promptly been sick as a dog, much to the amusement of her fellow reporters, and hadn't been able to close her eyes for a week without seeing that poor woman's face.

Since then, there'd been dozens of murders to investigate, some more gruesome than others, and over the years, she'd learned to handle each death as she came to it. She'd never thrown up again, but she hoped she never got so jaded that she accepted cold-blooded killing without a blink of an eye. Especially when the victim was a kid like Bryan Fitzgerald, who should have been home laboring over his homework instead of lying cold and dead out in the middle of nowhere.

Questions of how and why and when pulling at her, she flipped open Dillon's cellular phone and quickly called the sheriff.

Thirty minutes later, Sydney and Dillon stood at the bottom of the quarry and watched as Riley Whitaker and his men investigated every inch of the cliff path and the surrounding terrain with high-powered flashlights. There hadn't been a murder in the county in all the years that Riley had been sheriff, and he and his deputies were grim-faced as they examined the area and tried to make sense of it. But there was no sign of foul play, and a healthy sixteen-year-old boy just didn't drop dead without a reason.

An ambulance had arrived a few minutes earlier to take Bryan Fitzgerald's body away, but it was still another fifteen minutes before Riley reluctantly admitted they weren't going to find anything in the dark. Making his way down the cliff path, he crossed to where Dillon and Sydney waited, his expression grave.

"We didn't find anything," he said flatly, "but I didn't expect to. The boy wasn't killed here."

Her tape recorder whirling, Sydney frowned. "How do you know? I thought there was no sign of foul play."

"I'm no coroner, but from the condition of the body, the boy was probably killed soon after he disappeared a week ago. I searched this place myself four days ago, and it was clean."

"Which means somebody dumped the body here some-time since then so it would be found," Dillon concluded, his gray eyes lifted to the rough cliff wall as if it held the an-swers to all their questions. "I don't like the sound of that. It's almost as if whoever did this is taunting you, just dar-ing you to catch them."

Already picturing the headlines and the panic this was going to cause, Sydney gave Riley a sharp look that warned him she wouldn't be put off. "*Do* you have any suspects? Or have any idea what Bryan Fitzgerald died of?"

"No," he said. "We'll have to wait for the coroner's re-port for cause of death. As for suspects, you know I can't tell you anything about an ongoing murder investigation, Syd. As soon as I'm ready to make a statement, though, you'll be the first to know. Okay?"

It wasn't okay—she just wanted his thoughts on the mat-ter—but after dealing with Riley Whitaker for the past four years, she knew he rarely allowed himself to be pushed into saying something he shouldn't. Needling him tonight, when he was just coming to grips with the fact that he had a mur-der somewhere in his county, wouldn't get her anywhere.

Gracefully accepting defeat, she turned off her tape re-corder. "Then there's no point in me hanging around here.

I've got to get back to the paper and get this written up for the morning edition. You are going to contact the Fitzgeralds tonight, aren't you?''

He nodded, his mouth compressing into a thin white line just at the thought of the unpleasant task. "As soon as I leave here." Glancing around for one of his deputies, he called out, "Joe, walk Sydney to her car, will you?"

Surprised, she objected. "That's not necessary."

"Whoever killed that boy is still walking around free," Dillon reminded her before Riley could say anything. "It doesn't pay to be careless."

Only a fool would have argued with that, and Sydney O'Keefe was apparently no fool. Without another word, she let Joe Sanchez escort her to her car, which was still parked near the quarry entrance.

As they disappeared into the dark, Dillon knew he hadn't seen the last of the lady. "She's going to be a problem," he told Riley irritably. "Why didn't you warn me about her?"

Riley chuckled. "Because Sydney's one of those women that can't quite be described with words. I take it she made an impression."

"Oh, yeah." Annoyance flickering in his eyes, he said, "She told me she was very good at what she did and nothing got in her way when she smelled a story. Then she proceeded to do what she damn well pleased."

Not surprised, Riley made no attempt to hold back a grin. "That's Sydney, all right. If she'd gone into law enforcement instead of journalism, she would have given J. Edgar Hoover himself a run for his money. So just get prepared. She'll be snapping at your heels every second you're looking for Juan Martinez."

"So you still want me to continue the investigation?"

His smile fading, Riley nodded. "With one boy dead, we've got to conclude that the other one is in serious trouble. And you know yourself that the longer it takes to find him, the less chance he has of being found alive. I can use all the help I can get.''

''The parents may change their mind about me looking for their son after this. This probably isn't just a runaway anymore and they might feel better if one of your deputies took up the search. I'm not in law enforcement anymore—''

''I can deputize you if necessary, but I don't think it is. I know the Martinezes and I know they're going to want the best man looking for their son. That's you.''

Dillon had no use for false modesty—he knew his capabilities. And though he didn't doubt that Riley's men were good, he knew he could find that boy. He only hoped it was in time. ''I'll do what I can.''

Chapter 2

Her eyes on the copy on her computer screen, Sydney studiously tried to ignore the man comfortably sprawled at the desk directly across from hers, but it wasn't easy. With his size-thirteen feet propped on the corner of his paper-strewn desk, Blake Nickels was not a man who liked to be ignored. His copy long since written and approved, he had an hour to kill before he met his girlfriend, Trina, for a late supper, and Sydney knew he was just itching to spend that time teasing her. Giving her grief was his favorite pastime, and if she so much as looked at him, he'd be off and running.

A minute passed, then another. Fighting a grin, Sydney could practically feel his impatience. He wouldn't, she knew from experience, be able to stand the silence much longer. Any second now...

"I can't believe it," he drawled casually, smirking. "The great Sydney O'Keefe missed a deadline. Has anyone called the AP? This is news."

Her fingers frantically flying over the keyboard, Sydney grinned but couldn't take time to spare him a glance. She and Blake had sat across from each other for the past four years, trading taunts and insults on the way to developing a relationship that was more like that of brother and sister than co-workers. Good friends, they could say practically anything to each other—and frequently did.

"You're going to be history if you don't button those thin lips of yours, Nickels," she warned. "Can't you see you're in the presence of genius? So stuff it. I'm trying to concentrate. This one could get me a Pulitzer."

His amused snort of disdain told her what he thought of that. "Pardon me if I don't ask for your autograph, but in case you haven't noticed, Harry's already got the front page set and the press warmed up. Face it, Red. Nobody's going to see your masterpiece until the day after tomorrow, and by then it'll be old news."

Usually at the very mention of his irritating nickname for her, she rose to the bait like a trout to a fly, but not tonight. Finishing up, she saved the copy, then pushed back from her desk, the look she shot him playfully pitying. "You're just jealous because nobody ever raves over the sports page. Trust me, sweetie, Harry's going to stop the presses for this one."

His green eyes mocking, Blake just grinned. "In your dreams, honey child. You've been sniffing the ink fumes again, haven't you?"

Laughing softly, Sydney ignored him and headed for Harry's office, knowing her boss would be going over the layout right up until the second the presses started. Knocking lightly on the jamb of the door that was never shut, she quickly stepped into the small, unpretentious office that had been Harry's domain for the last twenty years. Seated at his desk and almost hidden behind his computer monitor, his glasses slipping down his nose and his bald head shining in the glare of the overhead light, he looked like a little old gnome hard at work.

"Harry, the Fitzgerald boy was found tonight—"

"I know." Glancing up, his sharp brown eyes met hers over the top of his glasses. "When I saw you rush in, I knew you wouldn't be here this time of night unless you had a headline. I've already read your copy and given it the go. Has Riley notified the boy's parents?"

"I believe he's doing that now."

"Then I don't have to rearrange the front page a third time. Good work."

"Thanks," Sydney said, grinning.

Harry wasn't one to gush praise, which was just fine with her. She'd won her share of accolades and awards in Chicago and had learned, to her regret, that such things weren't worth the paper they were written on when a jealous coworker decided to shred your reputation.

After four years, the sting of betrayal had faded and she was able to look back at the past with some degree of objectivity. She no longer had the urge to scream when she thought of Beth Jenkins, but she would never forget her deceit or the smug look of satisfaction in her eyes when she'd accused her of stealing her story. To this day, Sydney still didn't know how she could have been so blind where Beth was concerned. She'd trusted her...and paid the price. And the irony of the whole situation was that, unlike Beth, Sydney had never needed awards to confirm that she was a good reporter. She'd already known it.

Disillusioned, forced to resign, she'd cleaned out her savings and left Chicago without a backward glance, everything she owned piled in the U-Haul trailer hitched to the back of her Jeep. She hadn't known where she was going, just that she never again wanted anything to do with the cutthroat competition of a big-city paper. Then she'd found herself in New Mexico and passing through Lordsburg. To this day, she didn't know what had possessed her to check out the local paper, but the second she'd stepped inside the small storefront operation, she'd felt like she was home.

At first glance, it hadn't looked as though it had a lot going for it. The printing presses were old and cantankerous, the desks scarred, the computers older models and the cheapest money could buy. But Harry and his wife, Marge, hadn't been out to set the world on fire with their style of journalism; they just wanted to make a decent living and put out a paper they could be proud of. As straightforward and unpretentious as homemade bread, they'd accepted her version of what happened in Chicago as the gospel, warned her they couldn't pay her what she was worth and that they could up and retire and move to Vegas, where all the action was, whenever the mood struck them. Deciding to chance it, she'd snapped up their offer and had never regretted it.

They still jokingly talked about Vegas, but a lot of other things had changed in the past four years. She'd welcomed the peace and slower pace of small-town life, but she was too good at what she did to be content with writing about the garden club and VA dances for long. Gradually, the paper evolved from a six-page weekly that depended on the wire services for any real hard news to a daily that had been judged one of the best in the state. And for that, Sydney knew she had Harry and Marge to thank. They gave her the freedom to write whatever stories she could dig up, and she loved it.

Leaving Harry to the last-minute fine-tuning of the copy before he started the presses, she stepped back into the city room to find Blake waiting expectantly. Arching a brow at her, his smile quirky, he said, "Well? He shot you down, didn't he? I tried to tell you—"

"I believe his exact words were *'good work,'*" she cut in smoothly, grinning. "And you know what that means—two-inch headlines and a byline. Harry always did know a good story when he saw one." Chuckling, she stopped at her desk only long enough to pick up her purse and tape recorder, then she was breezing out the door with a teasing little wave that she knew he positively despised. "Nighty-night. I want to check in with the sheriff before I head home. Tell Trina hi for me." Daring to wink at him, she hurried out just seconds before the wadded-up piece of copy he threw at her fell harmlessly to the floor.

She was still grinning when she stepped outside, but the coldness of the night quickly reminded her of the quarry... Dillon Cassidy...and the moment she'd stumbled over poor Bryan Fitzgerald's body. Sobering, suddenly chilled, she buried her hands in the pockets of her jacket and cast a surreptitious glance up and down the street. There wasn't a soul in sight in either direction, which wasn't surprising. Downtown closed up and pulled in the sidewalks with the setting of the sun.

Normally, the emptiness of the streets wouldn't have bothered her. Whenever she worked late, she usually walked around the corner to the sheriff's office without giving it a thought. Lordsburg wasn't crime-free, but most of its troublemakers were limited to drunken cowboys and kids bent on mischief. She wouldn't have classified any of them as vicious, but a boy was dead and whoever had dumped his body at the quarry was in all likelihood responsible. As much as she hated to admit it, Dillon Cassidy was right. It didn't pay to be too careless. So instead of rushing over to the sheriff's office on foot, she drove.

She expected to find Riley filling out paperwork, but he was in the break room instead, downing coffee like shots of whiskey and evidently finding no pleasure in it. His mouth

was bracketed in deep lines, his eyes haunted. Glancing up
at her entrance, he rose and reached for another mug.
Pouring her a shot of the thick strong coffee without asking if she wanted any, he then plunked the mug down on the
table in the middle of the room, pulled out a chair for her
and took a seat across from it.

"Sit down, Syd," he said tersely. "I imagine you're here
to ask how the Fitzgeralds took the news."

Under normal circumstances, she would have taken im-
mediate exception to his harsh tone, but the fight he was
spoiling for was with a killer, not her. Dropping into the
wooden chair opposite him, she reached for her coffee. "I
don't have to ask," she said quietly as she wrapped her fingers around the mug. "I can see by your face that it was
hell."

Just that quickly, all the hostility went out of him. Sighing tiredly, he slumped in his chair. "You got that right. You
should have seen them, Syd. They just sat there and looked
at me like they didn't understand a word I said. Then they
thanked me for coming out and telling them the news myself! It was awful. I kept waiting for them to cry or scream
or even call me a damn liar—I know that's what Becca and
I would do if someone came to us with that kind of news
about Chloe or Grant."

Since it was a well-known fact that he absolutely adored
his six-month-old son and his adopted daughter, Sydney
didn't even want to imagine how he and his wife, Becca,
would react to that kind of tragedy. "I'm sure they were in
shock. They probably fell apart after you left."

"I hope so. No one should keep that kind of pain locked
up inside them. And I know they cared about him. They
were very upset when I told them the county's resources
were limited and I couldn't keep looking for a runaway that

didn't want to be found. That's why I brought Dillon in on the case.''

At the mention of the intimidating stranger who had tried to interfere with her investigation of the story, her ears picked up, an interest she assured herself was strictly professional sparking in her eyes. "I'm glad you brought him up. It's not like you to bring in an outsider on a case.''

Pushing his coffee away with a grimace of distaste, Riley shrugged. "Like I said, the funds just weren't available to track down what appeared to be two runaways, but I couldn't just drop the investigation and tell the worried parents tough luck. So I approached Dillon about the case, and he agreed to continue a private investigation.''

"But why? Who *is* Dillon Cassidy? *What* is he? What's his story? And don't tell me he doesn't have one," she added quickly. "Everyone does, and all you have to do is look at that man's face to see that he's been to hell and back. How do you know him?''

"We're old friends.''

"From the DEA.''

It wasn't a question, just a clever statement of fact that would have given her one of the answers she wanted if he'd made the mistake of letting it pass. He didn't. Giving her a chiding look, he grinned. "Nice try, Syd. But if you want any information on Dillon, you're going to have to ask him yourself. He'll tell you what he wants you to know.''

"If he's got nothing to hide, why should he care what you tell me about him?" she asked shrewdly.

His grin broadening, he leaned back in his chair and surveyed her with laughing eyes. "I don't know. You'll have to ask him.''

If she hadn't been a woman who prided herself on her professionalism, she would have hit him then and enjoyed every second of it. They'd worked closely together over the past four years—he *knew* how it irritated her when he clammed up. Letting her breath out in a huff, she said, "Look, I'm not going to sell the man's story to the *National Enquirer*. I'm just curious. You must trust him an awful lot if you thought he could find Bryan Fitzgerald and Juan Martinez when no one else could."

For a moment, she thought he wasn't going to comment, but then something flickered in his eyes. "Let's put it this way," he growled. "Dillon Cassidy could track a spider across the desert. If one of my kids had just up and disappeared off the face of the earth without a trace, he's the man I'd call. And that's all I'm going to say."

Frustrated, she recognized the determination in those steady eyes of his and knew when she'd hit a brick wall. Not sure why it was so important to her to discover Dillon Cassidy's secrets, she rose to her feet and walked over to the sink to dump out the coffee she'd barely touched. "Then maybe I will talk to him myself. Where's he live?"

"Out Highway 21, second drive on the right after the tracks. He won't be happy to see you."

Glancing back over her shoulder, she arched a brow at him. "Then why did you give me his address?"

He laughed shortly, the hard angles of his face folding into a rueful grin. "Damned if I know. Maybe because he spends too much time alone out there, and it's time someone shook him up a little."

"And you think I can do that?"

"Hell, yes! Don't you?"

Not the least insulted, she chuckled, her eyes dancing impishly. "Of course. I like to think it's one of my better talents, but it's not always appreciated. Not that I let that stop me."

"Tell me something I don't know, Syd."

Grinning, she headed for the door. "See you around, Riley."

The minute she reached the end of the long rocky drive that came to an abrupt end at Dillon Cassidy's house, Sydney knew she shouldn't have come. Not tonight. It was late, and the small frame house looked as uninviting as the cold night. A security light by the detached garage provided a wide pool of weak yellow light, illuminating a weathered picket fence that leaned like a drunken sailor and a yard that was bare of trees and plants and anything that even came close to resembling grass. It was stark, lonely, depressing.

Wondering what a friend of Riley Whitaker's was doing hiding away in such a desolate spot, Sydney approached the deep shadows of the porch, refusing to be intimidated by the dark. This wasn't the first time she'd gone alone into the night after a story; it wouldn't be the last. And it wasn't as if she had anything to fear from Dillon Cassidy. He might have a tendency to be overbearing, but she wasn't going to spend the rest of her life with the man, just interview him. Squaring her shoulders, she stepped up to the door and knocked firmly.

After her encounter with him at the quarry, she hadn't expected him to welcome her with open arms, which was a good thing. Because the minute he flipped on the porch light and pulled open the front door, the lines of his hard-edged face tightened at the sight of her. Suspicion glinting in his gray eyes, he stood in the doorway in jeans and a T-shirt and made no move to invite her inside. "What are you doing here? How did you find out where I lived?"

Reminding herself that she'd known this wasn't going to be easy, she let his hostility roll right off her and dredged up a rueful smile. "We got off to a bad start at the quarry and

I wanted to apologize. I talked to the sheriff and he gave me your address. Could I come in for a minute?"

Common courtesy demanded that he step aside and invite her inside, but that sixth sense that had never failed him was screaming in his ear that furthering his acquaintance with her could be nothing but a mistake. Rudely standing his ground, he said coolly, "Apology accepted. Next time, call and save yourself the trip out here. Now, if you'll excuse me—"

"Oh, but I thought we could talk, get to know each other better," she said hurriedly, before he could shut the door.

"Why?"

"Because..." Floundering, she shrugged. "Because finding that boy tonight wasn't a pretty sight, and I thought you might want to talk about it."

It sounded good, but Dillon wasn't buying it. "Why don't you just cut to the chase, Ms. O'Keefe? It's late and it's been a bitch of a day. We both know you didn't come out here to apologize, so quit beating around the bush and just tell me what you want. Okay?"

To her credit, she didn't so much as blink at his bluntness. Drawing herself up to her full five foot four inches, she met his gaze unblinkingly. "You'd make a good human-interest story as a follow-up to the death of the Fitzgerald boy. Any man that Riley Whitaker would trust to handle one of his cases has to be pretty special, and my readers would like to know more about you. I know you and Riley worked together in the DEA—"

"Did he tell you that?"

He gave her a piercing look, one that had intimidated more than a few street-tough smugglers, and dared her to lie to him. And for a moment there, Dillon actually thought the little snoop was going to try. There was a gleam in her eyes that he didn't trust, the subtle, almost unconscious lift of her chin a blatant warning that she was a woman who had no problem with a dare.

Transfixed, Dillon stared down at her, admiration catching him by surprise, amusement threatening to drag a reluctant smile across his face. Damn if she didn't have spunk! He liked sass and guts in a woman... or at least he had before he'd ended up with a bullet in his back. Now he couldn't take a chance with anything in skirts, especially one who made a living sticking her nose into other people's secrets. Even if she was the prettiest thing he'd seen in a long time.

Irritated that he'd even noticed her looks, he jerked his thoughts back to the conversation. "Well?" he demanded.

"No." She fairly spat the admission at him.

His smile was smug. "I thought not."

"But he said the two of you once worked together," she added triumphantly. "And since you're not from around here and it's a matter of public record that Riley's only other job before moving to Lordsburg was with the DEA, it stands to reason that you were both agents. He wouldn't bring just anybody in on one of the most unusual cases to hit this county in years."

Obviously confident that she now had him right where she wanted him, she arched a brow at him. "So just exactly what did you do for the DEA, Mr. Cassidy? And why did you quit? You're hardly old enough to retire. What happened?"

The questions flew at him like bullets, reopening wounds he was trying his damnedest to heal. Damn her, why was she hounding him? She couldn't know about the shooting in the jungle the night Santiago was captured. The DEA had made sure the story never made it out of South America, and she'd already admitted that Riley hadn't told her anything. She was just fishing, looking for something to fill the pages of that precious paper of hers, and she couldn't possibly know the damage a human-interest story about him could cause. True, the odds of Santiago ever coming across a copy of the *Hidalgo County Gazette* were slim to none, but even from prison, the man was as dangerous as a cornered rattler. Dillon had no intention of underestimating him.

"No comment," he said curtly, and reached for the door.

This time, she made no move to stop him. "You can put me off for now," she warned him, raising her voice as he shut the door in her face, "but not forever. You hear me, Cassidy? You're hiding something, and I intend to find out what it is."

Great, he thought crossly as he heard her stomp down the porch steps to her car. This was just great! From the moment he'd arrived in town, he'd been careful to keep a low profile and mind his own business... until Riley had asked for his help. Now, thanks to that one little favor he'd agreed to do, he had Sydney O'Keefe to deal with. Another newshound he might have been able to put off, but he'd read her work. There was no question that she was a talented writer with a nose for headlines in a place where they were few and far between. And she'd decided that he was news. God help him!

By the time school started the next morning, news of the discovery of Bryan Fitzgerald's body had raced through the streets like a hot summer wind, and the halls were abuzz with speculation about the murder. Teenagers gathered in clumps at their lockers, their voices hushed, their eyes troubled as they discussed how such a thing could have happened in their slow-moving, easygoing town.

Slowly making his way through the crush of students, Dillon hardly noticed the wary glances and sudden silence his presence created when the students realized there was a stranger in their midst. The boys he'd seen at the quarry last night had to be here somewhere. He'd been there since the janitor opened the doors at seven, and at first he hadn't had any trouble checking out the kids who straggled in early. Then the school buses had pulled up out front and unloaded, and in the mass of chattering humanity that had streamed inside, he hadn't been able to get a good look at the face of every boy in the crowd. And he was running out of time, dammit! In five minutes, the bell would ring and the halls would clear. Where the hell were those kids?

"Well, well, if it isn't the elusive Mr. Cassidy."

Glancing sharply up from his thoughts, Dillon stiffened at the sight of Sydney making her way through the crowd toward him, looking hardly older than a teenager herself in faded jeans and an oversize hooded sweatshirt that fell to her thighs, swallowing her slender figure whole. A grin, full of delight, tipped up the corners of her mouth, and in her eyes was an impish spark that he immediately distrusted. He might have been able to avoid her questions last night, but there was no door to shut in her face now and she knew it.

Swearing, he didn't wait for her to reach him, but turned back toward the foyer at the main entrance. "I don't have time to talk to you now, Sydney. I'm working—"

"I know. You're looking for the boys from the quarry. So am I." Catching him in four quick strides, she hurriedly moved into step at his side. Her blue eyes cutting to his, she grinned at the scowl he directed at her. "Isn't it lucky that we ran into each other this way?"

"Yeah, it's a real riot."

Chuckling at his dry tone, she explained, "No, I mean it. You're obviously not having any better luck than I am at finding those kids, but together we might just hit paydirt. And in the meantime, you can answer some questions for me."

"Not in this lifetime or the next," he retorted coldly, returning his gaze to the teenagers crowding the hall. "I said all I was going to say last night."

He expected her to argue with that—she'd already proven herself to be nothing if not tenacious—but she only shrugged as if the matter was of no concern to her, then, like him, turned her attention to the kids hurrying to their first class. "I figured you'd say that, and that's okay. It's a free country and you don't have to say anything you don't want to. I just thought it was odd that you own a ranch but no cattle. Why is that?"

"No comment."

Undaunted, she said airily, "In fact, you don't seem to have any means of employment, and you're too young to be retired. So how the heck do you support yourself? Did you're grandma die and leave you a chunk of change or what? Not that it's any of my business, of course, but—"

"But why let that stop you, right?" he mocked, arching a taunting brow. "I take it it never has before."

"Now, now, don't get tacky," she soothed in an irritatingly calm voice. "We all have our jobs to do, and I'm just doing mine. Anyway, this isn't about me. *You're* the one with the secrets."

She smiled up at him so sweetly, Dillon didn't know if he wanted to snatch her into his arms and kiss her or throttle her. And that threw him. When had he started thinking about kissing the lady? When had he started thinking about her, period? She might have the soft, classic beauty of an old-fashioned Gibson girl, but she was as sharp as a knife and so stubborn that it was all a reasonable man could do not to shake some sense into her. Not his type of woman at all, he decided.

So why was he so fascinated with her? She knew exactly what she was doing to him. He could see the wicked sparkle in her eyes, the amusement the little witch made no attempt to hide. There was no doubt about it—she enjoyed pushing his buttons, and he was letting her!

Disgusted with himself, he jerked his gaze from hers…just in time to catch a glimpse of what looked like one of the bikers from the quarry turn the corner toward the stairs to the second floor. "Excuse me," he said curtly to Sydney. "I've got work to do."

Hurriedly pushing his way through the throng of students, he took a quick step around the corner and intercepted the boy just as he reached the stairs. Quickly introducing himself, he said, "Hold up a minute, will you, son? I'm a private investigator, and I need to ask you a few questions."

His eyes huge in his suddenly chalky face, the boy looked quickly around for a way out. "Uh—I've g-got class—"

"If you're late, I'll be happy to talk to your teacher," Dillon assured him, urging him away from the flow of traffic near the stairs. "This is too important to put off. How well do you know Juan Martinez?"

"I don't know him at all!"

Practically shaking, the boy was obviously scared out of his mind…and lying. Knowing he'd get nothing out of him if he frightened him too much, Dillon struggled to be patient, but it wasn't easy. One kid was dead and the second one could be in serious trouble if he didn't find him soon. "Look, son, you're not in any kind of trouble. I just want to talk to you. What's your name?"

For a minute, he didn't think the kid was even going to give him that much before he grudgingly admitted, "Tommy Gordon."

"Okay, Tommy, I'm going to be straight with you. I know you ride dirt bikes out at the old quarry, and that's okay with me," he said quickly when the boy looked ready to bolt. "I don't own the property and I didn't track you down to talk about trespassing. But since you hang out there and Bryan Fitzgerald did, too, you must have run into each other there occasionally. Right?"

Still suspicious, Tommy stared at him for a long time, fear darkening his eyes. "I don't know. Maybe. Maybe not."

So much for doing this the easy way, Dillon thought, gritting his teeth. "Okay," he said with a sigh, forcing a smile, "let's try this a different way. Let's say you did know Bryan. The night he disappeared, maybe he showed up at the quarry with another friend. Juan Martinez. So you must know him, too."

"I never said that," Tommy said quickly, alarmed. "I never said I knew either one of them."

"True, but if you did and you were friends, you'd want to help Juan if you could," Dillon pointed out easily, not pressing the issue. "Friends help friends, and Juan could be in serious trouble about now. The kind that could get him killed. So if you were worried about him and afraid he was going to end up like Bryan, you'd tell someone who was concerned about him what you knew, wouldn't you? Because you're a good friend."

Watching the conflicting emotions flicker across the teen's still-baby-faced features, Dillon waited expectantly. He knew the look of a witness who wanted to spill his guts, and it was stamped all over the boy's face. He was dying to talk—all he needed was the sympathetic ear of somebody he could trust. A few more seconds and—

The bell rang suddenly, the sound sharp and shrill, and just that quickly, Tommy clamped up tighter than a bank vault. His gaze darting past Dillon to the hall that had emptied without his noticing, he said hoarsely, "Oh, God, I'm late. I gotta go!"

"Wait!" Swearing, Dillon grabbed the boy's notebook and quickly jotted down the number to his cellular phone. "This is my number," he said, shoving the notebook back into the kid's hand. "If you can think of anything that can help me find Juan Martinez, call me anytime, day or night."

Not making any promises, the teenager bolted past him and up the stairs like a scared rabbit, his notebook clutched to his skinny chest. Watching him until he was out of sight, Dillon knew a lost opportunity when he saw one. The only reason he'd been able to get anything at all out of the kid was because he'd caught him off guard. Once he calmed down, he'd realize that the next move was his. If he didn't want to talk to Dillon, he didn't have to. And there wasn't a damn thing Dillon could do about it.

It had, Sydney decided a few minutes after the tardy bell rang, been a raunchy morning all the way around. She still didn't know how Dillon had managed to elude her. One second she'd had him cornered, and the next he was gone, pushing his way through the crowd before she could stop him. She'd gone after him, of course, but then she'd thought she caught sight of one of the kids from the quarry. By the time she'd trailed him to his class and realized she'd made a mistake, the halls had cleared and Dillon was nowhere to be found.

Torn between irritation and amusement, she imagined he was probably feeling pretty pleased with himself right about now. The dog had given her the slip without answering a single one of her questions. Chuckling softly to herself, she shrugged. So he got lucky. If he made the mistake of thinking he was always going to evade her so easily, he was in for a rude awakening. His little stunt only stirred her interest more and proved he had a story to tell. Before it was over with, she'd find out what it was.

But for now, she needed to do some follow-up on the missing Martinez boy. With the finding of Bryan Fitzgerald's body, the whole complexity of the case had changed, and she wanted to talk to the Martinez family again. Climbing into her car, she headed for the south side of town.

As expected, she found Manuel and Elaina Martinez frantic with worry over their son. Elaina had obviously been crying and her husband looked as if he had aged ten years since Sydney had last spoken to him. Seated at the kitchen table, his face haggard and drawn, he spoke of his son as if he were in the next room, safe and well, but there was a tragic sadness in his dark eyes that told Sydney he had already accepted the worst. Now he was just waiting for the horrible news from the authorities.

Her heart breaking for him and his wife, Sydney hated to intrude, hated to push questions on them when they were in so much pain. She had a job to do, of course, but she took no pleasure in it at times like this. Promising herself she was going to keep it brief, she took the seat Elaina offered her at the kitchen table.

"I know you must be sick of questions," she began as she pulled out her miniature tape recorder and set it on the table between them, "but I just have a few. You said in our last conversation that Juan took a duffel bag with him when he left. Do you have any idea what was in it?"

Sniffing, his mother nodded. "Two pairs of jeans, three long-sleeved shirts and underwear. And the thirty dollars he took from Manuel's wallet." Tears welled in her eyes, spilling over onto her weathered cheeks. Wiping them away with a trembling hand, she said, "I still can't believe he did that. He never stole from his father in his life."

His own eyes glistening, Manuel added, "That's why we were so sure he'd run away. But now I don't know. After the Fitzgerald boy was found last night, nothing makes sense."

"Did Juan ever threaten to run away before?"

"No, never!" Elaina exclaimed. "He's a good boy. Headstrong like his father, and a little spoiled, but all boys are at that age. If he was unhappy enough to run away, no one knew what he was planning. Not even his girlfriend."

"His girlfriend?" Sydney echoed, startled. "What girlfriend?"

Elaina frowned in confusion. "Lisa Hunter. Didn't we mention her? She and Juan are hardly ever out of each other's sight."

This was the first Sydney had heard of the girl—she was sure of it. "And she hasn't heard from him? If they're that close, he must have contacted her."

Not liking that suggestion at all, Manuel stiffened, his lined face folding into a disapproving frown. "Lisa would never keep something like that to herself. She knows how worried we are about Juan. She would have called us immediately if she'd heard from him."

Privately, Sydney wasn't so sure of that, but that wasn't for publication. Carefully concealing her excitement, she didn't push the issue. "I'm sure you're right, Manuel. She sounds like a good kid. In fact, I'd like to talk to her. Do you have her number?"

Elaina rattled it off, only to caution, "But she's in school right now and has cheerleader practice afterward. You probably won't be able to get in touch with her until later this evening."

Already rising to her feet, Sydney quickly stuffed her recorder into her purse. "That's okay—I've got a jillion other things to do this afternoon, so that will be perfect. Thanks."

She hadn't lied—she really did have a long list of things to do that afternoon—but they were all piddling tasks that she was able to fly through without much thought. By four o'clock she was finished and staring at the clock. She told

herself she knew how to bide her time and wait for a story
to break. But as the seconds ticked by with maddening
slowness, she knew there was no way she was going to be
able to just sit there and wait till that evening to call Lisa
Hunter. Giving in to the inevitable, she reached for the
phone.

Twenty minutes later, Sydney couldn't believe her luck.
Lisa had not only been home because cheerleader practice
had been canceled, but she'd promised to meet Sydney at the
City Diner just as soon as she could get there. Seated halfway down the row of booths that lined the windows, she
watched a petite blond teenager walk in the door and knew
immediately that she was Lisa. Dressed in a fuzzy aqua
sweater and tight black jeans just as she'd promised, she was
cheerleader cute and confident, with every hair in place.

"Hi," Sydney greeted her, smiling as she motioned her
into the seat across the table from her. "Thanks for coming
so quickly. Would you like something to eat?"

"Just a Coke, please," she told the waitress as she slid
into the booth seat. Looking nervous for the first time since
she'd walked in the door, she fiddled absently with the strap
of her purse as she set it in her lap. "You said this was important," she began hesitantly, her large blue eyes, dark
with worry, searching Sydney's. "Is it about Juan?"

Sydney nodded. "Actually, I just learned this morning
that you two were friends or I would have talked to you right
after Juan disappeared. Have you heard from him?"

The quick question caught the girl off guard, just as Sydney had hoped, but before she could take advantage of the
moment, the waitress returned with Lisa's drink. By the time
she'd deposited it and a straw on a table, the teenager had
had time to compose herself. Instead of answering, she met
Sydney's gaze unblinkingly. "Why would you think that?"

"Because according to Juan's parents, you two are very close. And I don't think he would just run away without a word to anyone, not if he's as good a kid as his parents say he is." Giving that a chance to sink in, she sat back and surveyed the girl shrewdly. "This isn't just a runaway story anymore, Lisa. Bryan Fitzgerald is dead and Juan's missing. Does he know something about Bryan's death?"

"No!"

Her answer was just a little too quick and sharp with panic. "Then why did he run?" Sydney pressed. "There had to be a reason. I was hoping you might know what it is."

Expecting a denial, she was shocked by the sudden tears that filled the girl's eyes. "He w-wouldn't tell me," she whispered brokenly. "He just said not to tell anybody where he was going." Sniffing, she jerked a paper napkin from the chrome napkin holder and wiped her wet cheeks. "If something happens to him—"

Her face was stark with terror, and with a jolt, Sydney suddenly heard what she'd just admitted. "Oh, Lord, you mean you know where he is? Honey, I know you're trying to protect him, but he could be in serious trouble!" Leaning forward, she gripped the girl's tightly clenched hands where they rested on the table. "This isn't a game, Lisa. Bryan is already dead and I know you don't want Juan to end up the same way. Where is he? You've got to tell me."

She hesitated, her teeth biting into her bottom lip, smudging her lipstick, before she finally blurted out, "I'll tell you, but only if you promise not to tell anyone where he is. Swear."

Sydney didn't hesitate. "I can write his story without ever mentioning that. I swear. Where is he?"

"At my uncle's in Tucson." Having given that much, there was little point in keeping the address to herself. She watched Sydney hastily scribble it in a small notebook she carried in her purse, her expression troubled. "Please tell me you're not going to Tucson. Juan was afraid he was being followed—"

Glancing up quickly from her notebook, Sydney frowned. "Did he say why?"

"No. I just know he was constantly looking over his shoulder. If someone was trying to find him to hurt him and they followed you to my uncle's..." Shivering at the thought, she pleaded, "Please be careful, Ms. O'Keefe. If something happened to him or you because I opened my big mouth, I'd never forgive myself."

Normally, Sydney would have laughed at the suggestion that she couldn't take care of herself, especially after thriving on the streets of Chicago for years. But the girl's fear was real and soul deep. Giving her a reassuring smile, she patted her hand. "Don't worry. Nothing's going to happen to either one of us. I'll be careful. I promise. I'll call you just as soon as I get back to town and let you know how it went. Okay?"

The girl would still worry; they both knew it. But something in Sydney's tone must have calmed her fears. Releasing a slow breath, she nodded and slipped out of the booth. "Okay. I'll be waiting to hear from you."

Already picturing the headlines that would accompany her story, Sydney grabbed her purse and started digging for the money to pay the check for Lisa's Coke. She'd fill up her car, stop at the grocery store for extra batteries and tapes for her recorder, then head for Tucson, she decided. She could be there in—

"Well, well, look what we have here," Dillon said, slipping into the empty booth seat across the table from her. When she glanced up, startled, he grinned. "Lois Lane. And she looks like she just got a hot tip. Care to tell me what it is?"

Chapter 3

"Don't smoke," she retorted with a smirk, her heart lurching at the sight of him. Telling herself it was just from surprise—she hadn't seen him walk in—she made a move to slide out of the booth, her smile deliberately dismissing. "Now, if you'll excuse me, I've got things to do—"

That was as far as she got. Lightning quick, his leg shot out to block her exit, his booted foot settling on the seat mere inches from her hip, pinning her in. When her eyes flew to his in surprise, he merely grinned and settled back for a chat, his gray eyes alight with satisfaction. "I don't think so, darlin'. We need to talk."

Her gaze lifting from the sight of his foot next to her hip to his crooked grin, Sydney felt her throat go dry. He had, she thought dazedly, the kind of smile that should have carried a warning label—it was that dangerous. And any woman who trusted it was just asking for trouble. Suddenly wondering why he was being so chummy when he'd wanted nothing to do with her last night and just that morning, she frowned at him suspiciously. "About what?"

"The identity of the cute little blonde, for one thing. And don't try to pass her off as a friend," he warned. "She couldn't be sixteen if she's a day, and I don't think you get your kicks by hanging out with the high school crowd. So who is she? And what does she have to do with the Fitzgerald and Martinez boys?"

For all of two seconds, she actually considered telling him. After all, it wasn't as if he were another reporter who would steal her story. But Riley had charged him with the responsibility of finding Juan, and if Dillon thought she was a threat to the boy's safety, he'd never let her near him.

Leaning back in the booth, she decided to play it safe. Giving him a maddening half smile, she lifted a delicately arched brow. "Who said she had anything to do with the case?"

So she wanted to play games, Dillon mused. He hadn't thought he was in the mood for it—since he'd tracked down the Gordon kid at the high school earlier, he'd run into nothing but one dead end after another, and he was getting damned frustrated. But there was something about the mischievous glint in her eyes that he found impossible to resist.

He should have looked away then and reminded himself why he was there. He'd been sitting in his favorite booth, the last one at the back that gave him an unrestricted view of the diner and all its patrons as they came and went through the front door, when he'd seen Sydney walk in, then greet the teenager that joined her at her table. There was no question that she'd uncovered something interesting—even though she'd been sitting with her back to him, he'd sensed her barely contained excitement as the little blonde had confided something to her before she'd left. He'd joined her solely to find out what that something was, but instead of grilling her as he should have been doing, he couldn't stop looking at her.

If he was a man who believed in such things, he would have said her aura was sprinkled with the dust of a million diamonds. Her eyes had a sparkle, her cheeks a becoming wash of color, her mouth a tempting curve that drew his gaze like a magnet. Even with the width of the table between them, he could feel the energy that set the air around her humming...and the heat that curled, uninvited and unwelcome, low in his gut.

Amused in spite of that, he found himself fighting hard to hold back a grin. "Nice try," he drawled, "but I wasn't born yesterday. That little-girl innocent act might play well for the local cowboys, but after talking to cows all day, they're liable to believe just about anything. I'm not. Who is she?"

Flashing her dimples at him, she grinned. "Don't you wish you knew."

His eyes locked with hers. "There are ways of finding out," he warned softly.

"Oh, really?" Not a spark of fear shone in her dancing blue eyes. "What are we talking about here? Chinese water torture? Thumb screws? Is this when you bring in the whips and chains?" Leaning forward, she propped her elbows on the table and rested her chin in her palms, her eyes widening with a sudden thought. "Don't tell me you're into S and M?"

Lord, she was full of sass! His mouth twitching, his eyes locked with hers. "Don't beat around the bush, sweetheart. If you want to know about my sex life, just ask."

That got her. Fascinated, he watched the heat climb in her cheeks and her eyes shy from his. Who would have thought it? Sydney O'Keefe shy? He wouldn't have believed it if he hadn't seen it with his own eyes.

But between one heartbeat and the next, she recovered. Straightening abruptly, she leaned back in her seat and grinned. "Thanks for the offer, but I think I'll wait for the movie. I like popcorn with my epics."

He laughed, he couldn't help it. Damn the little minx. She actually dared to wink at him! "I'll remember that," he said dryly. "In the meantime, I believe we were talking about the little blonde—"

"No, *you* were talking about the little blonde," she corrected sweetly. "I don't believe I mentioned her name."

"My point exactly," he retorted. "Who *is* she? You might as well tell me, Sydney. I'm not letting you out of here until you do."

The words were hardly out of his mouth when the cellular phone he never went anywhere without rang. Totally unfazed by his threats, Sydney leaned across the table to confide softly, "Don't look now, but I believe you're ringing."

He was, Dillon decided, going to kill her. Scowling, he pulled the phone from his pocket and flipped it open. "Cassidy here," he growled into the mouthpiece.

"Uh...Mr. Cassidy, this is Tommy G-Gordon."

To his credit, Dillon didn't drop the phone, but every muscle in his body tightened in expectation. Dammit to hell, why did the kid have to call now, when Sydney was right across the table from him and blatantly eavesdropping? Talk about lousy timing! If Tommy was calling with the information he was hoping for and Sydney caught the slightest hint of it, he'd never be able to shake her loose.

Silently cursing the Fates, he said carefully, "It's nice to hear from you, Tom. What can I do for you?"

"I—I've been thinking about what y-you said this m-morning," he stuttered. "You know . . . about Juan . . ."

"Yes?"

For a long moment, there was nothing but a nerve-racking silence that seemed to stretch into infinity. Dillon could almost smell the boy's fear and the doubts tearing at him. It had taken all day for him to work up the courage to call, but the boy was still obviously scared spitless. One wrong word from Dillon and he knew he would lose Tommy—and his information—forever. Fighting the urge to plead with him not to hang up, he couldn't do anything but wait.

"If s-something happened to him," he finally said shakily, "and I didn't tell anyone where he w-was, it would be my fault, wouldn't it?"

"I don't know that I would put it that way," Dillon replied cautiously, frowning. "But if you give me that information, I'll do everything I can to see that that doesn't happen."

Hesitating, the boy drew in a deep breath and finally, reluctantly blurted out, "He's in Tucson . . . at a friend's uncle's house—2315 Adams. That's all I know."

The line went dead then, the drone of the dial tone a steady buzz in Dillon's ear. Putting the phone away, Dillon's thoughts jumped ahead to the drive to Tucson. He could be there before dark and possibly have Juan Martinez safely back with his parents by midnight—

"Problems?"

He hadn't for a minute forgotten Sydney's presence . . . or her occupation. The last thing he needed at this phase of the investigation was a pushy reporter sticking her nose into things and scaring the kid off before he had him in protective custody. Forcing an easy smile, he shrugged. "Nothing worth worrying about," he lied, "but we're going to have to continue this little interlude some other time. I've got to go—I've got an appointment."

"Isn't that a coincidence?" she purred smoothly, her mouth curling at the ironies of fate. "So do I." Rising to her feet as soon as he slid from the booth, her gaze lifted to his. "Guess I'll see you around."

Not if I see you first. The words weren't spoken aloud, but Sydney could read them in his eyes as clearly as if they were spelled out in lights. Amused, she noted that he motioned for her to precede him after she paid the bill for Lisa's Coke, as if he were afraid she was going to follow him.

Grinning, she could have told him there was no need for him to be paranoid—she had her own fish to fry—but she decided he was too sure of himself as it was. From what she'd seen of Dillon Cassidy, he didn't appear to be a man who spent a lot of time looking over his shoulder. Thinking he had a woman on his tail, tracking his every step, just might shake him up a little.

Pleased by the thought, she pulled out of the diner parking lot and turned left. A quick glance in the rearview mirror assured her that Dillon had turned his midnight blue Suburban the opposite direction, for which she sent up a heartfelt prayer of thanks. He'd already made it clear that he didn't approve of her sniffing into the case. If he had even a suspicion of what she was up to, he'd do whatever he had to to stop her, even if that meant calling in the sheriff, and there was no way she was letting that happen. She was the one who had tracked down Lisa Hunter and got her to talk, and if Juan really did turn out to be in Tucson, she'd notify Riley herself. *After* she got her story. And that was going to be a lot easier to do with Dillon tied up with an appointment. He'd never even know when she left town.

A grin flirting with the corners of her mouth, she pulled into the Kwik Stop and filled up, then hurriedly bought batteries and several cassettes just in case she needed extras. Twelve minutes later, she was back in her car and turning onto Main Street. The radio was blaring and her thoughts were already locked on the tough questions she intended to ask Juan when she caught up with him. Without sparing it a glance, she went right through the Yield sign where Main intercepted the access road of Interstate 10. Distracted, she never saw the dark Suburban that had the right of way until a horn blared like a blast from hell.

She never remembered floorboarding the brakes, but suddenly her tires were screaming and her fingers locked in a death grip on the steering wheel as she struggled for control. The Suburban was right in front of her, dark and threatening, impact only seconds away. Horrified, she wrenched the wheel to the right and knew in her heart it was too late. Slamming her eyes shut, she braced for the crash.

But when her Wrangler shuddered to a stop, there was no collision. Stunned, she opened her eyes to find her front bumper just inches from the Suburban's passenger door. And glaring at her from the other vehicle's driver's seat was Dillon. Muttering curses, he unsnapped his seat belt with a savage jerk. Then, in the next instant, he was out of the Suburban and heading right for her, his long legs quickly eating up the distance between them.

Sydney only had time to shakily alight from her own vehicle before he was on her. "What the hell do you think you're doing?" he thundered. "That was a Yield sign, lady. I realize that word's probably not in your vocabulary, but you damn well better learn it. You almost hit me!"

Flushed, more than willing to take the blame when she was in the wrong, she said, "I know, and I'm sorry. I wasn't paying any attention—"

He snorted contemptuously. "You got that right. You were too busy trying to follow me."

Sydney couldn't have been more surprised than if he'd accused her of drunk driving. "Following you?" she echoed, choking on a startled laugh that held little humor. Of all the insufferable egos! Cocking her head to the side, she surveyed him with barely concealed irritation. "You're really something, you know that? You seem to have this misconception that I can't do jack squat without you to track down a story for me. So let me let you in on a secret. I'm damn good at what I do, Cassidy. If I was following you, you wouldn't even know it. Now, if you'll excuse me, I have an appointment."

It was the second time in less than an hour that she'd tried to dismiss him, and as far as Dillon was concerned, it was two times too many. Irritated, he should have let her go anyway. He could deal with her sass another time—right now he needed to get to Tucson. But even as the thought registered, something just snapped. "Not so fast, lady," he growled, and reached for her.

Snaring her wrist, he caught her before she'd taken two steps and dragged her back in front of him, intending to find out what the devil she was doing here, her bumper just inches from his Suburban, if she *wasn't* following him. But the second his fingers closed around the delicate bones of her wrist, he couldn't seem to think of anything but how close she was, how soft her skin was, how sweetly intoxicating her scent was.

Staring down at her, caught in the trap of her startled eyes, he saw that she felt it, too. The sharp tug of attraction, the unexpected heat of desire. The knowledge was there in the blush that warmed her cheeks and the faint, frantic, enticing fluttering of her pulse at the base of her throat. She swallowed, and it was suddenly his mouth that was dry, his blood roaring in his ears. Unconsciously, his fingers tightened around her wrist.

Entranced, Sydney felt his touch all the way down to her toes. Shaken, she couldn't remember the last time a man only had to lay his hand on her to rob her of breath and speech. What was she doing? This was Dillon Cassidy, for God's sake! The man who would, if he could, stand between her and a story that was the biggest thing to happen in Lordsburg in more years than most people cared to count. Was she really going to just stand here and let him turn her knees to water with nothing more than a heated look and hot touch?

The fuzziness abruptly clearing from her brain at the mortifying thought, she jerked free of his hold, then could have kicked herself for not being a little more subtle when knowing amusement suddenly glistened in his eyes. Damn the man, he already had an ego the size of Texas. If he discovered he could make her heart jump in her breast with nothing more than the brush of his fingers, she'd never hear the end of it.

Stepping back, she was disconcerted to discover how much effort it took to summon a taunting smile. Annoyed, she quipped, "I don't know how they treat women where you come from, Cassidy, but around here, men don't grab women. Not if they want to keep their fingers."

"I'll try to remember that," he said dryly. "Now, why don't you tell me what brings you to this part of town if you're really not following me?"

"I told you—"

"I know what you told me. Now I'd like the truth. I've got an appointment, and you claim you do, too. I head for the I-10 West on ramp and surprise, surprise, you do, too. And I'm supposed to accept that as just coincidence? I don't think so."

Put like that, Sydney had to admit that he had a point. If she hadn't been so rattled by the near accident, she would have seen it sooner. Her gaze slipping past him to the interstate entrance ramp a half a block away, there was no question that they were headed in the same direction. Toward Tucson. And Juan Martinez.

So he had the boy's address. She shouldn't have been surprised. Riley had warned her he could track a spider across the desert, but he'd conveniently forgotten to mention how damn deceptive the man was. Now that she'd had time to think about, there'd obviously been more to the phone call he'd gotten at the diner, but he'd been so casual about it, she hadn't suspected a thing. Idiot! she chided herself. How could she have missed what was right in front of her nose? One minute he'd been grilling her about Lisa Hunter and the next, he'd claimed he had to be somewhere else. That alone should have tipped her off that something was up. No one on the trail of a story walked away from one lead unless a stronger one called them away. So what else had he learned about Juan Martinez? And from whom?

Surveying him speculatively, she said, "I know you're probably not going to believe this, but I really wasn't following you. I just happen to be going to the same place you are."

He didn't so much as blink. "Sure you are. And where is that?"

"Tucson," she said succinctly, and had the satisfaction of seeing his eyes narrow slightly.

Still, he wasn't convinced. "That's obvious. Where in Tucson?"

After the way they'd competed with each other for information, Sydney couldn't blame him for being suspicious, but they couldn't continue to play games when one boy was dead and another one was possibly in grave danger.

"You want the exact address? Fine. 2315 Adams." When he swore softly, she swallowed an *I told you so.* "Now that we've established that we're both good at what we do, don't you think it's more practical for us to work together and start pooling our information instead of constantly trying to one-up each other?''

It was a logical suggestion. The only problem was that Dillon didn't want or need her help. He worked alone and that was just the way he liked it. If he let her tag along, she'd just slow him down and get in his way.

But as he opened his mouth to reject the idea, common sense pointed out that if he didn't cooperate with the lady, she could cause him a hell of a lot of problems. He could just see it now.... Both of them rushing to Tucson, each trying to reach the boy first. They'd scare the poor kid out of ten years of his life and possibly lose him completely if he decided to take off again. It could take months to find him again.

"All right," he agreed. "You want information—I'll tell you what I know. The kid's staying with a friend's uncle in Tucson. I'm heading up there now to talk to him and see if I can convince him to come home. As soon as I get back, I'll give you a call and let you know how it went. Okay?''

"Okay?" she gasped, insulted. "You call that working together? In case you've forgotten, I have the kid's address, too. I don't need your permission to talk to him. So what's it going to be? The choice is yours. Either we go together or I go by myself, but I'm going to Tucson.''

She had him and she knew it. He either agreed to work with her or he chanced letting her blow the case for him. And she called that a *choice?* Like hell!

Every instinct he possessed cringed at the very idea of letting her tag along with him—he was having a hard enough time ignoring her as it was. Spending more time with her would only compound that problem. But if she was with him, at least he'd know where she was and what kind of mischief she was up to.

Annoyed that he'd let her manipulate him so easily, he said tersely, "If I agree to work with you—and that's a big if—we need to get some things straight right now. This is my investigation and I'm in charge. You're just along for the story."

He expected an outburst, but she had herself well in hand. Her mouth twitching, she settled back against the fender of her Wrangler and crossed her arms over her chest. "What century are you living in, Cassidy? This is the nineties. Women don't take orders from men anymore."

"Nobody said anything about taking orders," he began, frowning.

"Good. Because I ask my own questions, and if I don't like the direction you're going with this, you'd better believe you're going to hear about it. If you can't handle that, then you'd better speak up now and we can part company right here."

She'd do it, Dillon thought, wanting to shake her. She'd race off to Tucson by herself and never stop to think of the danger she could be in. Whoever killed Bryan Fitzgerald was still out there and, for all they knew, just as determined to find Juan Martinez as they were. If she got in his way or stumbled across him by mistake, he'd eliminate her as easily as he had Bryan.

Something twisted in him at the thought, something that he didn't allow himself to examine too closely. He just knew he couldn't let her go off by herself. "We can take the Suburban," he said grimly, and just that easily, they struck a deal.

He followed her back to her house, where they left her Jeep, then waited for her to join him in the Suburban before retracing their steps back to the interstate. The sun had set, and although the western sky was still light, the long shadows that were creeping across the desert landscape were quickly lengthening. Long before they reached Tucson, it would be fully dark.

Excitement skittering along her nerve endings, Sydney shifted restlessly in the passenger seat, hardly able to sit still. Too late, she wished they'd taken her Jeep instead of Dillon's Suburban so she could have passed the time driving. Just sitting had never been easy for her, especially when she was hot on the trail of a story. Given the opportunity, she would have flattened the accelerator and damned the consequences. Dillon, however, seemed to feel no such urgency.

Glancing at him from the corner of her eye, Sydney saw that his grip on the steering wheel was easy, his foot steady on the accelerator. The speedometer never moved off sixty-five. Stifling a sigh, she tried to remind herself that she couldn't ask any more of him than the legal limit. But if Sydney hadn't known better, she would have sworn they were crawling. Frustrated, she ordered herself to be patient.

Ten minutes later, when Dillon suddenly lifted his foot from the accelerator and flipped on a turn signal for the upcoming rest area, Sydney glanced over at him in surprise. "What's wrong?"

His eyes directed straight ahead, he said, "Nothing. I just thought you might need to stop."

Puzzled, she almost pointed out that they'd hardly been on the road thirty minutes, but she only said, "Thanks, but I'm fine. In fact, I can't wait until we get there. Don't stop on my account."

After that, she thought he'd just cruise on through the rest area and reenter the interstate, but to her surprise, he stopped in front of the building that housed the rest rooms and vending machines and switched off the motor. "Since we're here, I might as well get something to drink. Would you like something?"

"No. Nothing. Thanks."

If he noticed her terse tone, he gave no sign of it. Swinging open his door, he carefully eased out of the Suburban. "I'll be right back."

His back ramrod straight, his pace leisurely, Dillon moved as if he had all the time in the world. If Sydney hadn't seen it with her own eyes, she never would have believed it. For two days now, they'd been tearing Lordsburg upside down looking for Juan Martinez, and now that they knew where he was, Dillon was stopping for a Coke of all things! What the devil was going on?

Drumming her fingers against her armrest, she tried to curb her impatience as she waited for him to rejoin her, but it was another ten minutes before he returned to the Suburban. By then, her temper was simmering. The minute he slipped behind the wheel and started the motor, she turned on him. "Tell me something, Dillon. Do you plan on reaching Tucson tonight?"

With the darkness broken only by the faint illumination of the dash lights, his expression was lost in shadows. "Don't worry," he said shortly. "I'll get you there."

Pulling away from the rest area, he quickly accelerated, and within seconds, they were racing toward Tucson, this time at a speed that Sydney could find little fault with. Still, something was wrong; she could sense it. Dillon sat like a stone behind the wheel, tense, hardly moving, speaking only when spoken to, and then his answers were limited to one or two terse words.

Had he changed his mind about working with her? she wondered, studying him in the dark. Was that what his silence was about? Was he hoping she would become so uncomfortable that she would change her mind and tell him to forget it? Not bloody likely, she thought grimly. She wasn't out to make friends with him, just get a story.

Her mouth compressed into a flat line, she forced herself to relax, her eyes trained straight ahead on the dark road that stretched into a straight line all the way to the horizon. If he wanted silence, she could give it back to him in spades.

Then he stopped again.

Unable to believe he was actually pulling over and braking to a stop on the side of the road, Sydney cried, "Now what? Dammit, Dillon, what's going on?"

The muscles of his lower back burning like the fires of hell and his teeth tightly clenched on a groan he refused to utter, Dillon didn't dare open his mouth to answer her. Taking time only to throw the transmission into Park, he threw open his door and escaped out into the night.

With the growing darkness, the air had turned noticeably cooler, but it could have been snowing and he would not have noticed. His face lifted to the star-filled sky, he slowly, carefully, expelled his breath and waited for the pain to ease. But he'd sat too long without moving and his back burned like someone had stuck a knife in it.

He should have stopped sooner, he berated himself angrily. Every passing mile had cost him, but like an idiot he'd thought he could make it without having to stop again. He should have known better. He was lucky if he could make it from town to his house without having to stop and stretch his legs. How the hell had he expected to make it all the way to Tucson?

"Dillon? Are you all right?"

Caught up in the haze of pain that fogged his thoughts, he hadn't heard Sydney's approach, hadn't even heard her get out of the vehicle. Glancing down at her, he found her standing hesitantly at his side staring up at him, her face pale and etched with concern in the starlight.

He tried to drag up a smile but couldn't manage much more than a grimace. "Yeah, I just need some fresh air."

"Are you sure? You don't look so good."

He imagined he looked like hell—he certainly felt like it. And there was no way he was going to be able to climb back into the car with her without giving her some sort of explanation. Motioning to Sydney to precede him to the front of the Suburban, where they were in less danger of being hit, he was relieved to feel the sharp bite of pain near his spine ease slightly.

"It's nothing serious," he told her huskily, lying through his teeth. "I injured my back a couple of months ago and I can't sit in one position for too long without it stiffening up on me."

Instead of easing her mind as he had hoped, the explanation only stirred up her curiosity and deepened her concern. "If you're in that much pain, it must be pretty bad. Have you seen a doctor? What did he say? Surely there's something he can do to at least make the pain bearable."

Silently cursing himself for not coming up with another explanation, Dillon shook his head. "It's no big deal, just something I have to learn to live with. Don't worry about it—I don't."

"But—"

"I don't want to talk about it," he said bluntly before she worked up a full steam of questions he had no intention of answering. "Why don't you wait in the car? I only need a few minutes to work the kinks out, then we can be on our way."

Watching every nuance of his expression, Sydney knew in her gut that he was leaving something out, but the harsh lines of his face didn't encourage further conversation. His chin had that granite set to it, the one that warned her not to push him, the one that invariably challenged her to do just that. But the pain darkening his eyes was real, and the thought of him hurting that badly tugged at her heartstrings in a way she hadn't expected.

Disturbed by the thought, she asked, "Would it help if I drove?"

"Not really. Driving gives me something to concentrate on besides my back."

Sensing that he wouldn't be comfortable being chauffeured around by a woman, she wasn't surprised by his answer. "Then I guess I'll get back in the car. Let me know if you change your mind."

He didn't, of course, and within minutes, they were back on the road. Blatantly watching the stiff way he held himself, Sydney could do nothing but shake her head. Stubborn man. Didn't he know it wasn't a weakness to admit that you needed help once in a while? If they put the back seat down, he could stretch out and be much more comfortable, but she didn't even suggest it. If he wouldn't let her help him drive, there was no way he was going to lie down.

How he made it all the way to the city without stopping again, Sydney never knew. His back had to be killing him—his fingers had a death grip on the steering wheel and even in the poor light, she could see the beads of sweat that had popped out on his brow. Just watching him hurt.

Then the lights of Tucson appeared on the distant horizon, glowing like a beacon in the night, and there was no question of slowing down, let alone stopping. Within minutes, they had reached the city limits and Dillon was glancing at her for directions. "I assume you know where we're going?"

She nodded. "The northeast side. Take the next exit."

* * *

The house where Juan Martinez was hiding out was a simple, unassuming white frame home that sat in the middle of an older neighborhood that was showing the signs of age. Around the corner, the nearby strip centers were going to seed, and respectable businesses that had once been the lifeblood of the community were slowly moving out, leaving space for cheap bars and saloons and the type of riff-raff that always brought a neighborhood down.

Pulling up in front of the house, Dillon cut the motor and lights, then took a quick but thorough inventory of their surroundings. The street was quiet and dark, with the nearest streetlight half a block away at the corner. From what he could see, most of the backyards appeared to be fenced, but it was the shadowy alley those fences bordered that could present a problem. As far as Juan was concerned, he and Sydney were strangers. If he felt threatened by their unexpected presence, the alley presented a perfect escape route.

Turning back to Sydney, he said, "Since we're not exactly expected, I suggest we play it safe. You take the front door and I'll cover the back."

"You think Juan'll try to give us the slip?"

He shrugged. "There's no telling. According to what you told me about your conversation with his girlfriend, he's terrified of something. He could freak out the second we knock on the door, and we didn't come all this way to lose him now. Let's go."

Her heart in her throat, Sydney stepped onto the narrow front porch as Dillon made his way to the back, the unlocked gate making no more than a faint clinking noise as he opened it, then closed it behind him. Two houses down, a dog barked, and Sydney suddenly had this horrible image of someone spying Dillon skulking around in the dark and calling the police. Quickly knocking on the door, she prayed Dillon was ready.

The man who answered the door was small and wiry and pushing sixty. He had the bearing of a former Marine—shoulders back, spine snapped straight, confidence visible with every breath he took—and Sydney had only to look at him to know why Juan would have run to him for help. He didn't look like the kind of man who would back down from a fight.

Making no effort to open the screen door that separated them, he surveyed her with eyes that missed little. "Yes? What can I do for you?"

"Mr. Hunter? I'm Sydney O'Keefe." Pulling her press pass from her purse, she flashed it for him. "I spoke to your niece this afternoon in Lordsburg and she gave me your address. I wonder if I might come in and talk to you for a minute?"

He didn't budge. "My niece?"

Not the least affronted, Sydney gave him high marks for being so cautious. "Yes. Lisa told me about Juan, Mr. Hunter. His parents are worried about him—"

He didn't let her finish. His expression shuttered, he moved to shut the door. "You made the long drive from Lordsburg for nothing, Ms. O'Keefe. I have no idea what you're talking about."

"Wait! Dammit—"

"We appreciate your efforts, Mr. Hunter," Dillon said from behind her, suddenly joining her on the porch, "but as you can see, they're not necessary. We mean Juan no harm."

Whirling, Sydney gasped at the sight of the frightened, defiant boy at Dillon's side. "He decided to cut out the back way when he heard you wanted to come in," Dillon told her.

"I suggested he might want to at least hear us out before he took off again."

Glancing past her to the man who had pulled the door wide the second he'd spied Juan, he met his suspicious gaze head-on and introduced himself. "I know this probably sounds like a line of bull to you, sir, but the sheriff of Hidalgo County asked me to look for Juan, and no one's going to hurt him while I'm around. If you don't believe me, I'll give you Sheriff Whitaker's phone number and you can call him yourself."

His piercing gaze jumped between Sydney and Dillon. Tony Hunter liked to think he was a shrewd judge of character. If the somber man at Juan's side had wanted to harm him, he could have done it when he intercepted him in the backyard. Unlocking the screen door, he pushed it open. "Please come in," he said. "We've obviously got a lot to talk about."

His host may have accepted their story, but apparently Juan was keeping his own counsel. The minute everyone was seated in the simply furnished living room, he said coldly, "I don't care who sent you, I've got nothing to say."

His chin was thrust out belligerently, his dark eyes rebellious. Exchanging a speaking glance with Sydney, Dillon sat back and said lightly, "Fine. If you don't want to tell us why you ran away, that's your choice. We're certainly not going to hold a gun to your head or anything."

"Of course not," Sydney added indignantly. "You have your reasons, whatever they are, and you're entitled to your privacy. We'll just assure your parents and the sheriff that you're fine and keep your whereabouts to ourselves."

The boy blanched. "My parents—"

"They've been worried sick about you," she continued as if he hadn't spoken. "When Bryan Fitzgerald turned up dead, your mother was so afraid the same thing was going to happen to you that the doctor had to give her a sedative. But she's fine now," she assured him airily, deliberately laying it on thick. "I'm sure she'll stop worrying once she learns that you just ran away because you weren't happy at home anymore."

He winced as if she'd slapped him. "It wasn't like that."

"No? Well, you have your reasons, whatever they are. Just as long as whoever killed Bryan Fitzgerald isn't after you, we can go home with a clear conscience." Gathering up her purse, she turned to Dillon. "If we want to get back in time to make a report to the sheriff and Juan's parents tonight, we'd better get going."

"Wait!"

At the boy's strangled cry, Dillon lifted a dark brow. "Is there a message we can give your parents for you, son?"

"I..." He looked around the living room, but his eyes were unfocused, locked in horror on another night, another house. "I had to run," he whispered hoarsely. "I wasn't supposed to go to the quarry—I didn't even have a bike. But I liked to watch the other kids and I was on my way there that night when I ran into Bryan." He swallowed convulsively. "He was on his way to the quarry, too, but first he had to stop at the old Stanton place. A guy he met at the Teen Canteen was going to give him some drugs."

"Give?" Dillon asked sharply. "Are you sure about that?"

He nodded. "That's what he said. I didn't want any part of that kind of garbage, but it was on our way, so while Bryan went inside, I waited outside."

When he hesitated, Sydney touched his arm. "It's all right, Juan. You can tell us the rest of it. What happened next?"

"I got curious and looked in the window." Blinking, as if coming out of a trance, he looked at her in growing horror. "Whatever he gave Bryan, it killed him—" he snapped his fingers "—just like that." Tears suddenly flooded his eyes. "I must have made a noise...I don't remember. But suddenly this guy was coming toward me." Unable to sit still, he jumped up as if he were going to bolt any second. "I ran. I had to. He told me he was going to kill me. How could I go home?"

Chapter 4

The boy's story was a variation on a theme Dillon had heard a million times before, and he didn't like this version any more than he had liked the others. Kids and drugs, in over their heads and at the mercy of low-life pushers who were no better than pond scum. Where was it going to end? It was because of kids like Juan that he'd gotten into the DEA in the first place. And it was because of victims like Bryan Fitzgerald that he'd known the day was coming when he would have to make a choice between the job and his own sanity. A man could only deal with so much death and greed before he became as inured to it as the bastards he was trying to catch. But before he could make the final decision to get out, Carlos Santiago had made it for him by shooting him in the back.

"You don't have to hide out like a fugitive on the run, son," he told the boy huskily. "The DEA can keep you safe until this is all over. I know some people in the Tucson office. Why don't you let me call them for you?"

For a moment, he thought the boy was going to jump at the chance, but then the hope that flared in his dark eyes faded and tears trailed silently down his thin cheeks. "I can't. If word got out I went to the DEA, my parents could be in danger."

"No one's going to know but us," Sydney said quickly. "You don't have to worry about this hitting the morning papers because that's not going to happen."

"And your parents will be protected," Dillon added. "The Tucson office will send someone to Lordsburg to pick them up and bring them to a safe house where the three of you can be together. All of you will be safe, Juan. I promise. I used to work for the DEA, and I know what I'm talking about. You're a valuable witness...the *only* witness that can identify the pusher who killed Bryan. The agency's not going to let anything happen to you or your parents."

Tony Hunter, silent until then, said, "You know you're welcome to stay here as long as you like, Juan, but I can't protect you the way government agents can. And if Ms. O'Keefe and Mr. Cassidy found you this quickly, there's a good chance Bryan's killer will, too."

He spoke nothing less than the truth, and they all knew it. Agitated, the boy turned back to Dillon, his dark eyes pleading for reassurance. "What if he's watching my parents' place? He could follow them—"

"The agent that picks them up will be prepared for that. He'll know how to lose a tail and won't go to the safe house until he's absolutely sure that no one's following him. You can trust him, son."

"Why can't *you* do it?"

Surprised, Dillon was taken aback. "Collect your parents? Because I'm not an agent anymore." And he couldn't guarantee that he could keep anyone safe, not when the bullet in his back could take him out at any moment. Ignoring the bitterness that leaked like acid into his gut, he said stiffly, "The best thing you can do for yourself and your parents is put yourself in the hands of people who have been trained to deal with this type of thing. I was more of a field operative. So what do you say? Should I call them for you?"

When it came to choices, the boy really had none. Unable to hide his apprehension, he swallowed thickly. "I—I guess you'd better."

When Juan left the security of the small house for an unknown destination thirty minutes later, he looked vastly relieved. Pete Salazar, the agent who accompanied him, was hard-nosed and tough. The minute he'd introduced himself to Juan, he'd assured him that he was more than qualified to protect him. He had a black belt in karate and was a crack shot. No one, not even the president himself, was getting near Juan without his okay.

Standing on the sidewalk watching the taillights of Salazar's car disappear into the night, Dillon thanked God that the boy hadn't asked how long he would have to stay in the safe house. He was safe for now, but the son of a bitch who had killed Bryan Fitzgerald was still out there, still free. Until he was captured, none of the kids of Hidalgo County were completely safe. Especially Juan Martinez.

Turning to Tony Hunter, who had walked out to the Suburban with him and Sydney, he held out his hand. "Thank you for your cooperation, sir. I'm pretty sure that I can speak for the Martinezes when I say that they're extremely grateful to you."

"I don't know about that," he countered ruefully, returning his handshake. "Once they hear the whole story, they'll probably be more inclined to string me up for not insisting that Juan call them. But he was so terrified that any contact with him would put them in danger, I couldn't take the chance that he might be right."

"I'm sure they'll understand," Sydney said. "After all, what's important here is that he's alive. And that's mainly due to the fact that you took him in and kept him safe. That's more than a lot of people would have done."

"It's the only way I could sleep nights," he said simply. "But I must admit, I'm glad he's in the hands of professionals now. My nerves are shot!"

Thanking him again for his help, they left soon after that and headed back to Lordsburg with Dillon once again behind the wheel. He still had the long drive to get through, but his thoughts weren't on the pain that was sure to come but rather on Juan and what he had told them about Bryan Fitzgerald's death. It just didn't make sense. A pusher was out to make money—he didn't give *anything* away. And he didn't build up his business by killing off potential customers. So why did he give the boy something so lethal that it had killed him almost instantly?

As if she read his mind, Sydney shifted in the seat so that she was half-angled against the passenger door to face him. "You know, something's not right here. The Fitzgerald boy was probably after some crack, but it doesn't sound like that's what he got. What kills that fast?"

"High-dollar stuff," he said promptly. "And you don't usually buy that kind of trash on the streets, at least not in a one-horse town like Lordsburg."

"But Bryan didn't buy anything," she reminded him. "What I can't figure out is why a pusher would give something that expensive—and deadly—away. Unless his goal was something other than profit." Like murder. Expectation tightening the muscles of her stomach in that old familiar way that warned her there was a story here—a *big* one—she shivered. "I don't like the sound of this."

"I don't, either," Dillon said, reaching for his cellular phone. "I'd better call Riley."

The minute his friend came on the line, he said, "I've got good news and bad. Which do you want first?"

"The good," Riley retorted. "I've got a feeling I already know the bad."

"Juan Martinez is at a DEA safe house, presumably in Tucson...though I didn't verify that with the agent who escorted him there," he quickly added. "His parents will be joining him later this evening and the three of them will stay there until it's safe for them to return home."

Quickly and succinctly, he then gave him the bad news, sticking to the high points when he repeated Juan's accounting of Bryan Fitzgerald's death. "It sounds like the kid dropped dead immediately," he concluded.

"I'm not surprised," Riley said grimly. "I just got the coroner's report on Bryan. There's no question that the kid O.D'd on some exotic drug nobody's ever seen in these parts before. The coroner said he never had a chance."

In all his years in the DEA, Dillon had only run into such a sophisticated drug a few times, and then only in major cities like Miami and New York. How the hell had something that rare found its way to a town that was so small it didn't even have its own hospital?

When he asked Riley that same question, he didn't have an answer, either. "I know just about every dopehead in the county, and believe me, if any of them was into this kind of garbage, I'd know it."

"So you think an outsider's responsible? Maybe some sleaze just passing through on his way to L.A.?"

"I wish to hell I could say yes, but at this point, who knows? Up until now, we've been looking at this thing every way but the right way." Disgusted, he sighed heavily. "Stop by my office as soon as you get back in town. We've got a lot to talk about.''

Sydney expected him to give her a quick recap of Riley's side of the conversation the minute he broke the connection, but he only absently returned the flip phone to his pocket, his eyes never leaving the interstate as they left the lights of Tucson far behind. Lost in his thoughts, he didn't even seem to be aware of her at his side.

Staring at his hard-edged profile in the dark, she should have been thoroughly irritated with him—he had to know she was dying to know Riley's reaction to the latest developments in the case—but she found herself distracted by the man himself. He had the kind of dark good looks that were complimented by the night. With his gray eyes thoughtful and a day's growth of beard shadowing his lean, square-cut face, he was rugged, sexy. A phantom figure touched with mystery.

And she'd never been able to resist a mystery.

Horrified by the thought, she cursed the sudden pounding of her heart and ordered herself not to be an idiot. Dillon Cassidy was the type of man she avoided like the plague—bossy and opinionated, he had no respect for the work she thrived on and only suffered her presence because she hadn't given him much choice. She'd do well to remember that.

Hugging that thought to her as though it were a shield that could protect her heart, she straightened in her seat and deliberately broke the silence that threatened to stretch into eternity. "Well? What was that all about?"

Dragging his attention from the road, he glanced over at her, the furrowed lines creasing his forehead easing slightly as his eyes met hers. "Riley got the coroner's report back on Bryan Fitzgerald."

"And?"

"The cause of death was some fancy designer drug."

After their discussion earlier, Sydney wasn't surprised by that announcement, but her stomach knotted at the thought of something so deadly being available to kids on the streets of her town. "Riley thinks the pusher was just someone passing through?"

"That's what he's hoping. But these days, drug lords are pushing their operations into small towns all over the country—there's no getting away from it. Until we know more about Bryan's killer, we can't rule out anything."

Her mind working furiously, Sydney frowned. "I still don't get it. No matter who this guy is, he had to know what kind of drug he was dealing with. Which means he knew exactly what he was doing when he gave it to Bryan. He meant to kill him. But why? It sounds like he didn't even know him."

Dillon wasn't surprised that she'd immediately jumped on the one point that had been nagging him ever since he'd heard Juan's account of the murder. There'd never been any question that the lady was sharp as a tack. "It could have been a simple case of an overdose," he began.

"But you don't think so."

It wasn't a question but a flat statement of fact. He didn't bother to deny it. "No."

"So what do you think? You were with the DEA. And don't look at me like that," she said when he shot her a scowl. "I'm just curious. You were the one who told Juan you worked in the field. I imagine your work must have brought you into close contact with more than your fair share of scumbags over the years. What kind of mind-set do these characters have? Are they completely amoral?"

"Sydney—"

Ignoring his warning tone, she said reflectively, "I don't know how you stood it. The constant danger must have been incredibly nerve-racking. Is that why you retired? Because you were sick of putting your life on the line for something that never seemed to get any better?"

Casting her a quick glance, Dillon had to admit that she was damn clever. In the dark, warm confines of the front seat, she sounded like an old friend, the kind he could discuss just about anything with. Her tone invited confidences, her eyes secrets. If he hadn't been so aware of who and what she was, he could have easily made the mistake of trusting her.

"Why does anybody leave a job they love?" he countered, then neatly turned the tables on her. "Why did you leave Chicago? You worked for the *Daily News,* didn't you? From what I heard, you were the best reporter they had. So how'd you end up in Lordsburg? You get fired or what?"

He was teasing, hoping to distract her from her own line of questioning, and couldn't have been more surprised when she answered seriously, "Something like that."

Stunned, he jerked his gaze from the road only long enough to see if she was pulling his leg. "You're kidding."

She laughed, but the sound didn't hold much humor. "That's what I said. But it was no joke."

She told him then about Beth Jenkins, the woman she'd considered her closest friend at the paper, the Judas who had set her up, then stabbed her in the back. "Looking back on it, I can't believe I was so stupid. I knew how ambitious she was, how she'd do just about anything to get her byline on the front page. But she was like a sister to me. Or at least I thought she was. Boy, was the joke on me."

"She framed you."

"Oh, yeah." She laughed shakily. "And like a fool, I walked right into it. She'd just sat down to write a story on a murder trial she was covering when she supposedly got a tip on a big political scandal that was about to break wide open. Writing the story itself wasn't going to take all that long, but her notes from the trial were on tape and needed to be transcribed. I offered to do it for her since I was at loose ends, and she agreed.''

Already suspecting what was coming next, Dillon took his foot off the accelerator as they approached the exit for a rest area. Staring out at the night, Sydney hardly noticed. "Let me guess," he said. "She didn't have a hot tip at all, did she?"

"Evidently not. I took her tape recorder to my desk and was working on her notes, and the next thing I know, she's back with my editor and shrieking that I'm stealing her story."

"And he believed her?" Dillon demanded incredulously as he braked to a stop under a light. "Good God, that had *setup* written all over it. Was the man blind or what?"

"You'd have to know Beth," she said dryly. "She could cry real tears at the snap of a finger, and she played the scene for everything it was worth. He wasn't the only one who believed her."

The muscles of his back were as tight as the strings of a steel guitar, demanding that he move, but something in Sydney's tone warned him there was more to this story than the betrayal of a friend. Shifting in his seat so that he was angled toward her, he frowned at the disillusionment that took all the sparkle out of her blue eyes. In the short time he'd known her, she'd irritated him, angered him, intrigued him... always with a glint in her eyes. He found, to his chagrin, that he missed it.

"Like who?" he demanded, not liking the direction of his thoughts. "Friends? Family? Lovers?"

"Fiancé," she corrected. "Now ex-fiancé."

So there had been a man in her life. He shouldn't have been surprised—she was a damn good-looking woman—but just thinking about her with some muscle-flexing idiot irritated the hell out of him. And for the life of him, he didn't know why. Giving her a hard look, he said, "You dumped the guy."

"You're damn right I dumped him," she said with a laugh. "And then I got the evidence I needed to clear my name."

He nodded. He'd expected nothing less from her. "Good for you."

Surprised, she lifted a delicately arched brow, a teasing grin tugging at the corners of her mouth. "Excuse me? For a minute there, it sounded like you actually approved of something I've done. But that couldn't be right—you don't like reporters. I guess my ears were playing tricks on me."

Fascinated by the mischief dancing in her eyes, he drawled, "Cute, Ms. O'Keefe. Real cute."

"And now flattery. My goodness, I don't know if I can stand the shock of it." Her hand pressed dramatically to her heart, she flashed her dimples at him. "It must be the stress of this case. It's getting to you, isn't it? Maybe you should let me drive for a while. You can't be at all well."

She was flirting with him, the little minx, and enjoying every second of it. Unable to take his eyes from the laughter skimming her delicate features, he told himself not to take her seriously. She was just teasing, getting back some of her own for him slamming the door in her face when she turned up uninvited on his doorstep last night. It didn't mean a damn thing.

But even as the logic of such reasoning registered, she suddenly seemed too close, her smile too inviting, the Suburban—in spite of its size—too intimate. He had this crazy need to reach for her, to haul her close and trace the curve of her mouth, to taste her. Just once, a voice in his head tempted. What could it hurt? All he had to do was touch her—

Suddenly realizing his fingers were itching to do just that, he drew back as if stung, silent curses ringing in his ears. He had a damn bullet in his back that might as well have been a time bomb, and one day when he least expected it, it was going to shift and he wouldn't be worth a damn to anyone, especially a woman. He knew that, accepted the inevitability of it. So what the devil was he doing sitting here thinking about kissing Sydney O'Keefe?

Fumbling for his door handle, he said hoarsely, "You're right. My back is burning like a house afire. I need to walk." Breaking out of the Suburban like a man escaping the bowels of hell, he slammed the door behind him and walked away as quickly as his tight back muscles would allow.

He needed some breathing space and the cold night air helped. But after ten minutes of solitary pacing, he still couldn't draw in a breath without the remembered scent of her filling his lungs and tormenting his senses. It was damn frustrating and there wasn't a hell of lot he could do about it. His back was feeling better and he couldn't stay out there all night. Disgusted, he returned to the Suburban.

The easy teasing they'd shared was a thing of the past after that. Dillon slid behind the wheel without a word, the dome light revealing the stern set of his mouth and a cold reserve in his eyes before he shut his door, enclosing them in darkness once again. Then they were racing toward Lordsburg, and neither one of them could seem to think of anything to say.

The pressure of his foot on the speedometer consistently keeping the needle hovering nearly ten miles over the speed limit, Dillon told himself he couldn't get her home fast enough. Their bargain was complete—Juan was safe. Once he dropped her off at her house, he could finally wash his hands of the lady for good. It couldn't happen too soon as far as he was concerned.

But after his back forced him to stop one more time, then the lights of Lordsburg finally came into view, the relief he expected to feel just wasn't there. Instead, he found himself thinking that there was little chance that he would enjoy her company again. Oh, they'd see each other in passing. Lordsburg wasn't New York or Chicago, where you seldom saw a familiar face on the street. Everyone was extended family in one way or another, and most people were friendly to a fault. He'd run into her at the grocery store or gas station—in such a small town, it was inevitable. But they wouldn't talk, not really. Like strangers, they'd throw up a hand in greeting, and that would be about it.

As he pulled up before her house and parked, he found that particular image damn disturbing. Then she turned to him, her expression far more somber than usual. Unwittingly, she echoed his thoughts. "Well, I guess this is it." The porch light she'd left burning picked up the rueful glint in her eyes. "It was . . . interesting."

That was one way to describe it. "I guess I'll read all about it in the morning paper."

She glanced at the clock on the dashboard. "Maybe. I'll have to hurry . . . ."

That was his cue to say good-night and let her go. It was what he should have done. But when the silence started to hum and she hesitated, her eyes locked with his as she felt behind her for the door latch, he knew he wasn't going to be able to let her go that easily. It was stupid and he didn't doubt that he was going to regret every second of what he was about to do, but there were some things a man had to do to be able to sleep at night. And kissing Sydney O'Keefe was one of them. Cursing his curiosity, he reached for her.

He saw her eyes widen, heard her breath catch in her throat and found himself grinning. He hadn't planned it, but it was payback time for her earlier teasing, and the lady wasn't expecting it. Lifting a dark brow, his eyes glinted down into hers. "Surprised?" he murmured.

Recovering quickly, she didn't try to pull away but returned his gaze steadily, her blue eyes dancing with naughtiness. "I'll let you know in a few minutes."

It was an out-and-out challenge, one that no man with any blood in his veins could refuse. His fingers tightening to draw her closer, he murmured, "You do that," and covered her mouth with his.

He'd meant to knock the little tease out of her shoes with a kiss that would curl her toes—it was no more than she asked for. But the second his lips touched hers and his arms closed around her, a need he had been trying to ignore for hours hit him from the blind side. Heat shuddered through him, warming his skin, pooling in his loins, clouding his brain, making it impossible to think, to remember why he shouldn't be doing this. Nothing mattered but holding her, tasting her.

His tongue dipping and swirling with hers in the dark wetness of her mouth, he never consciously ordered his hands to move, but suddenly they were in the soft fire of her hair, holding her still before him so he could take the kiss deeper even as his lungs were straining for air. His heart beat a roar in his ears, all he could think of was the urgency burning in his blood. He didn't want it to end. Not yet.

He was a man who knew how to kiss.

Somewhere in the far distant recesses of the gray matter that usually kept her out of trouble, the thought blinked like a warning light, but Sydney was in no shape to heed it. Aside from a rare peck on the cheek from one of the cowboys she occasionally shot pool with, it had been four years since she'd been kissed. But if *this* was a kiss, then what she'd experienced before, she was quickly learning, had been nothing more than the press of one mouth to another. Lord, what was this man doing to her?

Her head was spinning, a need unlike anything she'd ever known burning deep in the core of her. She wanted to sink into the sensations, into him, to melt like chocolate in the sun and lose herself in his passion. Her heart pounding heavily in her breast, she crowded closer and told herself this was crazy, sheer insanity. Any second now she was going to come to her senses and end this madness.

But *he* was the one who abruptly decided enough was enough and broke the kiss. Brought back to earth with a jolt, she opened her eyes to find herself draped all over him, the windows of the Suburban fogging, and his gray eyes, dark and disturbing, searching hers, seeing all the way to her soul.

"Well?"

The deep, husky timbre of his voice slid down her spine like the stroke of his hand. Her brain still mush, she looked up at him in confusion. "Well, what?"

A sudden grin tugged up one corner of his mouth, amusement crinkling his eyes. "You said you'd let me know if I surprised you," he reminded her. "I guess I did."

He was altogether too cocky, too pleased with himself. And the kiss that had just shaken the ground under her didn't seem to have affected him at all. Irritated, mortified to realize that she still had her arms draped around him, she pushed him away and scrambled to her side of the bench seat, silently cursing herself for a fool. What in the world had gotten into her? The man didn't even appear to like her, and most of the time she wasn't exactly crazy about him, either. He was moody and far too secretive, and the last time she let her guard down with a man, she got hurt. That wasn't a mistake she intended to repeat...even if he did kiss like a lover straight out of her dreams.

Hot color burning her cheeks, she struggled for nonchalance and failed miserably. "I wouldn't let it go to your head if I were you," she said tartly. "It's nothing personal. I don't have much of a head for liquor, antihistamines or long drugging kisses. They wipe me out every time."

His grin deepened. "Oh, really? You have this response to every man you kiss, do you?"

"You're darn right," she retorted flippantly. "Sorry if that bruises your ego, but I believe in being honest with a man. It was just a kiss, no big deal. Nothing to lose any sleep over."

It was an out-and-out lie and they both knew it. Wicked laughter gleaming in his eyes, Dillon gazed speculatively at her mouth. "You sure? Maybe we should try it again."

He made her laugh—drat the man—and that made him far too dangerous. Quickly gathering up her things before he could tempt her into changing her mind, she pushed open her door. "Nice try, Cassidy," she tossed over her shoulder with a grin. "But I'm not interested. If you want to run an experiment, go find yourself a lab rat. Science isn't my thing."

She was gone in a flash, hurrying up the walk to her front door without a backward glance. Watching her disappear inside, Dillon couldn't help but chuckle. All that sass in such a tempting package. The lady was something else. And if she hadn't bolted when she had, he would have had no choice but to haul her back into his arms and kiss her again just to prove that she wasn't nearly as indifferent as she tried to pretend.

And that could have been nothing but a mistake. She was too tempting, too bewitching, too damn provocative. And in spite of all his denials to the contrary, he wanted her...much more than he should. He could admit it now that she wasn't within touching distance. And thank his lucky stars that the little bargain they'd made to work together was now null and void. Because if he'd had to spend much more time alone with the lady, he had a feeling he'd have been hard-pressed not to do something stupid...like give in to the fire she lit in his blood with just that flirty grin of hers.

Riley was waiting for him at the sheriff's office, killing time doing paperwork. The minute he spied him in the doorway, he pushed to his feet. "I was beginning to wonder if you were going to make it back tonight. You okay?"

"Yeah." The pain in his back more persistent than usual because of the long hours driving and the too few breaks he'd taken, he shook his head at the chair Riley pulled over for him. "Thanks, but I need to move around. I've been sitting down too much as it is."

Riley could relate to that. It was pushing midnight, and his workday had started at nine that morning. Moving to the coffeepot, he poured them both a cup, gave Dillon one, then sank tiredly into the chair behind his desk. "Okay, tell me more about this pusher. Juan said Bryan met him at the Teen Canteen?"

"Actually, I think he ran into him outside the Canteen," Dillon replied, taking a cautious sip of the steaming coffee. "According to Juan, Bryan was riding by on his bike, heading for McDonald's, when this character asked him where the nearest garage was. He claimed his transmission was acting up and he was stuck here until he could get it fixed. They got to talking, and that's when the guy mentioned that he had this fantastic nose candy and if Bryan wanted to try it, he could stop by the old Stanton place and have a snort for free.''

Riley's jaw tightened. ''When are these kids going to learn that nothing's free in this world? Everything's got a price. I hope to God Juan got a good look at this character.''

Dillon nodded. ''Oh, yeah. Listen to this—he's got red hair, a beard and an eye patch. If he was stupid enough to hang around, he ought to stand out like a sore thumb.''

Riley arched a brow. ''An eye patch, hmm? Well, that's different. Any chance it was a disguise? I've been here twelve years and thought I knew everyone there was to know in these parts. The last time I saw anyone with an eye patch was in *Lonesome Dove.*''

''Your guess is as good as mine,'' he said with a shrug. ''The kid claimed it looked real, but it was getting dark and he was outside the Stanton house looking in.''

''I'll check with José at the garage tomorrow to see if he's had any strangers in needing transmission work or even seen anyone who meets that description. But the chances of anyone new to town knowing about the Stanton place are pretty rare. It isn't exactly on a main thoroughfare, and it'd be pretty hard to stumble across it by accident since the house isn't visible from the road.''

As restless as Dillon, Riley rose to his feet to pace, his coffee forgotten on his desk. ''You realize this has all the makings of a first-class nightmare, don't you? We don't have a clue who this bastard is, where he comes from, even if he's still in the county, which I hope to God he's not. Because if he's setting up an operation here, he's got some other agenda in mind than making money or he never would have killed poor Bryan. And I've got to tell you, that scares the hell out of me. There's a lot of naive kids in this town.

If this jackass decides to offer some of them the same nose candy he gave Bryan, there's going to be hell to pay.''

His face somber, the bullet in his back a constant reminder of just what drug lords and their underlings were capable of, Dillon didn't want to think about the kind of disaster Riley was talking about, but he'd learned a long time ago that burying your head in the sand only made a problem worse. "I talked to Pete Salazar about the DEA coming in on the case, but the Tucson office is understaffed and overworked, and we'd need a hell of a lot more than an isolated overdose to get someone out here. So it looks like we're on our own, at least for now.''

Riley nodded, not surprised. "Then we'll hit the ground running first thing in the morning. I'll meet you at the Stanton place at eight and we'll go over it inch by inch and see what we can turn up. Not only did the bastard meet Bryan there and kill him, at some point he had to take his body out and dump it at the quarry. Unless he's damn good at covering his tracks, he's bound to have left at least one clue.''

Following the directions Riley gave him to the Stanton place, Dillon pulled up at the barred entrance to the deserted ranch just after dawn the following morning. He hadn't slept worth a damn, thanks to a particularly annoying strawberry blonde and a kiss he couldn't forget, and work was the only thing he could think of to get her out of his head.

Leaving his Suburban parked by the side of the two-lane road, he approached the ranch entrance on foot and searched the gravel drive for signs of recent use. According to Riley, the ranch itself had been abandoned years ago, which explained the broken-down fences, washed-out drive and general air of disrepair about the place. What that didn't explain was the tire tracks in the dirt near the cattle guard.

Squatting down, Dillon pulled a notebook from his jacket pocket and quickly sketched the tread pattern. There were, he knew, several ways the tracks could have gotten there. Anyone could have pulled over at the ranch entrance to turn around. The only problem was that the tracks didn't begin and end at the pavement—they came from the other side of the gate and couldn't have been over a week old or the last rain would have washed them away.

The slimeball had been here recently—he could practically smell him. And his nose was seldom wrong, he silently acknowledged as he pushed to his feet. Ignoring the No Trespassing signs posted next to the locked gate, he ducked down and slipped between the fence's sagging rows of barbed wire that wouldn't keep a child out, let alone a psychotic drug dealer who appeared to be, for some ungodly reason, bent on murder.

"Damn!" Scowling at the Suburban parked on the side of the road, Sydney didn't have to ask where Dillon was. She'd known that he'd investigate the Stanton place just as soon as he got the opportunity, but she'd hoped to get in and out before he suspected she was anywhere in the vicinity. So much for good intentions.

Disgusted, she considered going back into town and coming back later, but dammit, she had as much right to be here as he did! And why should she have to come back just because he was here?

Because you don't want to face the man after the way you went up in flames in his arms last night, a voice snidely said in her head. *Face it, honey, he's got you running scared.*

"The hell he does," she muttered to herself. She didn't run from anything, especially a man—she didn't care how good a kisser he was! Pulling up behind his Suburban, she parked and grabbed her camera, then hurried over and squeezed through the fence before she could question the wisdom of her defiance. Her chin set at a don't-mess-with-me angle, she started walking.

The house where Bryan Fitzgerald had met his death turned out to be little more than a three-room shack that had been severely abused by time and the weather. Every window was broken, the porch had a tendency to lean and the front door was off its hinges. If anyone had lived there in the past twenty years, you couldn't tell it from looking at the place.

Approaching the rickety porch steps, Sydney hesitated, not liking the eerie silence of the place. Where the dickens was Dillon? There wasn't so much as a footstep in the dust that covered the warped floorboards of the porch to show that he'd been there. And that worried her more than she cared to admit. There was no doubt that he could take care of himself under normal circumstances, but there was nothing normal about this case. They didn't know what kind of weirdo they were dealing with, and with Dillon's back bothering him the way that it was, there was no question that when it came to any kind of physical confrontation, he would be at a definite disadvantage. If the killer had been here when he arrived . . .

Alarmed, she didn't even finish the thought, but bolted up the porch steps, her heart in her throat. She'd hardly taken two steps when Dillon suddenly filled the doorway, his expression less than welcoming. "What the devil do you think you're doing here?" he demanded. "This a crime scene. That makes it out-of-bounds to the press."

Her heart jump starting at the sight of him, Sydney felt her knees go weak with relief. He was okay. Thank God! Then his words registered like a cold slap in the face. The press? she fumed, resentment darkening her eyes. After kissing her senseless last night and steaming up the windows of his Suburban, now she was suddenly *the press?* Some nobody reporter he could dismiss with a scowl and a wave of his hand? She didn't think so!

Bristling, her eyes narrowing dangerously, she started toward him, knowing she was asking for trouble and heading straight for it anyway. She was just as disturbed as he was by the passion they'd shared last night, but there was no way she was going to just stand there and let him pretend it had never happened. A girl had her pride, after all!

Her mind made up, she walked defiantly up to the big lug, grabbed him by the ears and kissed him.

Chapter 5

The minute she touched him, the second her mouth settled on his, he stiffened. He didn't push her away, but he didn't respond, either, and for what seemed like an eternity, he just stood there, stiff as a poker, his mouth cold and immobile under hers. Undaunted, Sydney had no intention of letting him discourage her so easily...not after she'd spent the night loving him in her dreams. It was wild and crazy and nothing was ever going to come from it, but there were some things a woman couldn't walk away from without sampling it one more time, and like it or not, Dillon Cassidy was one of them.

Murmuring his name, a yearning she couldn't control seeping through her like warm honey, she leaned into him, her arms circling his neck as she changed the angle of the kiss and, just for a moment, indulged herself. He had, she thought with a sigh, the most incredible mouth. Giving in to temptation, she traced the sensuous curve of his bottom lip with her tongue, stroking him, teasing him, losing herself in the simple pleasure of tasting him.

And as much as he tried to pretend otherwise, he wasn't anywhere close to indifferent. At the first wet glide of her tongue, she felt his start of surprise, the sudden clenching of his teeth on a groan that was hastily swallowed. Encouraged, delighted by the thunderous pounding of his heart against her breast, her own head starting to spin, she daringly nipped at him.

Heat streaked through Dillon like a fireball, scorching him alive, shattering his dogged control. Sucking in a sharp breath, he never remembered moving, but suddenly his hands were at her shoulders, gripping her too tightly. He should have put her away from him then—he would have sworn that was his intention—but as he abruptly started to push her away, his fingers stubbornly refused to release her. Dammit to hell, what was he letting her do to him?

Furious with himself, with her, he glared down at her and told himself to let her go. He might as well have ordered the wind to stop blowing. His mouth flattening with irritation, he grated, "What the hell do you think you're doing?"

Not the least bit intimidated, she grinned up at him. "I thought it was obvious. I'm trying to shake you up, Cassidy. How am I doing?"

Stunned that she even had to ask, he almost laughed at the absurdity of the question. How the hell did she think she was doing? She had to know she was tying him in knots, and he didn't like it one little bit. The whole point of kissing her last night had been to satisfy his curiosity about the lady so he could put an end to this crazy attraction he had for her and get her out of his head once and for all. God, what a joke that was! She could make him ache with nothing more than that mischievous smile of hers, and he didn't even want to think about what she did to him when she kissed him.

Suddenly realizing that his fingers were tightening on her shoulders to pull her back against him, he swore under his breath and snatched his hands back like a kid caught snitching cookies. "If I wanted to be shook up, I'd live in L.A.," he growled. "So keep your kisses to yourself—"

"I think that's an excellent idea if we're going to get any work done today," Riley drawled suddenly from the drive. A crooked grin pushing up one corner of his mouth as he watched them jerk apart in surprise, he lifted a mocking brow. "Am I interrupting something?"

"No!"

"Yes!"

Sending Sydney a glowering look, Dillon repeated, "No, you're not interrupting a damn thing except me trying to reason with a bullheaded woman. Tell her this is a crime scene, Riley."

His lips twitching, he obediently repeated, "This is a crime scene, Syd."

"And I'm a reporter just doing my job," she retorted, returning Dillon's glare with one of her own. "If you've got a problem with that, tough!"

"What I've got a problem with is a pushy redhead—"

"My hair's not red!"

"But you're pushy as hell, right?"

Her chin jutted up at that. "I prefer *persistent,*" she replied snootily.

Feeling as if he were watching a boxing match that was about to get out of hand, Riley hastily swallowed a grin and gave a sharp whistle. "Hey, you two, time out! End of round one. Everybody go to a neutral corner."

They didn't move, but they did shut their mouths, the tension sparking between them as volatile as gasoline on a grass fire. There was obviously a heck of a lot more going on here than who had a right to be there, and Riley couldn't think of two people who deserved it more. But that was none of his business. Sticking to the matter at hand, he said calmly, "Now that we can hear ourselves think, it's my turn to talk. Yes, this is a crime scene, and no, Sydney shouldn't be here until we've had a chance to investigate it. But," he added, holding up his hand when Dillon started to put in his two cents, "ordering her to leave isn't going to do much good. She'll just come back later—"

"You're darn right," she retorted, her smile smug.

"And if she finds something, I want to be here when she does," Riley continued. "Besides, I've got a bone to pick with her about her story in this morning's paper."

Surprised, Sydney couldn't imagine what he had to complain about in her account of Bryan Fitzgerald's death. She'd been careful not to mention Juan's witnessing of the murder or his whereabouts. "What's wrong with that story? I stuck to the facts."

"I don't have a problem with your facts—it's the slant you put on the story. Granted, the sophisticated drug used to kill the Fitzgerald boy is news, but you blew it all out of proportion and made Lordsburg sound like Chicago."

"An innocent boy died, Riley. That alone is always going to stir up the public. The way that Bryan was killed only makes the story more sensational. I didn't have to embellish anything—whoever killed Bryan did that for me."

"I know that," he huffed. "But I just wish you would have tamped down the drug factor. I got calls before I even left the house this morning from people who took one look at the paper and thought a major drug cartel was moving into the area. They're scared, dammit, and when people get scared, they do stupid things."

Dillon frowned. "Are you afraid they're going to go looking for this character on their own?"

"This is the West," he said simply. "You won't find anybody out here who doesn't believe in the right to keep and bear arms and protect what's theirs. You put their kids in danger, and yeah, they'll go after whoever threatens them. But I mean to beat 'em to the punch. What have you found so far?"

"Just tire tracks in the drive," Dillon said, showing him the track design he'd drawn when he'd first arrived. "From what I could tell, no one's been in the front rooms in years. I was just heading for the back when Sydney walked up."

"Then let's check it out. Sydney, I don't have to warn you not to touch anything." Motioning for the two of them to precede him, he followed them inside.

The interior of the house was every bit as bad as the exterior. The roof had leaked in the two front rooms, causing major damage to the ceilings and walls and rotting the wooden floor. Wallpaper hung in dirty strips, shattered glass from the windows crunched underfoot and there was the distinct sign of rodents everywhere. In spite of that, Dillon and Riley went over the two badly damaged rooms systematically, examining every inch before they were finally satisfied that there was nothing there. That left the single large bedroom at the back where, according to Juan, Bryan had met with the pusher and died.

Standing in the doorway, Dillon stared at the empty room and saw nothing that indicated that a young boy had made the biggest mistake of his too-short life here. There were no heavy vibes, no signs of a struggle, nothing but some markings in the thick dust that covered the floor that suggested something...or someone...might have been dragged to the back door. And even that told him little. The footsteps of whoever had done the dragging had been wiped out by whatever was being dragged.

Stepping around him into the room, Riley hunkered down on his heels to study the telltale trail in the dust. It told its own story, but none of the details. "Damn!" he swore in disgust as he pushed to his feet. "Looks like we struck out. The bastard covered his tracks."

"So where do you go from here?" Sydney asked as Dillon followed the dusty path to the back door to examine the threshold.

"We keep looking," Riley said flatly. "And asking questions. There's no such thing as a perfect crime—the bastard's bound to have made a mistake somewhere. And when we find it, we find him. It's that simple."

"*If* he's still here," Sydney said. "Nothing else has happened since Bryan was killed, has it? There've been no reports of increased drug activity in the area, no strangers acting suspiciously. Maybe he took off after he dumped Bryan's body at the quarry. He had to know things were going to heat up around here once the murder was discovered."

Turning from the doorway, Dillon surveyed the scene, his mouth compressed in a flat line, and shook his head. "Whoever this guy is, he's not the type to get shook at the thought of a little heat. If he was, he would have taken off the second that boy dropped dead at his feet, not hung on to the body for a week before dumping it in plain sight. No, he's still here and playing games. He'll strike again before it's over with—he's probably planning it right now."

"Which means we're racing against the clock," Riley added. "I assigned every man I've got to the case the minute I read the coroner's report, but it's a big county and we're stretched so damn thin, it's a joke." Tilting his cowboy hat to the back of his head, he glanced ruefully at Dillon. "I know when I got you into this it was just supposed to be a simple case of tracking down a couple of runaways, but I still need your help, man. How do you feel about being deputized?''

Surprised, Dillon said, "You mean officially? I thought the county was low on funds."

"It is, but I can't keep taking advantage of your generosity, so they can damn well scrape together enough to pay you for your time or they can try finding this sleaze on their own."

Dillon almost told him to stuff the salary—his disability retirement from the government more than met his needs and he was just happy to have an excuse to get out of the house—but Sydney was all but taking notes, and the lady already knew more about him than he'd have liked. "If you want me to carry a badge, fine. But it's not really necessary. When I agreed to this, I knew it could be a long haul. Nothing's changed just because the case has taken a couple of dips and curves."

Sydney, holding her tongue, had heard enough. "Jeez, I wish you hadn't done that, Riley," she teasingly drawled in disgust. "Getting information out of him now is already like pulling teeth. He'll be impossible with a badge."

Chuckling, Riley grinned. "I'm sure you'll find a way to deal with him, Syd. You always have with me."

Unconvinced, she almost laughed at his reasoning. Of course she was able to deal with him! He was easygoing and accommodating and more than willing to let her do her job. And not once in all the years that she'd known him had he ever made her mouth go dry or her knees weak, let alone tempted her to kiss him. The same, unfortunately, could not be said about his best friend.

Ignoring the sudden, wild beating of her heart at the thought, she retorted, "Oh, yeah, I'll deal with him, all right. By going out and digging up the story myself."

Dillon whirled on her as if he couldn't believe he'd heard her correctly. "You can't be serious."

Her eyes narrowed at his tone. "Riley just said he could use all the help he can get," she reminded him. "And even you have to admit I'm pretty good at tracking down leads. I found Juan as fast as you did."

"I don't care if you found Jimmy Hoffa, this isn't a competition, dammit!" he snapped. "You're talking about hunting down a man who has already killed once, and that's crazy. This is a job for professionals, so why don't you back off and let us do our jobs? If you want something to write about, go cover the upcoming spring fashion show at the Tucson Mall this weekend. At least I won't have to worry about you getting killed there."

His cold words struck her like darts, cutting deep. Hurt, she told herself she could take criticism. She put herself on the line every day in the paper, leaving herself open to anyone who didn't like what she had to say, and she handled it just fine. But this wasn't just criticism. It was a casual dismissal of what she did for a living, of who she was... from a man who had, only moments before, been anything but indifferent in her arms. Granted, she'd instigated the kiss, but he'd wanted her...needed her.... She couldn't have been mistaken.

Resisting the need to hug herself, she stood proudly before him. "You don't have to worry about me, period, Mr. Cassidy," she said stiffly. "Believe it or not, I'm quite capable of taking care of myself. Now, if you'll excuse me, I'll get out of your hair."

Stepping past him, she heard him swear, but she didn't spare him a glance. She didn't dare or she might say something she'd regret. Or, worse yet, cry. And dammit, that was something she'd sworn she'd never do again over a man. Not after Adam and the buckets she'd cried over him. The disaster at work—Beth's betrayal—had thrown her for a loop, but it was Adam's lack of faith in her that had devastated her. It had taken her a long time to get over that, but she finally had, and there would be no more tears. Not over Dillon or anyone else.

So she headed for her car, fuming all the way down the rocky drive, clinging to her anger like a toddler hugging a security blanket, trying to convince herself she didn't care if she ever laid eyes on him again.

Getting the insufferable man and his kisses out of her head wasn't as easy as walking away, however. She tried throwing herself into the search for the redheaded pusher, using every minute she could spare away from her regular duties at the paper to scour the county for the man. But three days later, she was still unconsciously looking for Dillon everywhere she went, still waking each morning with hazy dreams of him warming her bed. He couldn't have been more of a distraction if they'd been attached at the hip.

Furious with him, disgusted with herself, she was in the mood for trouble when she went into the paper late Wednesday after investigating a four-car pileup on the interstate. Blake, busy knocking out a story about the local boys' high school basketball team, took one look at her and grinned. "Uh-oh. Somebody had a bad day. What's the matter, Red? Did Harry shoot down your latest masterpiece?"

Plopping down at her desk, she shot him a warning look that would have flattened a lesser man. "Don't start with me, Nickels. I'm not in the mood."

"No kidding? I would have never guessed." Far from discouraged by her attitude, he saved his own copy, then sat back with the expectant grin of a man prepared to enjoy himself. "Who's been giving you a hard time, sweetheart? Give Uncle Blake a name and I'll go beat him up for you."

Her mouth twitched; she couldn't help it. "Thanks, but I can fight my own battles. Haven't you got something better to do than pester me?"

"Not a thing," he laughed. "Trina's gone shopping in Tucson with her sister, and I'm footloose and fancy-free. Whatdaya say you and me and some of the guys go shoot some pool tonight?"

Hesitating, Sydney had to admit she was tempted. She and Blake and some of the cowboys from the Double R met every couple of weeks at the Crossroads Bar for a lively pool tournament, but it had been a while since they'd all gotten together. A night out with the boys did sound like fun. And it might be just what she needed to take her mind off Dillon and a few kisses she'd rather forget.

"I'll meet you at the Crossroads at seven," she said, making a snap decision. "Loser buys the beer."

"You got a deal, girl. Make sure you bring plenty of money. You're going to need it."

Grinning, she said, "You know, that boast might carry a little more weight if you'd ever beaten me. Should I warn you now or later that I'm feeling particularly lucky?" At his groan, she chuckled. "I'll have my money. You just make sure you and the guys have yours." Feeling better than she had in days, she was still smiling twenty minutes later when she finished her story and left to check out a report of missing headstones at the Catholic cemetery.

But that evening, she and the guys were barely into the first game of pool when she knew her friends weren't going to be able to distract her from thoughts of Dillon the way she had hoped. And she couldn't for the life of her figure out why. Blake, with his usual needling wit, kept her on her toes, and Ford and Harley, the Double R ranch hands, were crazy, outrageous flirts. She usually spent most of the evening laughing whenever she was with them. But not tonight.

The Crossroads, a favorite hangout for the local cowboys, was crowded and noisy, and cigarette smoke hung from the ceiling in a thick pall. The jukebox was blaring and the unceasing beat seemed to have taken up residence in her head. Her eyes tearing from the cigarette smoke, Sydney blinked, then took her next shot…only to scratch as the cue ball followed the six ball into the pocket.

"Well, darn!"

Blake exchanged a telling look with Ford and Harley before drawling, "Don't take this wrong, Red, but you're going to be buying a lot of beer tonight if you don't get your head in the game. You feelin' okay?"

"I've just got a headache," she said with a grimace. "It's nothing."

"Maybe not," Ford said, taking her pool cue from her. "But if we're going to beat you, it's not much fun if you're not up to snuff. Go get yourself a drink and relax while we finish this game. Then we'll start over again."

If her temples hadn't been throbbing sickeningly, she would have never agreed to ducking out of a game for such a sissy reason. But in her present condition, she wasn't much fun, and she hated being a wet blanket. "Okay, guys, you've got a deal. Thanks."

Weaving her way through the crowd of cowboys who were standing around the pool tables waiting for a chance to get in on a game, she made her way to the long bar that hugged one entire wall of the building and took a seat at the end near the entrance. The music still blared from the jukebox, but the smoke was less thick there due to the occasional gusts of cool night air that rushed inside whenever anyone pulled open the door. Settling her feet on the brass footrest that ran the length of the bar, she ordered a wine cooler and lifted the cold glass to her left temple as soon as the bartender set it down in front of her. Sighing in relief, she closed her eyes and let the coldness work its magic.

"Headache?"

The quiet question came from the man who sat on her right at the shadowy end of the bar. Barely opening her eyes, Sydney forced a weak smile. "No, thanks. I've already got one."

His chuckle was rough, as if he didn't laugh much. "Then how about an aspirin to go with it? My doctor gave me some samples of this new wonder aspirin that's not on the market yet, and it kicked my migraines just like that." He snapped his fingers right in front of her face. "I never would have believed it if I hadn't tried it myself. So what do you say? If you want one, I've got plenty."

The pounding in her head giving a fair imitation of jungle drums, Sydney was sorely tempted to jump at whatever help she could get. But aspirins—wonder drug or not—had a tendency to act up in her stomach, and she was already feeling miserable enough as it was. Regrettably shaking her head, she said, "Thanks, but I'd better not. I don't have much tolerance for drugs of any kind...especially aspirin."

"Suit yourself," he said with a shrug as he went back to his beer. "If you change your mind, just let me know."

"I'll do that," she promised and closed her eyes again, sure that if she just sat still long enough, the pain would ease.

But the bar seemed to be getting rowdier—and smokier—by the second. The noise intensified, along with the throbbing in her temples, and after another five minutes, all she could think of was getting out of there. Setting her untouched drink down with a snap, she excused herself when she drew a questioning look from the stranger next to her, then escaped outside.

The second she stepped out into the poorly lit parking lot, the cold night air swirled around her, pulling at her hair and whisking the cigarette smoke from her lungs. She'd forgotten her jacket and a shiver raced over her skin, but nothing short of a blizzard could have convinced her to go back inside anytime soon. Hugging herself, she lifted her face to the star-speckled night sky and dragged in a deep breath of relief.

She was still there ten minutes later, chilled but enjoying the silence that engulfed her, when the same guy who'd offered her an aspirin at the bar pushed open the door and stepped outside. His hat was pulled low, all but concealing his face in the darkness, but he saw her and nodded, then made his way to an old pickup almost lost in the black shadows at the far end of the crowded parking lot. Obviously comfortable with the night, he didn't turn his headlights on until he was half a mile down the road.

Marveling that he hadn't run off the road before he'd realized he was driving blind, Sydney turned away and gave serious consideration to going back inside. Her headache was almost gone and the guys were probably wondering what had happened to her. But she really wasn't in the mood for a night out after all, and it would be better for everybody if she just left. She'd just make her excuses—

A sudden shout from inside the bar ripped through the night. Smiling to herself, she wondered if Blake was the one who was exercising his lungs—one beer and he'd sing on the tables if anyone dared him. And the rest of the guys weren't much better. The later it got, the rowdier the crowd got—it happened all the time. But for reasons she couldn't begin to explain, her heart started to pound and she was suddenly afraid. Before she could stop herself, she was rushing toward the entrance.

Bedlam. The place had turned into bedlam. Men were shouting, somewhere near the pool tables a woman screamed incessantly and everybody seemed to be standing flat-footed, craning to see something near the bar. Her stomach starting to churn at the thought of what they were looking at, Sydney pushed through the crowd of tall cowboys.

All her attention focused on the men who blocked her path, she suddenly burst free of the crowd and almost stumbled upon the cowboy writhing on the floor before she had time to stop her forward motion. Alarmed, she froze in her tracks. He was choking.

"Give him room! Has anyone called the Rawlings Clinic? Dammit, somebody help me!"

Kneeling next to the downed man trying to help him breathe, Blake shouted orders as he struggled to loosen the cowboy's collar. But when he ripped the shirt wide open, it didn't help. His hands clutching his throat, his raspy breathing loud in the sudden silence, the stricken man arched up off the wooden floor with a keening cry that chilled the blood of everyone who heard it. A heartbeat later, he was dead.

For what seemed like an eternity, no one moved. As shocked as everyone else, Sydney just stood there, unable to drag her eyes from the dead man, unable to believe what she'd just witnessed. Then Blake slowly pushed to his feet, his usually smiling face haggard as he glanced dazedly around. "Somebody needs to call the sheriff. Harry, have you got something we can cover this poor man with?"

The bartender, jerking to attention, stuttered, "Y-yeah. I—I've got a blanket in my c-car. I'll go get it."

Shoving the phone across the bar to Blake so he could call Riley, he shot out from behind the bar like the devil himself was after him and rushed outside, returning seconds later with an old army blanket he quickly draped over the dead man. The second he straightened from the task, the crowd breathed a collective sigh of relief, and just that quickly, Sydney snapped out of the daze that had held her in its grip. What the devil was she doing just standing here like a ninny? As tragic as it was, a young, apparently healthy man didn't drop dead in the prime of his life without a darn good reason. This was news!

Grabbing her purse, she pulled out the small tape recorder that she depended on as religiously as some women depended on a man and went to work. "Can anybody tell me what happened?" she asked, easing her way through the crowd. "Somebody must have seen something."

She glanced around expectantly, but if anyone saw anything, they weren't willing to talk about it. Blank stares stared back at her, telling her nothing. Frustrated, she turned to Blake, who, as soon as he finished his call to the sheriff, signaled the bartender to pour him a straight shot of whiskey. "Blake?"

Swallowing the drink in a single gulp, he motioned the bartender for another. When he turned to Sydney, he couldn't tell her much more than anyone else. "Sorry, hon, but the boys and me were concentrating on the game and didn't notice anything until the guy fell off his stool and grabbed his throat. I thought he was choking, but the Heimlich maneuver didn't help. And I didn't know what else to do. The next thing I knew, he was dead."

"But there has to be a reason," she insisted. "Did he say anything? Does anyone even know his name?"

"He was a stranger," Harry said suddenly from behind the bar, the lines that furrowed his brow deeper than usual.

"Never seen him before. A quiet sort. He ordered a beer and just sat there nursing it for the last half hour."

"How was he acting before he started choking?" Sydney asked eagerly, setting her tape recorder on the bar. "Was he sick? Did you notice if he had any difficulty breathing?"

He shook his head. "No, nothing. 'Course, I was pretty busy and he was the quiet sort. He didn't draw much attention to himself." He started to shrug, as if to say that was all he could offer, when he suddenly added, "It seems like he did say something though, right before he fell. I was drawing a draft for Jimmy Taylor at the other end of the bar, so I couldn't hear him real good, but if I didn't know better, I'd swear he said aspirin." Scratching his gray head in puzzlement, he looked to Sydney for an explanation. "You think he had a headache or something? Maybe one of those aneurysm things?"

Sydney's heart stopped in midbeat. "Aspirin?" she repeated faintly. "Are you sure he said aspirin?"

"That's what it sounded like, but like I said, I was at the other end of the bar. Hey, are you all right? You're as white as a sheet! Sit down, girl, before you fall flat on your face. Blake, help her—"

"No! I—I'm fine." She swallowed thickly and sank unassisted onto the nearest barstool, her gaze carefully averted from the still, blanket-covered figure on the floor. She wasn't a lily-livered coward who got weak-kneed at the sight of a corpse—she wouldn't have survived a week covering the police beat on the streets of Chicago otherwise. But it wasn't every day that she had that close a call with death, either.

"My doctor gave me some samples of this new wonder aspirin.... If you want one, I've got plenty...."

The words echoed in her ears like a taunt from the devil, deceptively innocent, threatening. Her blood running cold, Sydney shivered...and thanked God that she was alive to

feel anything, even fear. Because every self-preserving instinct she possessed told her that if she'd accepted one of
those new wonder aspirin from the stranger next to her at
the bar, she would have been the one now lying dead on the
floor.

Glancing up to find Blake, Ford and Harley hovering over
her as if they were afraid she was going to pass out cold at
their feet, she smiled weakly. "Really, guys, I'm fine. I just
felt a little dizzy for a second, but it passed. Give me a minute to collect myself, and I'll be raring to go."

She was lying through her teeth and only had to look at
the faces of the three men who surrounded her to know that
she hadn't fooled anyone. A disapproving scowl darkening
his brow, Ford growled, "You're not going anywhere until
Doc Josey or Tate checks you out."

"You're damn right," Harley agreed in a low rumble that
was sandpaper rough. "So you just sit there like a good little girl and wait for the doc. She should be here any second."

But it was fifteen minutes before Tate Rawlings arrived
and by then, Sydney was too antsy to sit still. Someone had
tried to kill her. The thought throbbed in her head like a
smoldering ember. Pale and shaken, she paced, clinging to
the hope that Dr. Rawlings would take one look at the dead
cowboy on the floor and announce that he had died of natural causes.

But it was a vain hope, and she wasn't really surprised
when Dr. Rawlings did a quick examination of the body and
announced somberly, "I can't be certain without a blood
test, but this looks like a drug overdose. Does anyone know
if he had a history of drug use?"

"He was a stranger, ma'am," Harry replied from behind
the bar. "His driver's license says his name's Lawrence Osborn. He's from Silver City, but nobody here's ever seen

him before. We don't know what his habits were, but he did mention something about aspirin before he died.''

On her knees next to the victim, Tate frowned down at the still form one last time before covering it with the blanket and pushing to her feet. ''Aspirin, hmm? I've never heard of anyone dying from a reaction to it, but I guess stranger things have happened. We'll have to wait for the autopsy report to be sure. Has anyone called the sheriff?''

''I did,'' Blake volunteered. ''Right after I called your clinic. Somebody should be here any minute.''

The words were hardly out of his mouth when the sound of a patrol car pulling up outside, sirens blazing, easily reached the occupants of the bar. Seconds later, Dillon strode into the bar with Joe Sanchez, one of Riley's most dependable deputies, right on his heels.

Still seated at the bar, Sydney knew the second he spied her in the crowd. Recognition flaring in his eyes, he stopped in his tracks, shocked. Still jittery and trying to hide it, she was horrified by the need to walk into his arms and just let him hold her. What in the world was wrong with her? she wondered wildly. She wasn't some fainthearted damsel in distress looking for a man to come charging to her rescue. She could take care of herself.

Lifting her chin, she gave him back stare for stare, but when he finally glanced away, she took little satisfaction from the small victory. Then he was taking charge of the situation with the ease of a man who was used to giving orders. ''Joe, let's get this crowd out of here except for the witnesses.'' Turning to Tate, he offered his hand and introduced himself. ''You must be one of the Rawlings doctors. Riley's in Tucson for the evening and asked me to take over in case of any unusual circumstances.''

''Then this definitely qualifies,'' Tate replied. ''A thirty-year-old man doesn't drop dead without a reason.'' She gave him a quick rundown of what the bartender had told her, then her own diagnosis.

He nodded. The coroner would determine the exact cause of death, but his gut told him Tate Rawlings was right. Which made this the second O.D. in a matter of weeks in a part of the country where things like this just didn't happen. Grimly thanking the doctor for getting there so quickly, he turned to face the witnesses that Joe had rounded up and found himself face-to-face with Sydney. Disturbed, wondering what the hell she was even doing there, he avoided her gaze and said tersely, "We'll need to talk to each of you separately. Let's grab that table by the window, Joe, and get started. This could take a while."

That proved to be an understatement of the grossest proportions. Everyone who saw Lawrence Osborn fall off his barstool had to tell what they saw, and each version of the story was more or less the same. By the time Sydney took a seat across the table from him and Joe, Dillon thought he had heard it all. She quickly proved him wrong.

"Lawrence Osborn took some kind of fancy new aspirin that killed him," she announced before either he or Joe could say a word. "And he didn't have it on him when he walked in here."

"How do you know that?" Joe asked with a frown. "Did you talk to him before he died?"

"No, but I was offered that same aspirin and turned it down."

"What?" Slouched in his chair, Dillon straightened as if he'd been poked with a cattle prod. "What the hell are you talking about? Start over, and this time at the beginning. What are you doing here?"

He hadn't meant to ask that—her reasons for being there had nothing to do with the investigation, dammit—but the words just popped out. And before he could call them back, she said, "Blake and I met some of the cowboys from the Double R here to shoot pool. But my head was hurting, so I took a seat at the bar. That's when the guy sitting next to me offered me a new kind of aspirin."

Jealousy hitting him right between the eyes, Dillon heard "Blake" and nothing else. So she was out with that Nickels character she worked with, the sportswriter. If that wasn't just like a fickle woman, he didn't know what was. Get him in a lip lock one day, then three days later, go out with someone else. Irrational fury roiling in his gut, he told himself he didn't give a damn if she played pool or anything else with half the men in the county—what the lady did was her own business. Then the rest of her words registered, and his blood ran cold.

"What guy?" he demanded.

"The guy who left right before Osborn died," she said. "I went outside to get some air and saw him drive off in his pickup. He was hardly out of sight when I heard the shouting inside."

Dillon swore. He wasn't a man who believed in coincidence. He had two bodies and two men without faces who disappeared into the night. Every instinct he possessed told him that the pusher who killed Bryan Fitzgerald with a designer drug and the guy who'd loaned a wonder aspirin to the dead man on the floor were one and the same. And the slippery son of a bitch had just slipped through his fingers.

"What did he look like? Tell me everything you can remember. Would you recognize him again if you saw him? Did he have any distinguishing features? How tall was he?"

He threw the questions at her like a drill sergeant issuing orders, hardly giving her time to draw a breath before he was thinking of something else to ask. Flustered, she finally blurted out in exasperation, "Dammit, Dillon, if you'll let me get a word in edgewise, I'll tell you what I know. But it isn't much. He wore a tattered straw Stetson low on his ears. Other than that, there's not much else I can tell you.''

"Why the hell not? You sat right next to him. You must have looked at him when he offered you the damn aspirin.''

"Of course I looked at him. But he didn't look at me. He kept his head down and sort of stared at his drink. And in case you haven't noticed, there aren't a lot of lights in here, especially near the bar. He was just sort of odd looking. Okay?''

"Odd how?''

"I don't know." She frowned, trying to put her finger on what it was about the man that had struck her as weird. Images played before her eyes like a flashback and just that quickly it hit her. "His hands!" she said excitedly. "His hands didn't fit the rest of him. He was wearing a long-sleeved shirt, and with his hat pulled low, I couldn't see much of him, but I do know that his hair was black. Except on his hands.''

"So?''

"So the hair on his hands was a pale strawberry blond,'' she explained. "Like mine. I don't know about you, but that doesn't add up to me. A person is either a brunette or a blonde, not both. If the man was a natural brunette, then the hair on his knuckles would be dark, not blond. Which means he was either wearing a wig or he dyed his hair. Either way, he was trying to disguise what he really looked like.''

Chapter 6

His gray eyes as cold as ice, Dillon didn't need to hear more. There wasn't a doubt in his mind that the so-called aspirin that had killed the poor cowboy lying dead on the floor was some form of the designer drug that had put a quick end to Bryan Fitzgerald's too-short life. And Sydney had almost taken it. She could have been the one who died—the one he, when he walked in, found stone cold on the floor, her hands clutched to her throat in frozen horror. A giant fist closed over his heart at the thought, threatening to choke him. Then the rage hit him, red-hot. The slimeball wasn't going to get away with it. Not this time.

Reaching across the bar for the phone that Harry kept within reach behind the counter, he quickly called the sheriff's office. When the dispatcher answered, he said hurriedly, "Myrtle, this is Dillon. I need you to issue an APB on a sixties-model white Dodge pickup, partial license 7 GXY—"

"That's Cookie Barshop's truck," she cut in, surprised. "You got ESP or what, Cassidy? Cookie just called in not ten minutes ago. That old pickup is her pride and joy and it seems somebody stole it right out of her driveway, bold as brass. She could hardly talk, she was so mad—"

Wound up tighter than an eight-day clock, Myrtle could, Dillon knew, talk his head off if he gave her the chance. Struggling to curb his impatience, he waited for her to take a breath and said tersely, "I want you to send somebody out to her place to talk to her as soon as you can, Myrtle, but first I need you to get on the radio and issue that all points bulletin. *Now,* Myrtle. Okay? There's no time to lose."

Swallowing the rest of what she was going to say in a single gulp, she said, "Oh…yeah, sure, Dillon. It's as good as done."

Praying she was as good as her word, he hung up, then turned to find Joe Sanchez quietly talking with some of the witnesses who were still milling around. Giving the other man an abbreviated version of his conversation with Myrtle, he said, "I'm going after the bastard. He's probably gotten another vehicle stashed somewhere, and if we don't catch him before he ditches the pickup, we can forget catching him anytime soon. He'll go to ground wherever he's been hiding out and lay low until he's ready to kill again."

"Go on," Joe told him. "I'll hold down things here until the ambulance gets here."

Before the words were even out of his mouth, Dillon was heading for the door, pushing his way through the lingering crowd, every instinct he possessed urging him to hurry. Each second lost was time he wouldn't get back, not when he was trailing a cold-blooded snake in the grass who didn't leave many tracks. Rushing outside, he strode toward his truck as fast as his protesting back would allow and never noticed that Sydney was right behind him.

Tearing out of the parking lot, he headed west, just as Sydney had said the murderer had. The road stretched like a black ribbon before him, disappearing into the night in a straight line that he knew ran for twenty-five miles without so much as a twinge of a curve in it. The speedometer reached sixty, then seventy, and kept on climbing as he searched the distant horizon for the revealing glint of tail-lights, but the darkness before him remained unbroken. There wasn't so much as a security light to relieve the all-concealing night.

Since there were no side roads to turn down for at least another fifteen miles, there was no way the perp could have turned off. Which meant one of two things. He was either farther ahead of him than he'd thought or the bastard had only gone west to throw Sydney off, then retraced his route once he'd figured she'd gone back inside the bar. Either way, he could have already lost him. His jaw set in granite, he pushed the speedometer to eighty and switched his head-lights to bright, his anger growing hotter by the second.

Feeling as if he were crawling, he hardly noticed the dark, barren countryside that flew by his window in a blur. His hands tight on the wheel and his gaze trained straight ahead, he whizzed over a shallow bridge that crossed one of the countless arroyos that cut through the dry earth and kept on going. Nearly a mile down the road, his brain registered what his eyes had already noted...a flash of white that could have been a vehicle, almost hidden at the deep end of the arroyo. Muttering curses, he slammed on his brakes and swung into a U-turn while his tires were still screaming in protest.

* * *

The arroyo couldn't have been more than eight feet wide at its broadest spot. In the overall scheme of things, it wasn't much more than a wrinkle on the face of the earth. It was, however, just big enough to hold a stolen truck.

Braking to a stop in a cloud of dust, Dillon saw in an instant that the vehicle was the Barshop woman's Dodge, and it looked more than a little the worse for wear. Caught in the glare of the Suburban headlights, which stripped the shadows from the scene and painted it in stark black and white, the pickup had obviously been driven into the ditch at a high speed. Up to its axle in sand, it had come face-to-face with the rocky cliff at the far end and wouldn't be going anywhere soon under its own power without some major repairs.

Grabbing his gun from the glove compartment and a flashlight from under the seat, Dillon hit the ground running. But when he was still twenty yards away, he knew the driver was long gone. The driver's door was still open and there were deep tracks in the loose dirt next to the ditch where another vehicle appeared to have been parked recently. But it was the silence more than anything that told him he was alone. Nothing moved, not even the wind.

The bastard had gotten away. Again.

Swearing, Dillon slid down into the arroyo. Dammit, who the hell was this guy? What was he after? With questions buzzing around in his head like angry bees, he went over the truck with painstaking thoroughness, sure that there had to be something there that would give him a clue as to the identity of the killer. The killer who had walked away from his latest victim after casually leaving a tip on the bar for the bartender. But there was nothing, not even a strand of hair or a half-smudged fingerprint. The truck had been wiped clean.

Furious, frustrated, he was still swearing when Sydney drove up a few seconds later. "You wasted your time following me," he said flatly as he kneeled down in the dark to examine the tire tracks next to the ditch. "There's nothing here but the damn truck, and it's cleaner than a new penny."

"The tracks—"

"Were made by some type of four-wheel-drive vehicle," he concluded in disgust. Rising to his feet, he gazed off into the distance, but as before, there wasn't a spark of a light for as far as the eye could see. If the man he sought was out there somewhere, he had thousands of acres of darkness to hide in. "There's no telling where the bastard is now—there are cattle guards all along this road. He could have driven across any one of them and just disappeared into the desert."

"So you're just giving up?" Sydney asked incredulously. "You can't be serious! He can't be more than fifteen minutes ahead of you."

"Hell, no, I'm not giving up. But look around, dammit!" Exasperated by the criticism, he curtly motioned to their surroundings. "We could stumble around in the dark for the rest of the night and only cover a fraction of this damn desert by morning. And we still wouldn't catch the bastard. Not tonight. He knows where he's going and we don't, and you can bet that damn tape recorder of yours that he won't leave us a trail. Whatever else the sleaze may be, he's not careless."

"No, he's just a psychopathic killer who's struck twice in less than a month," she pointed out heatedly. "If I weren't so paranoid about taking medication—especially from a stranger—it would be me lying dead on the floor of the Crossroads now, not that poor cowboy who never knew what hit him. And, dammit, he's not getting away with it! I don't care if I do have to search all night, I'm going after him!''

"The hell you are!"

Later, when his head was clearer and he had a tighter grip on his churning emotions, he would kick himself for reaching for her. In his present state of mind, it was the wrong move. Images kept flailing him like a whip.... Sydney, still and unmoving on the dirty floor of the bar, not an ounce of color in her face, her beautiful blue eyes lifeless and dull, dead. It sickened him how easily it could have happened. And now she wanted to go after the slimeball? Like bloody hell! Damn her, hadn't she figured out yet that this wasn't a game of who could get the story first? A headline wasn't worth her life, and that was what it could come to, especially if she got in the killer's way.

Blind fury seizing him, he caught her before she could turn back to her car and snatched her up on her toes in front of him. He'd intended to give her a tongue lashing she'd never forget, but the hot words that nearly choked him wouldn't come. With her this close, he couldn't think, and suddenly the emotions squeezing his chest had nothing to do with her stubborn determination to get herself killed and everything to do with the furious need clawing at him for release.

Let her go.

The order echoed from a distant part of his brain like the only sane voice raised above the roar of a riotous crowd. But it was too late for anything that came even close to reason. He burned deep inside and, like it or not, she was the cause. Cursing her, wanting her, aching for her, dammit!—he hauled her into his arms.

Stunned, Sydney tried to remind herself that she despised men who used physical attraction to win an argument. She should have fought free of his arms and told him exactly what she thought of his tactics. It was no more than he deserved. But his mouth was too hot on hers, too hungry, the bold, seducing sweep of his tongue too knowing. He was a man who knew how to kiss and had no compunction about using that knowledge to his advantage. In spite of all her determination, she felt her will begin to waver and the starch in her knees dissolve.

No! she wanted to cry. But he touched a need in her she'd thought was long buried, and she found herself fighting her own desire as desperately as his. She couldn't take a breath without drawing in the fresh, clean scent of him, couldn't move without feeling the hard length of him against her. Her heart started to pound, her blood to warm, her mind to cloud. Aware of nothing but the heat of his mouth on hers, she kissed him back.

She couldn't for the life of her say how long that single, hot, soul-destroying kiss lasted—it could have been seconds, aeons. When he finally let her up for air, she was clinging to him, unable to remember her own name. His breathing as ragged and revealing as hers, he pressed slow, lingering kisses to the curve of her hot cheeks, the delicate skin just under her jaw, the pulse beating wildly in her throat. With nothing more than that, he made her throb.

Dazed, feeling as though she were teetering on the edge of a cliff, she promised herself she was going to put an end to this craziness at any second. But his hands... Lord, the man had wonderful hands! Sure and strong, yet incredibly gentle, they slowly swept over her back and slid down to her waist, his fingers blindly tugging the hem of her blouse free of the waistband of her slacks. Alarm bells clanged, warning her that she was playing with fire, but he nuzzled at her throat, distracting her with hot, openmouthed kisses, and she couldn't think. Then his hands were sneaking under her blouse, heating her skin, delighting her. Expectation drizzled through her like liquid fire, and in that moment she wanted him more than she'd ever wanted a man in her life.

That thought brought her up short as nothing else could. She wasn't a woman who was easily scared of anything, but suddenly she was shaking. Jerking back, she stared up at him in bewilderment. How did he keep doing this to her? After she'd discovered just how little Adam really loved her, she'd sworn there wasn't a man on earth who could ever tempt her again, and not once since then had she had any reason to think differently. Which was a good thing, she admitted ruefully, since the selection of available men in Lordsburg was nothing to write home about. The good ones were either taken or as leery as she of getting burned again. Resigned to the fact that if she ever did want a man in her life again, she'd have to go out on the interstate and rope down the first good one that came along as he passed through town, she'd decided a relationship wasn't worth the effort.

She'd thought she was okay with that, but now, looking at Dillon in growing horror, she wasn't so sure. He made her want more. With nothing more than a few kisses, he made her want all the things she knew she wasn't ever going to have, and for the life of her, she couldn't understand why. If ever there was a man who was all wrong for her, it was Dillon Cassidy. She was open and curious and loved people and their stories. Dillon, on the other hand, was a man with secrets who resented her probing. He'd made it clear that he didn't care for her job and just wanted to be left alone, and still he made her tremble.

Needing to think, she whirled toward her car. "I've got work to do—"

"Dammit, Sydney, you're not going after that bastard!"

"At the paper," she huffed, glaring at him when he stepped in front of her to block her path. "Not that it's any of your business, but I'm going to the paper. So if you don't mind..." She lifted a delicately arched brow at him and waited impatiently for him to get out of her way.

Staring down at her flushed face, the defiance that flashed like starlight in her midnight blue eyes, it was all he could do not to jerk her back into his arms. But if he touched her again, when he was still burning from kissing her, he didn't think he could be responsible for his actions. Damn, he felt as if he'd tangled with a buzz saw! Scowling, he silently stepped back and let her pass.

But even after she brushed past him without another word and climbed into her Jeep to head back to town, he found himself standing at the side of the road staring after her as the night swallowed her whole. He was beginning to want the lady too much, he realized, more troubled than he cared to admit. And if he wasn't damn careful, he was going to be in over his head before he knew what hit him. And that could only lead to heartache. Because with his back, he could never be anything but a liability to any woman.

A muscle jumping in his clenched jaw, he turned away, his gaze falling on the abandoned pickup. He needed to get a wrecker out here to haul the stolen Dodge back into town, then get back to the Crossroads to finish the investigation. But instead of making the call on his CB, his eyes kept drifting back to the road to town...and Sydney.

She was in danger.

The thought nagged at him, refusing to leave him in peace. Irritated, he tried to dismiss it as just paranoia, but the facts spoke for themselves. She was the only one who came even close to getting a good look at the killer. And as far as he knew, she was the only one who had talked to the bastard one-on-one and lived to tell about it. That alone just might be enough to send the murdering son of a bitch after her.

And there was the matter of her stories in the *Gazette*. Just thinking about them made Dillon uneasy. The lady might drive him right up the wall with her persistence, but he had to acknowledge that she was a damn good reporter. She'd hunted down the facts of the case as quickly as he had, then put them together in a series of attention-grabbing front-page stories that had alerted everyone in the county to the presence of a murderer in their midst. According to Riley, his office had been inundated with calls from anxious people who were sure they'd seen the killer. With all the watchful eyes out there, the man had to be feeling the heat.

Which meant the slippery bastard had at least two twisted reasons to want Sydney dead.

His jaw rigid, he strode over to his car and made the call for the wrecker. Seconds later, he headed back to the Crossroads, but he didn't stay long. The coroner had already been there and gone, and Joe Sanchez was taking a few last statements and just mopping up. There was nothing left for Dillon to do except run into town and leave a report for Riley.

But when he reached the quiet, lighted streets of Lordsburg, he turned left instead of right at the first light he came to and, without making a conscious decision, ended up at the *Gazette*. Swearing, he threw the Suburban into Park, calling himself seven kinds of a fool. If ever there was a lady who could take care of herself, it was Sydney. She didn't need him to watch over her—hell, she'd probably see it as an insult. Which was too damn bad. Because like it or not, he was going to stick around long enough to make sure she got home safely after she finished writing her firsthand account of the murder at the Crossroads. He would, he assured himself, have done the same thing for a stranger on the street.

Sure, Cassidy, a voice jeered in his head. *Tell another one. You're here because you can't stay away, and you know it.*

Muttering curses at the taunt that struck too close to the truth, he slammed out of the car and strode into the building.

"I'm telling you, Red, you can sit there and stare at the screen until the sun comes up, but you've got to punch a few buttons if you want to write a story," Blake Nickels teased from his desk. His grin mocking, his gaze narrowed on the haunted look in the depths of her eyes, he watched her like a hawk. "Lord, I knew you learned to write through those mail-order correspondence classes, but I'd have thought somewhere, someone would have taught you this stuff. I guess it's up to me."

Her eyes trained on the blank screen, Sydney didn't spare him a glance. "Don't flatter yourself, Nickels. I can write circles around you and you know it."

"Then how come my copy's been approved and yours is still stuck in your head? Time's awastin', Red. I can hear the presses warming up. You gonna fish or cut bait?"

Over the top of her computer monitor, her eyes met his. She knew he was trying to distract her from the horror at the Crossroads and didn't have the heart to tell him it was a wasted effort. Instead, she pretended, as he did, that nothing out of the ordinary had happened tonight.

"I might be able to get something done if there wasn't so much jabbering going on in here," she said pointedly. "I can understand why that might not bother you—you could work in the middle of a subway station during rush hour—but some of us are a little more particular when it comes to putting our thoughts on paper. Which is why some of us write top-notch news and some of us write the kind of copy that lines the bottom of the bird cage."

Delighted that he'd finally gotten a rise out of her, he only grinned. "My parakeet was just reading your stuff on the Martinez kid this morning. He liked it, but hey, he doesn't get out much so he's happy with whatever reading material he can get."

"Then he ought to love that trivia you call sports news," she teased. "Don't you have someplace to go? There must be a ball game or a bubble-gum-blowing contest where you're needed."

As far as hints went, it was about as subtle as a fist to the gut, but Blake had never had much use for subtleties. He was just relieved that the colorless, subdued Sydney who'd walked in the door thirty minutes ago was well on the way to being her old snappy self again. Now he could leave.

Pushing to his feet, his eyes dancing, he grabbed his cowboy hat and plopped it on his head. "Nope, but I can take a hint, Garbo. You want to be alone. Why didn't you just say so?"

Laughing, she tossed a wadded-up piece of paper at him, which he deftly caught on his way out. Then the door closed behind him and silence, thick and heavy, slipped uninvited into the city room. Left alone with her thoughts, Sydney shivered slightly, her smile fading. If the killing at the Crossroads was going to make the morning paper, she was going to have to hustle. Stirring to life, she sat up straighter.

But when she placed her fingers on the computer keyboard, a tangled weave of images scrambled her thoughts. Dillon reaching for her, the aspirin-pushing stranger brushing shoulders with her at the bar, Dillon's mouth hot and hungry on hers, Lawrence Osborn lying dead on the Crossroad's dusty floor, Dillon making her ache...

Dillon.

Dillon.

Dillon.

Every thought began and ended with him touching her, holding her, kissing her. The scent of him clung to her clothes, the feel of him to her skin—and she only had to close her eyes to find herself back on the side of the road by that abandoned old pickup and in his arms. It was driving her crazy. She couldn't work, damn him! No man had ever interfered with a story before, not even Adam—the day after she'd broken off her engagement to him, she'd written an award-winning piece about a Chicago judge caught in a blackmailing scheme.

But then again, she'd never met anyone quite like Dillon. Her fingers frozen on the keys, she silently admitted to herself that he was really starting to worry her. She wasn't a woman controlled by her hormones; she never had been. While other girls in high school were giggling and batting their eyelashes over the latest football heartthrob, she'd been up to her ears in the school paper. And college had been no different. She hadn't cared less that she could count on the fingers of one hand the dates she had her entire senior year.

A sound from the doorway intruded on her thoughts, and she turned, half expecting to find Blake standing there with a devilish twinkle in his eye and one last teasing remark on his tongue before he went home for the night. But the man standing there wasn't Blake and he wasn't smiling.

Dillon.

Sydney's heart lurched at the sight of him. Not forty minutes ago, she'd run from him, run from herself, unable to get away fast enough from the way he made her feel. Now here she was hoping he'd followed her because he couldn't forget that hot kiss on the side of the road any more than she could.

But with the first words out of his mouth, that hope shriveled up and died like a deflated balloon. "Don't pay me any mind. I'm just here to make sure you get home okay."

So he was there to protect her. She supposed she should have been flattered that he cared enough to be concerned, but God help her, it wasn't protection she needed from him. Something that came too close to pain squeezing her heart, she deliberately returned her gaze to her blank screen. "Then you made a trip over here for nothing," she retorted coolly. "I've been finding my way home without help since I was a kid. I'm sure I can manage to do it again tonight."

It was a clear dismissal that bordered on out-and-out rudeness. From the corner of her eye, she saw his mouth compress with annoyance, but the man had proven on more than one occasion that he could be as stubborn as she, and tonight was no exception. Sauntering over to the chair angled in front of her desk, he dropped into it and stretched out his legs as if he intended to stay all night if he had to. Over the top of her monitor, his gray eyes were mocking as they met hers. "Maybe so, but I think I'll stick around just to make sure . . . if you don't mind."

Mind? She almost choked. Hell, yes, she *minded!* But if she told him so, it would be just like him to ask why, and that wasn't something she was prepared to answer, not even to herself. Shrugging with an indifference that cost her more than he would ever know, she dropped her gaze back to her computer and this time kept it there. "Suit yourself. But it could be a while."

Having given him fair warning, she didn't spare him so much as a glance for the next thirty minutes. Determined to ignore him, she tried to concentrate, her fingers flying over the keyboard in search of an opening paragraph. But the result was only gibberish, and she found herself starting over again and again in growing frustration. All because of Dillon.

To her consternation, she was aware of every little twitch he made, and he wasn't even trying to draw attention to himself. He sat quietly, thumbing through a Steven King paperback he'd grabbed from a corner of her desk, and seemed to be ignoring her much more successfully than she was ignoring him. But then he shifted in his seat, a grimace of pain visible in the sudden clenching of his jaw, and she knew his back was tightening up.

"You don't have to stay," she said, shattering the tense silence. "I don't need help getting home."

"I never said you did," he replied. "But there is a murderer loose on the streets and it doesn't hurt to be too careful."

No one knew better than she just how true that was, and she could only nod, any further argument effectively shot down. "I'll try to hurry," she promised, and turned back to her writing.

Twenty minutes later, she was finished and ready to go. The story itself wasn't the best thing she'd ever done, but considering her volatile emotions, she was pleased with it. What she was not pleased with was Dillon trailing her to her car like she was a kindergartner who got lost between the front door and the curb.

Balking in the dimly lit parking lot next to the building, she looked around at the dark, deserted street. Devoid of life but for the two of them, not even a leaf moved. "This is ridiculous, Dillon. You must live thirty miles cross-country from me. There's no reason for you to follow me home when there's no one out but rats at this time of night. I'll be fine."

"Rats come with two legs as well as four," he drawled. "Let's go, Syd."

She went, but only because she was in no mood for an argument. It had, to put it mildly, been a difficult evening. She just wanted to go home and crawl into bed and forget the rest of the world existed. But all the way to her house,

Dillon was right behind her, the reflections of his head-lights in her rearview mirror a constant reminder of his nearness.

Her heart starting to pound, she jumped out of her Jeep the second she finally braked to a stop in her driveway, in-tending to wave a thank-you to send him on his way back to town. But he'd pulled up behind her and was already out of his Suburban and striding toward her.

"Where're your keys?" he demanded.

"Right here." Holding them up, she frowned in confu-sion when he took them from her. "Dammit, Dillon, I can unlock my own door!"

He didn't dispute the fact—he just stepped past her and shoved the key into the dead bolt, then held the door open for her, one corner of his mouth curling into a crooked grin when she just stood there, glaring at him. "I'm coming in, Sydney."

Her heart stopped in midbeat, irritating her no end, but she was damned if she'd let him know that he'd shaken her. Pressing her hand to her breast in a dramatic gesture, she drawled, "Be still my heart! And here I thought you didn't care."

Chuckling, he reached out to tug at one of the curls that lay on her shoulders, surprising them both with the ges-ture. "I just want to check the place out and make sure it's safe, smart mouth."

After what had happened at the Crossroads, she had to agree that she couldn't be too careful, but deep inside her heart, a self-protective voice cried out in protest. She didn't want him in her house, didn't want him among her things, didn't want to be haunted by the memory of his scent—of *him*—following her around from room to room.

"There are dead bolts on both doors," she began.

"And locks on the windows," he said, holding the screen door wider and patiently waiting for her to precede him. "But this is an old house. Window catches get rusty or even break, and no one usually notices. It won't take me a minute to look at them." His eyes, sharp and discerning, locked with hers. "Unless you don't want me in your house for some reason. . . ."

Put on the spot, heat climbing up her throat into her cheeks, singeing her fair skin with revealing color, she did what any self-respecting woman would have done in a similar situation—she looked him right in the eye and lied through her teeth. "Are you kidding? You know me. If I didn't want you in there, I'd say so. It is late, and I didn't want you to feel like you *had* to check the place out tonight. But if you're not concerned about the time, then I'm certainly not. Come on in."

Stepping past him, she waited until he followed her into the living room, then airily motioned to the rest of the small house that she'd bought soon after moving to Lordsburg four years ago. "Look around all you want. There's not much too see."

Her tone was casual . . . too casual . . . and didn't fool Dillon in the least. She didn't want him there any more than he wanted to be there, and it had nothing to do with her stubborn independence and everything to do with a hot kiss on the side of the road that neither of them had forgotten. It was there between them every time their eyes met. And just thinking about it made him sweat.

He had no business being here, he thought irritably. He should have called one of the other deputies to do this, but now it was too late and he was stuck. He'd do them both a favor by making a quick check and getting the hell out of there.

But he made the mistake of taking a quick look around, and just that easily, he was intrigued. He didn't know what he'd expected, but it wasn't this. Neat and cozy, with the kind of knickknacks and doodads that were noticeably absent in his own house, it was not the kind of place he would have pictured as belonging to a career woman. It was too warm, too domestic, crying out for kids and a husband and a dog or two. Without expending any energy at all, he could imagine toys scattered about, a man's pair of well-worn slippers by the overstuffed chair angled next to the small fireplace, and Sydney glowing with happiness as she puttered around in the kitchen fixing supper for her family.

But it wasn't just any man she cooked for, it wasn't just any man who fathered her children. In the blink of an eye, the fantasy changed and the man who was missing from the picture, the man she shared her life with and spent her nights loving, was him.

Which only went to show that he'd been working too hard, he thought angrily, snapping back to reality with a hastily swallowed curse. Because some things just weren't ever going to happen for him, and happily ever after was one of them. He'd accepted that the day he woke up in the hospital to learn that he'd been condemned to hell by the bullet in his back. Sydney might tempt the devil himself, but wanting her until he burned wasn't going to change a damn thing. His was a solitary existence—for life.

Vowing not to forget that again, he strode into the kitchen to check the lock on the back door. As Sydney had claimed, it had the same type of lock as the one on the front door and nothing short of a Sherman tank was coming through it without a key. The windows, on the other hand, were another matter.

Examining the latch of the double-wide windows that overlooked the backyard, Dillon could only swear and shake his head. It had been new once—around the end of World War II—and had no doubt been state-of-the-art for that time. But so had black-and-white TV's. Technology and criminals had changed, however. Any burglar worth his salt could snap that pitiful excuse for a security system in two simply by jimmying the sash with a screwdriver from the outside.

And unless Dillon was mistaken—and he prayed to God he was—every other window in the house had a latch just like it.

Chapter 7

Returning to the living room, where she was impatiently waiting for him, he said, "We're going to have to do something about your windows."

Surprised, she glanced over at the double set of paned windows that overlooked the front drive. "Why? What's wrong with them?"

"Everything!" Incensed that she'd been so careless with her own safety—anyone could have broken in in the middle of the night and knocked her senseless!—he strode across the room and jerked back the curtain to show her the problem. "Look at that latch! My aunt Mabel could snap that thing off with one hand tied behind her back, and she's eighty-three. Dammit, Sydney, these things should have been changed years ago!"

Wound up and just getting started, he would have said more, but the sudden flare of headlights flashed against her front windows as a car pulled into the drive, cutting him off.

His eyes flying to hers, he asked sharply, "Are you expecting anyone?"

"No, of course not. It's nearly midnight!"

At another time, he would have been amused by her quick, indignant reply, but now he was too busy trying to figure out who the devil her unexpected visitor was. He didn't think it was the lowlife from the Crossroads—if he'd have come after her, he'd have made damn sure she didn't see him until it was too late—but Dillon wasn't taking any chances.

Quickly dropping the curtain, he pulled her back from view. "Check the dead bolt," he said quietly as he positioned himself next to the window that gave a clear view of the front porch. In the sudden silence, tension thickened like a cold fog.

Standing well back out of sight, Sydney gasped at the sight of the gun Dillon suddenly pulled from beneath his jacket. "What are you doing?" she gasped.

"Making sure that's not trouble coming up the walk," he replied, using the barrel of the .38 to carefully lift one edge of the thin curtain that covered the window. The set of his shoulders rigid, he peered out at the man who was already starting up the porch steps...only to laugh shortly and shove his gun back into the shoulder harness concealed under his jacket. "It's Riley."

"Thank God!" Relief flooding her in a dizzying rush, Sydney released the breath she hadn't even realized she was holding. She wasn't the type to jump at shadows, but for a second there, her knees were knocking loud enough to beat the band. And she hadn't liked the feeling one little bit! She'd never cowered behind a locked door in her life and she wasn't about to start now just because a murderer had gotten a little too close to her for comfort!

Moving to the front door, she unlocked it and pulled it open before Riley even knocked. "I guess I don't have to ask what you're doing here at this time of night," she said by way of greeting as he stepped inside. "You heard the news."

He nodded. "As soon as I got back from Tucson. I stopped by the office before going home and Joe filled me in on the details." Glancing past her to Dillon, he said, "I figured I'd find you here when you weren't at your place. We've got a problem."

Actually, they had two, Dillon almost quipped, but something in his friend's unsmiling face warned him he wasn't talking about the two homicides they now had on their hands. His eyes searching Riley's, he said, "Why do I have the feeling that I'm not going to like this? What is it?"

Hesitating, Riley shot a warning glare at Sydney. "This goes no further than this room for now, Syd. I'll have your word on that."

"If this is about the case, I've already agreed not to reveal anything concerning the ongoing investigation," she said with a frown. "But when this guy's caught, I'm coming out with the full story."

"Of the murders," he agreed. "But you'll have to clear the rest of this with Dillon. It's his story."

His gut twisting with apprehension, Dillon was liking the sound of this less and less. "Spit it out, Riley. I can handle Sydney. What's going on?"

"I got a call from Quinn Powell while I stopped by the office," he said reluctantly.

At the mere mention of his former supervisor, a man they'd both worked with at the DEA, Dillon braced for a blow. Quinn wasn't the kind to go to the trouble to track him down to talk about old home week—unless he had bad news. "And? What did he want?"

"Carlos Santiago escaped from prison. He's got every available man out hunting for him, but he thought you'd want to know."

Dillon took the news like a punch to the gut. Sucking in a sharp breath, he could only manage one word. "When?"

"Almost four weeks ago."

"Four weeks! Son of a bitch! And Powell just now decided to call? What the hell's he been waiting on?"

"He didn't want to worry you, especially when he thought the bastard was headed for the jungles of South America. But he and his men have exhausted every lead, and there's been no sign of Santiago anywhere. Powell's afraid he's headed for New Mexico."

If the rage choking him hadn't been so intense, Dillon would have laughed bitterly. Not only had Santiago headed for New Mexico, he was already there. He had to be—it was the only thing that made sense. From the moment the bastard was taken into custody after the shoot-out in South America, Santiago had vowed on his mother's grave to one day come after the one man above all others he blamed for his incarceration—Dillon Cassidy. Covered in his own blood at the time, Dillon hadn't doubted he'd do just that if he got the chance. The sleaze had a history of getting revenge, no matter what, and he wasn't going to forget his grudge against the only man who had ever sent him to prison.

God, why hadn't he seen it sooner? he thought furiously. All the signs were there: the designer drugs that few men in that area had the knowledge or skills to concoct, the irrational murders by a pusher who should have been trying to build business, not kill it. Even Sydney's description of the blond hair on the arms of the man who had tried to give her aspirin at the Crossroad fit. Santiago was as pale as his Spanish ancestors, and if he hadn't been sure the coke-selling son of a bitch was safely locked away, Dillon would have suspected him long before now.

"Did you tell him the worthless piece of trash is already here?" he asked Riley. "That there's a good chance he's already killed two people just to let me know he's in the neighborhood and I could be next?"

"What?" Sydney gasped, startled, glancing back and forth between the two men. "What are you talking about? Who's this Santiago character?"

"A drug lord Dillon was responsible for putting away," Riley answered before Dillon could open his mouth.

A muscle working in his jaw, Dillon had no intention of discussing the past in front of Sydney, but the present was another matter. "She saw him, Riley. Sat close enough to him to talk to him and rub shoulders with him. He had a hat pulled low over his face, but as far as he knows, she can identify him. We've got to get her out of here."

"Get me out of here?" Sydney repeated in growing confusion. "What are you talking about? I already told you that the guy at the Crossroads left before I did. Even if he is this Santiago jerk, there's no way he could have followed me home."

"Dammit, Sydney, you don't understand!" Dillon grated. "Santiago's not some two-bit pusher who doesn't have the brains to track a chicken across the road. He's a bloodsucking, amoral murderer who'd just as soon squash you like a bug as look at you . . . especially if you make the mistake of sticking your nose in his business."

"He's right, Syd," Riley added grimly. "Santiago's so low, he's got to look up to a worm. And he's got no use for reporters. I don't think that he offered you that aspirin by pure chance tonight, not when it's common knowledge that you and Dillon have been working together. If for no other reason than that, he'll come after you."

Dillon had heard enough. "Go pack a bag," he told Sydney. "You can't stay here. And you might as well call your boss while you're at it. You won't be going back to work until Santiago is back in custody."

Stunned, Sydney could only stare at him. "You can't be serious!"

His somber expression as unyielding as stone, he looked her dead in the eye. "Do I look like I'm joking?"

No, Sydney had to admit. There was nothing the least bit humorous in his set expression. He looked like a man who had seen hell and had not only lived to tell about it, but would never smile again. And for reasons she wouldn't let herself put a name to, that broke her heart. There was an emptiness in his eyes that seemed to go all the way to his soul, a loneliness he made no attempt to fight, and something told her Santiago was to blame. How, dammit? What was it that Dillon wasn't telling her?

Frustrated, suddenly furious with him and Riley for keeping her in the dark, she plopped her fists on her hips and snapped, "I'm not going anywhere until I get some answers. Neither one of you is the type to run from anything, especially a piece of trash who deals drugs for a living. Yet you're both ready to bundle me up and run for cover like the devil himself was hot on our trail. Now, are you going to tell me why or do I have to guess?"

He hadn't meant to tell her—ever. But the woman could teach a mule a hell of a lot about stubbornness, and all he could think of was that she was standing there wasting precious time arguing when even now, Santiago could be setting up an ambush right outside her front door.

Snarling a curse, he turned on her, gray eyes blazing. "You want the truth? Well, here it is, lady. You hit the nail on the head when you called that blond-haired bastard a devil, because that's exactly what he is. Thanks to him, I've

got a bullet lodged next to my spine that's going to paralyze
me one of these days. That's right," he growled when her
eyes widened with shock. "I set off metal detectors in air-
ports, sweetheart. And I live every day wondering if it's going to be the last one I can walk. So don't try to tell me what
kind of man Santiago is. *I know!*"

Horrified, Sydney couldn't have managed a word if her
life had depended on it. Helplessly, she looked at Riley and
prayed that he'd tell her this was Dillon's idea of a sick joke.
But she'd never seen him so somber.

"It's true," he said when Dillon muttered a curt *"Talk to
her,"* then stormed outside to cool off. "Dillon was the one
who brought Santiago down, but not before the scumbag
shot him in the back. The doctors did everything they could,
but the bullet was too close to the spine and they didn't want
to chance causing more damage by trying to move it. If it
ever shifts…" He shrugged, his silence saying everything his
words didn't.

"That's why he got out of the DEA, isn't it?" she asked
hoarsely. "He was no longer physically able to handle the
job."

Riley nodded. "He'd been thinking about retiring but the
shooting pretty much forced the issue. And even without the
injury, his effectiveness was virtually blown. Santiago had
a long reach, even from jail, and put a bounty on his head.
With every lowlife from Maine to Brazil on the lookout for
him, just stepping out of his house in the morning would
have been a risk. So the agency let it be known that he died
on the operating table after the shooting. Powell—Dillon's
supervisor—and the rest of the suits in power thought it was
the only way to keep him safe."

"But Santiago found him anyway." Staring out the open
front door to where Dillon stood on the porch, Sydney
blinked back sudden tears and had to fight the need to go to

him. He wouldn't appreciate her concern and was too proud a man to easily accept sympathy from her or anyone else, not when his stiff posture all but shouted *back off*.

"Because he's a loose cannon with a lot of power," Riley said curtly. "A psycho without a conscience who'll do anything to strike back at anyone who dares to oppose him. And that's what makes him dangerous—there's no predicting what he's going to do next. So you'd better do as Dillon says and pack a bag. You can't stay here. If Santiago doesn't know where you live yet, it won't take him long to find out."

Every independent instinct Sydney had cried out in protest at the thought of being driven from her home like a scared rabbit by a lowlife like Carlos Santiago. But Dillon and Riley knew this man, knew the type of violence he was capable of. If he really was the man who had offered her that aspirin at the Crossroads, he hadn't blinked an eye at killing. Just thinking how close she'd come to being his next victim made her skin crawl. For reasons known only to himself, he'd let her get away, but she doubted that that was any accident. If he was clever enough to track Dillon halfway across the country to a town that was hardly bigger than a dot on the map, then she had to believe that he'd known exactly who she was when he'd offered her that aspirin. Which meant that if he meant to destroy anyone connected with Dillon, he'd be back . . . for her.

Chilled by the thought, she shivered. "I'll get my things," she said huskily, and grabbed a suitcase from the hall closet before hurrying into her bedroom to pack and call Harry at the paper.

"I hate to leave you in the lurch this way," she told the older man as soon as she explained the situation to him a short while later. "I can't even tell you when I'll be able to come back in."

"So we'll see you when we see you," Harry said with a shrug she could picture all too easily in her mind. "Just don't take any chances. I mean it, Sydney. No story is worth getting killed over. This Santiago character sounds like a nasty son of a gun, so lay low like the sheriff and Dillon suggested. We'll manage to get by until it's safe for you to come back."

"I'll keep a journal and send you updates," she promised. "The readers'll love it."

"Now, wait a minute, girl. I don't know if you should do that," he began. "It could be risky—"

If the situation hadn't been so serious, she would have laughed at that. She was taking a risk, all right...by going off with Dillon into the boondocks. "It'll be great," she assured him quickly before hanging up. "I'll be in touch when I can."

Fifteen minutes later, her suitcase and laptop computer stored in the small back seat of her Jeep, she stood next to Dillon as Riley finished giving them directions to an old house in the desert where they would be safe until Santiago was in custody. "It used to be the old Henderson place, but the family died out except for some cousin in California who finally sold it to the Rawlings family several years ago. The house has stood empty ever since old man Henderson died ten years ago, but according to Gable, it's still in pretty good shape. And it's ten miles from the highway, so you don't have to worry about anyone spotting you from the road."

"What about the Double R cowboys?" Dillon asked. "They're bound to notice us. All it would take would be for one of them to let something slip while he and his buddies were playing pool at the Crossroads one night, and our cover would be shot to hell."

"Gable's already thought of that," he assured them. "The whole north section of the ranch is fenced with cedar post and he wants to replace it with steel. It'll take nearly every man on the Double R to get that done before the spring roundup starts, and the few that will be left to tend to the cattle will be his oldest hands. You can trust them not to talk."

"What about Dillon's clothes?" Sydney asked suddenly, frowning. "And food? If the house has been empty all this time, don't we need to get supplies?"

"It's too dangerous to go back to my place for anything," Dillon answered for him. "Santiago's bound to have it staked out. I'll just have to make do with the clothes on my back."

Riley eyed him speculatively, sizing him up. "We're close to the same height. I'll see what I've got in my closet and send it out with Joe Sanchez, who's going to be guarding you until this is over. As for food, there's not much I can do about it tonight since the grocery stores are already closed. Joe's going to bring some breakfast stuff from his house and whatever else you need to get you through the night when he meets you at the Henderson place within the hour. That'll have to last you until I can get out there first thing in the morning with more supplies. Okay?"

Sydney wanted to say, no, it wasn't okay. Nothing about this entire setup was okay with her—how could it be when she was supposed to hole up in the desert for God knows how long with a man who made her blood throb?—but how could she object when, right this very minute, Santiago could be plotting their deaths?

"That should cover things for now," Dillon agreed, slapping Riley on the back. "Thanks, man. I appreciate your help. We'll take the back roads and drive around for a while to make sure we aren't followed. If you need to get in touch with me, I've got my cellular.''

It had already been agreed upon that Sydney's Jeep with its four-wheel drive would be more maneuverable in the desert than Dillon's heavier Suburban, so without quite knowing how she let herself be talked into such madness, Sydney found herself handing the keys to Dillon and taking the passenger seat like an agreeable little woman. She had, she decided, lost her mind.

Within seconds, they had left Riley and her house behind and were racing into the dark. Too late, Sydney realized she never should have agreed to taking the Jeep instead of Dillon's much-larger Suburban. The Jeep had always been more than big enough for her, but Dillon's legs were longer, his shoulders wider. He seemed to take up all the available space, and every time he moved, even if it was to shift, she found herself holding her breath in anticipation of his touch. But he somehow managed to stick to his side of the vehicle, and in the growing silence, she was sure he must have heard the frantic, disappointed pounding of her heart.

You're in trouble, Sydney, old girl. Big trouble. If you can't take a drive with the man without getting all hot and bothered, how the devil are you going to share a house with him for who knows how long without going quietly out of your mind?

Wincing at the caustic inner voice of reason that needled her, she reminded herself that they weren't two lovers sneaking off in the night to a secret hideaway in the desert. Fate had thrown them together into a nightmare, not a fairy tale. Oh, it had all the elements—good guy and bad guy and a girl—but regardless of what happened, there would be no happy ending for Dillon. He had a guillotine hanging over his head, and he'd made it clear he wasn't letting any woman close enough to him to get hurt when it came crashing down on him without warning. Only a fool would allow herself to forget that, and she was no fool.

Suddenly chilled, she hugged herself, wishing they'd hurry up and reach the old Henderson place. But Dillon wasn't taking any chances that they were somehow being followed. Driving the maze of ranch roads that crisscrossed the high desert, he turned without warning, backtracked when he thought it was necessary, and occasionally, to her horror, drove without lights, using the weak glow of a hunter's moon to light his path. Only when he was satisfied that there wasn't another car anywhere in the vicinity did he follow Riley's directions to the abandoned house.

They bounced over a poorly marked gravel road for what seemed like forever before they came to the dark, hulking shadow that had to be the Henderson homestead. Joe Sanchez hadn't arrived yet, and in the glare of the Jeep headlights, the place looked downright spooky, sitting as it was, right in the middle of a pasture, miles from anything.

There was no yard, no trees, nothing but dust and dirt and the eerie creak of the broken-down windmill that turned lazily with the wind. Decades of exposure to the extremes of the New Mexican weather had stripped the wood siding of paint and turned it as gray as an old woman, and the windows were bare and curtainless. Sydney had never seen a more desolate sight in her life.

But it was a long way from the highway and anyone trying to sneak up on them by avoiding the drive would have ten miles of desert to travel over first. And for no other reason than that, she was prepared to love the place.

Which was why she didn't so much as blink when she followed Dillon through the back door after he found the light switch. In the sudden light that flooded the big, old-fashioned kitchen, every flaw was painstakingly revealed. The ceiling was stained from a leaky roof, the linoleum cracked and curling at the edges, the cabinets coated with a horrible avocado paint.

Glancing around, she nodded. "This is going to work out just fine. It's nothing fancy, but I've worked in a lot worse conditions, and as long as we've got electricity, water and indoor plumbing, I can put up with just about anything."

Setting her things down on the rusty chrome dinette table in the middle of the room, Dillon only grunted and lifted a skeptical brow. Only an eternal optimist could have described the place as "nothing fancy." It was in need of some major renovations, but that was the least of their worries now because they wouldn't be staying all that long. He and Riley hadn't spoken of it, but they'd both known this place would, at best, provide only temporary shelter. Literally, within weeks of breaking out of prison, Santiago had tracked him all the way across country. Once the son of a bitch realized that he and Sydney had gone into hiding, it wouldn't take him longer than a few days to run them to ground if they were foolish enough to stay in one spot. So they would move as much as they had to until he could arrange to have Sydney safely spirited away to someplace safe, preferably miles from Lordsburg. Then he would deal with the bastard in his own way, and this time *he* would be the one who tasted the sweetness of revenge.

In the meantime, they had the night to get through. Wondering where the hell Joe Sanchez was, he said gruffly, "According to Riley, there are two bedrooms, one on each side of the living room. You want the east one or the west one?"

"The east," she said promptly. "I like the morning sun."

He could have told her that was something he didn't need to know. She could have preferred flannel sheets to silk, cold winter mornings to warm summer ones, sleeping in on Sundays. There'd been nights lately when he'd thought of her and such things for hours, torturing himself. But that was when they had been separated by miles, not a single room that could be crossed in a matter of seconds.

His body tightening just at the thought of her availability, he cursed himself for ever agreeing to such an insane plan. The house was, thankfully, larger than he'd expected, but even a mansion wouldn't be big enough, not when he had to share it with Sydney. Picking up her things again, he growled, "Lead the way."

Not surprisingly, the east bedroom was in just as bad a condition as the rest of the house. There was dust everywhere and a rag rug on the floor that had definitely seen better days. The old iron bed needed paint, but it seemed sturdy enough, if you didn't mind a mattress that tended to sag in the middle.

Dillon took one look at it and wished he hadn't. He knew that later, in the loneliness of his own room, he would picture her there, cocooned in the middle of the bed, her hair tousled and loose about her shoulders, her soft, tempting body relaxed in sleep. Was she a heavy sleeper or a light one? Would she wake instantly if he crawled in beside her or only murmur in her sleep and roll toward him to snuggle close?

Bothered by the need to know, he muttered a curse under his breath and set her things on the floor just inside the door. "I'm going to check out the rest of the place while you get settled in," he said stiffly, turning to beat a hasty retreat. "Holler if you need anything."

He was gone before she could open her mouth, and Sydney had to admit it was for the best. The house was too quiet, their isolation too complete, their awareness of each other too strong for either of them to be comfortable in the other's company for long. She'd seen the way his eyes had lingered on the bed and had felt her own heart jump in response. The mattress needed to be pulled out onto the porch for a good beating, then turned, but her throat had closed up just at the thought of asking him to help her.

He wasn't here to set up house with her, she reminded herself sternly. And she couldn't let herself fall into the trap of thinking that he was or she'd never be able to walk away from here—and him—with her heart intact.

Her chin set stubbornly, she moved to the bed and started tugging on the mattress. It was heavier than she'd expected and hard to get a handle on. Muttering curses, she tugged and pushed and still only managed to drag it half off the bed. Finally climbing onto the rusty springs, she balanced herself precariously, shoved her shoulder under the mattress and finally sent the blasted thing sliding to the floor. Dust immediately rose in a cloud, mushrooming around her.

She was still coughing, tears streaming down her face, when Dillon appeared in the open doorway. "What the devil are you doing in here? I could hear you all the way out in the barn."

"Trying to g-get the mat-tress outside to beat the d-dust out of it," she choked out.

"Why bother?" he retorted, a crooked half smile tugging up one corner of his mouth as his amused eyes skimmed over her dirty face and clothes. "You've already done it in here."

Wrinkling her nose at him, she started to tell him to save the smart remarks for the peanut gallery, but the sudden glare of headlights flared in the distance and her heart jolted in alarm. "That better be Joe Sanchez coming up the drive or we've got trouble," she said, nodding to the curtainless window.

Dillon swore and reached for the light switch, immediately plunging the bedroom into darkness, but the precaution wasn't necessary. In his patrol car, Joe Sanchez flicked on his lightbar for just a second, silently identifying himself, before quickly dousing it. In the darkness, Dillon let out a slow breath and turned the ceiling light on. "It looks like backup's here. I'll go help him unload."

A husky man of medium height, Joe Sanchez was a likable, easygoing guy who never seemed to be in a hurry. A typical good old boy, he talked as slow as he moved, always had a twinkle in his black eyes and was the last person anyone would ever mistake for a tough-as-nails cop. Appearances were deceptive, however, and Joe was, in fact, one of Riley's sharpest deputies. He had eyes like a hawk, especially at night. If anyone could spot Santiago trying to sneak up on them in the dark, it was Joe.

Parking in the barn next to Sydney's Jeep, he climbed out of his patrol car with lazy grace and greeted Dillon with a grin. "When Riley said this place was a little wild, he wasn't kidding. I thought I was going to lose an axle on that drive. Is the house as bad as it looks?"

"Close," Dillon said, chuckling. "But Riley swears the roof doesn't leak, so I suppose that's some consolation. Let me help you with some of that stuff."

The trunk of the patrol car was packed solid with everything from sheets and blankets to food from Joe's own kitchen to the jeans and shirts that Riley had tossed in for Dillon. Sydney came out to help them carry it all in, then Dillon got Joe to help him carry her mattress out on the porch, where she beat the stuffing out of it with the old broom she found in the kitchen closet. By the time the mattress was back on her bed and she'd given Dillon's the same cleaning, it was going on two in the morning.

Exhausted, his back tight and crying out for a rest, Dillon finally climbed into bed a few minutes later. After his years with the DEA, when he'd learned to grab a few winks where he could, he should have gone right to sleep. Joe would be on guard the rest of the night, and if he saw any-thing the slightest bit suspicious, he only had to fire his service revolver into the air to bring Dillon running. There was nothing to worry about.

Except the lady sleeping in the bedroom on the other side of the living room. And Santiago.

In spite of the bullet in his back, he wasn't afraid of the slippery drug lord. He knew how the scumbag's mind worked, how he thought, and if it was just his own safety he had to be concerned with, Dillon knew he could handle him one-on-one. But there was Sydney to worry about. Sydney, who, after years of working the streets of Chicago, thought she knew the criminal mind but didn't have a clue as to what Santiago, with all his power and money and lack of con-science, was capable of. He'd come after her, hurt her, for no other reason than to hear her scream.

He wanted her safe, dammit. Away from here. Away from him. But he knew her well enough by now to know that she wouldn't go quietly. Hell, she'd pitch a fit at the mere sug-gestion that she walk away from any story, especially one this hot. So if she wouldn't leave, he would.

The thought came to him so suddenly that it didn't reg-ister at first. When it did, he knew it was the only solution to an untenable situation. By leaving, he would draw San-tiago's attention away from Sydney to himself, where it be-longed. And it would put some physical space between them, which at the moment, he badly needed.

Satisfied that he'd made the right decision, he lay on his back staring at the water-stained ceiling of his bedroom as the tension slowly eased out of him. But it was still another hour before he was able to relax enough to fall asleep. And then he dreamed of Sydney, and the images that haunted him had nothing to do with Santiago.

When they came face-to-face the next morning in the kitchen, he was edgy and irritated, and she didn't help matters by greeting him with a grin and cheery good morning. "Did you sleep well?"

Sleep? He almost laughed. How the devil was he supposed to sleep when she kept wandering in and out of his dreams like she owned them? And did she have to look so damn good at seven-thirty in the morning? The sun was shining and so was she, her hair glinting with red and gold as it fell in waves to her shoulders. Frustrated, he found himself battling the need to touch her just to see if she was as soft as she looked.

"Dillon?" Her blue eyes starting to crinkle with barely suppressed humor, she waved her hand in front of his face. "Hey? Are you in there?"

Lost in his thoughts, he jerked back to awareness to find himself staring down at her like a man struck dumb. Heat rose uncomfortably in his face. Good God, was he blushing? His brows snapping together in a fierce frown, he turned away to grab a disposable cup from the counter and pour himself a cup of coffee from the pot on the stove. "Yeah," he rasped in a voice as rough as the gravel road that led to the house. "But don't expect all cylinders to be working until after I've had some coffee. And maybe not even then."

"Ah," she said, smiling as the light dawned. "You're not a morning person."

Grunting, he took a long sip of the scalding liquid and tried not to notice the curve of her mouth, but it was impossible. Heat burned in his middle, and it had nothing to do with the coffee. Heading for the back door suddenly, he said shortly, "I'm going to go out and spell Joe. I imagine he's ready for some sleep."

From the corner of his eye, he saw the smile fall from her face and wanted to kick himself for being such a bastard. But he didn't turn back and apologize. Letting the screen door slam behind him, he found Joe standing in the shadow of the barn, a pair of binoculars lifted to his eyes as he slowly studied the back half of the property one last time before the end of his shift.

Only when he was convinced that the desert was as empty as it appeared did he drop the field glasses and turn to Dillon. His gaze taking in his unshaven face and tired eyes in a single glance, he smiled. "I won't ask if you had a rough night—you look like a bad stretch of road, man."

"Oh, God, another morning person," Dillon groaned. "I'm surrounded by them."

Chuckling, Joe pulled the binoculars from around his neck and handed them to him. "I think that's my cue to cut and run. It's been quiet as a church out there," he said, nodding to the endless stretch of arid grasslands that surrounded the house and barn on all sides. "Santiago would have to be crazy to try anything during the day, but from what Riley says, the man's a few doughnut holes short of a dozen, so go figure. Holler if you need me."

"Don't worry, I will," Dillon assured him and sent him off to bed. Knowing there was no such thing as being too cautious, he lifted the binoculars to recheck the land Joe had just inspected and satisfied himself no one was about. Only then did he move to the house to take up a position on the front porch to wait for Riley and acquaint himself with the lay of the land between the house and the highway ten miles to the north. He was still there fifteen minutes later when he spied Riley's patrol car slowly making its way over the pothole-laden drive.

More convinced than ever that the decision he'd come to last night was the right one, he announced his intentions just as soon as he'd given his friend a report on the lack of activity during the night. "We need to talk," he said flatly, leading the way to the barn, where they wouldn't be overheard. "This isn't going to work."

"What?" Riley demanded, frowning as they entered the shadowy interior of the building. "You just said you had a quiet night."

"We did, but dammit, Riley, you can't expect me to sit around here twiddling my thumbs while you and your men put your lives on the line looking for Santiago! And don't tell me that's your job," he added quickly when he opened his mouth to do just that. "The bastard was my problem before he was yours, and he wouldn't be here at all if it wasn't for me. So I'm going looking for him."

"The hell you are!"

"And I want you to take Sydney into protective custody," he continued, ignoring Riley's explosive growl as if he hadn't spoken. "It's the only way I can be sure she'll be safe and not go out looking for the damn man herself."

"You can't be serious."

"Dammit, Riley, this isn't a joke! I know how this jerk thinks—"

"And he knows you," Riley replied. "He knows you'll come looking for him just like you did before. Only, this time, he wants you as badly as you want him and he won't wait around for you to find him. Why should he? He wants revenge and he can get that by taking you out with a high-powered rifle the second you show your face in public. And he won't bother with shooting you in the back again, either. This time he'll shoot to kill."

He was right and they both knew it. Snarling a curse, Dillon hit a support post with the flat of his hand, but the sharp sting did little to relieve his mounting frustration. "I want to help," he said tersely. "And I can't do it by sitting around here watching the grass grow."

"You can't go after him, either." Riley hated to bring up the subject of Dillon's back but knew of no other way to make him see reason. "I'm sorry, man, but you know yourself you're in no shape for this kind of thing. That damn bullet could move at any time and you'd be a sitting duck. Santiago would kill you, and I'd have to come after him. Then we'd both be dead when Becca got through with me. Is that what you want?"

Against his will, Dillon had to smile at the thought of his friend's spunky wife taking her much-larger husband to task. If anyone could do it, it was Becca. "It wouldn't hurt you to be brought down a peg or two, but I'd just as soon not be the cause."

"Then stay here and watch Sydney yourself," he retorted. "The agency's sending two agents from Tucson to help me with the case, but Syd's the one who can be a real handful. If she gets it in her head that she's missing out on the best part of this story, it's going to take more than Joe to stop her from taking off like a bat out of hell. I'd feel a lot better knowing that you were here to help."

Dillon could have argued that there would be no need to watch over Sydney if he got busy and tracked Santiago down himself, but he and Riley went back a long way and he recognized the unyielding set to his friend's jaw. He wasn't going to budge on this and would, in fact, put Dillon in protective custody himself if he thought he was about to do something foolish. Not intending to give him the chance, Dillon gave in—for now—and told him what he wanted to hear.

"All right, we'll play it your way and see what the DEA can do. I just hope they don't send you a couple of rookies."

Chapter 8

Standing just outside the wide double doors of the barn, the cup of coffee she'd poured for Riley cooling in her hand, Sydney hadn't meant to eavesdrop. When she heard the car in the drive and seen the two men head for the barn, she'd just intended to bring Riley some coffee and catch up on the latest news. The second she realized they were arguing, she'd stopped, not wanting to intrude. Then she'd heard her name.

Resentment sparkling in her eyes, she was half tempted to storm inside and give Dillon Cassidy a piece of her mind. The rat! So he thought he'd talk Riley into locking her up in protective custody, then take off after Santiago himself, did he? Just let him try it! He might have fooled Riley into thinking he was willing to play it his way for a while, but she knew bull when she heard it. Dillon wasn't the type to sit on the sidelines for long. Santiago was his fight, and every instinct she possessed told her he was going after him. And she

was going with him—come hell or high water. He just didn't
know it yet.

Silently retreating to the house, she was puttering around
the kitchen when Riley came in with the groceries he'd
brought. He was in a hurry to get back to work tracking
down Santiago and couldn't stay to chat, which was just fine
with Sydney. He knew her too well. If he'd have stopped to
take one good look at her face, he would have instantly
known something was up. He didn't, however, and left almost immediately with the promise to be back when he
could.

After that, there was nothing left for Sydney to do but
wait. Over the long course of the day, Dillon only came inside for food and bathroom breaks, and Sydney gave him
the distance he seemed to want. But he was never out of her
sight for long. She watched him from the windows of the
house, watched him study every inch of the surrounding
territory and the movement of the sun in the sky. Separately, they both waited for the night.

She had to give him credit—if she hadn't overheard him
in the barn, she would have never guessed he was plotting
anything. He lounged in the shade of the porch as though
he didn't have a care in the world, while inside, she paced
like a nervous expectant father, unable to sit still. By the
time Joe finally woke and took the next watch, she was
ready to climb the walls. Dillon only laughed at the deputy's jokes and seemed totally resigned to an extended stay.

But when it was time for bed and they both retreated to
their separate rooms and the house was shrouded in darkness, Sydney knew the time had come for Dillon to make his
move. A quick glance out the window assured her that Joe
was making his rounds—a mere shadow in the darkness, he
silently patrolled the perimeter of the ranch compound.

Relieved, she quietly let herself out of her room and crossed the living room to Dillon's.

Slipping quietly into his room, she would have sworn she hadn't made a sound. But he was standing by the bed, throwing clothes into a plastic grocery bag, and whirled the second she stepped across the threshold. A large, threatening shadow in the darkness, he snapped, "What the hell do you think you're doing?"

Startled, she froze, her heart jumping into her throat and irritating her no end. "Going with you," she retorted, carefully keeping her voice as low as his. "And don't try to pretend you don't know what I'm talking about. I heard you in the barn with Riley—he may have swallowed that bull you were feeding him about playing it his way, but I know better. You're going after Santiago yourself and I'm going with you."

"Think again, sweetheart," he snorted, turning his back on her to resume his hurried packing. "I work alone."

Not surprised by his attitude, Sydney closed the door behind her and leaned back against it, prepared to wait him out if she had to. Short of physically removing her, which she didn't think he could do with his back, there was no way he was getting past her without her cooperation, and that was going to cost him.

Cocking her head, she studied him in the darkness. "You have got to be the stubbornest man I've ever met. You've got a bullet in your back that could take you out of the hunt at any time, and you still think you can go after the man who put it there by yourself. Do you have a death wish? Is that what this is all about?"

"No, of course not!"

"Then you'd better take me with you. I'm pretty good with a gun, and I can help get you to safety if your back freezes up."

No! Every self-preserving instinct Dillon possessed cried out in protest. He couldn't get her out of his head as it was—going into sure danger with her would only make it worse. He wanted her safe, dammit, not tagging along after him.

But she had a point, he silently acknowledged, swearing under his breath. One that he couldn't dismiss as easily as he'd have liked. Santiago was just like a coyote, sniffing out a weakness in his prey and using it to his advantage. If he caught scent of the least vulnerability, he'd be on him so fast that he wouldn't have time to so much as pull his gun before he'd tear him to shreds. With Sydney along, it would be two against one. And she could cover his back. If she could shoot half as good as she did everything else, they'd at least be able to hold their own.

But he didn't like it. He didn't like it at all.

Wondering how the hell he'd let her talk him into such insanity, he warned, "This isn't going to be any picnic. I'm going to be on the move and roughing it. So if you're going to cry about no hot water or even a bathroom, you'd better stay here. I don't have time for whiny babies."

Her blue eyes flaring at that, she shot him a resentful look. "I never whined in my life. I don't plan to start now."

"Good. See that you don't." His voice hardly louder than a murmur, he told her of his plan to slip out when Joe came in for a bathroom break. "Take only what you need and bring it in here when you've got it all together—we'll leave through the window. If we're lucky, Joe won't even know we're gone until he notices your Jeep is missing. By then, it'll be too late to stop us."

Nodding, Sydney soundlessly pulled open the door. "I'll be right back."

She was as good as her word, silently returning a few minutes later with a bundle of clothes, her laptop and a smaller bundle of nonperishable items she'd pilfered from the kitchen. Just making out the inquiring lift of Dillon's eyebrow in the thick shadows, she explained, "Food. I've got a feeling we're going to be a long ways from a McDonald's."

"Light-years," he agreed, and moved to the window to wait.

It seemed as if half the night passed before they heard the back door open and Joe quietly make his way to the bathroom. Her nerve endings tingling with expectation, Sydney instantly grabbed her things from where she'd laid them on the bed and quietly hurried across the room. Dillon was already at the window, carefully easing it open. Motioning for her to wait, he silently unlatched the screen and climbed through the opening. A heartbeat later, after handing her things through the opening, she landed with a nearly soundless thud next to him. In the darkness, their eyes met, then they were racing for the barn.

Feeling like a kid playing hooky, Sydney nearly choked on a laugh as she helped Dillon push the Jeep out of the barn. The keys were still in the ignition, but they didn't want to alert Joe to their leaving any sooner than they had to, and the sound of a motor roaring to life would certainly bring him running. So they pushed it as far as they dared, then jumped inside when the slight downhill slant of the drive was enough to start the vehicle rolling.

Her eyes dancing, Sydney glanced over her shoulder at the dark house. "Still no sign of Joe. Do you think he heard us?"

"If he didn't, he soon will. Hang on, I'm going to start her up."

Shifting into second, he popped the clutch, and the motor immediately roared to life. In the quiet of the night, there was no doubt that the sound easily carried to the house. Knowing Joe was going to come running any second, Dillon hit the gas and sent them surging forward. Seconds later, they were bumping over the rough drive like a runaway mine train barreling down a mountain.

Clinging to her seat, Sydney laughed and hung on for dear life as they left the ranch house far behind. The carefree sound warmed Dillon's insides like warm honey and for just a second, he found himself forgetting everything but the woman at his side. She was enjoying this, he marveled, grinning. Just like a kid sneaking off in the dark to paper the trees in a stranger's yard. There was always the danger of getting caught, but she wouldn't worry about that until it happened. The fun was in the doing.

God, how long had it been since he'd felt that mad rush of exhilaration? he wondered. That high that came from daring to take a chance, and to hell with the consequences? Lord, he'd almost forgotten what it felt like, but just listening to Sydney's husky laughter brought it all back. And just for a second in the darkness, he could almost believe that she could give him back all that he had lost when Santiago put that damn bullet in his back.

But then his cellular phone rang just as he reached the ranch entrance and turned onto the highway, and reality ripped through the illusion like a rusty knife. Knowing Joe would have called his boss the second he realized they were gone, he reached for the phone and said dryly into the receiver, "Don't waste your time, Riley. You're not going to talk me out of this."

"Of all the stupid, idiotic, self-destructive . . ." Running out of adjectives, Riley switched to curses, uncaring that he was turning the airwaves blue. "Damn it to hell, you crazy son of a bitch, you told me you'd give me some time, and I'm holding you to your word! You hear me? So get your skinny butt back to that ranch and stay there before you get yourself killed!"

Holding the phone slightly away from his ear, Dillon couldn't remember a time he and Riley had ever argued about anything, let alone yelled at each other. He didn't want to lose his friendship, but there were some things he couldn't do, not even for a friend. "Sorry, but I can't do that."

"Dammit, Cassidy, don't make me pull rank on you! You're still my deputy—"

"Not anymore I'm not," he cut in. "I just quit." And without another word, he hung up.

Sitting quietly at his side, Sydney said wryly, "Well, that sounded like it went pretty well. How ticked was he?"

"On a scale of one to ten? About a thirty-five."

Wincing, Sydney didn't have to ask if he was kidding. She knew Riley. "I had a feeling you were going to say that. Now what do we do?"

"Find a place to spend the rest of the night, then talk strategy." Shooting her a quick look, he said, "You'd better not be hoping for a hotel 'cause it ain't gonna happen. From here on out, we're roughing it, lady."

"I can take anything you can, Cassidy. Besides, I've got my pup tent and sleeping bag in the back, so I'm ready for just about anything."

"You brought a tent?"

She chuckled at his incredulous tone. "Believe it or not, it's one of the tools of the trade. I never know when I'm going to have to sit on a story overnight, so I started carrying the tent just in case."

"Well, I'll be damned." Shaking his head over her foresight, he peered through the windshield. "That definitely changes our options. This is more your neck of the woods than mine. Any idea where we are?"

"On Rawlings land," she said promptly. "It stretches halfway to Mexico."

"Where's the ranch headquarters? We don't want to chance stumbling across any of the family."

"Oh, you don't have to worry about that. The old homestead, where Gable and his wife, Josey, live, is about twenty miles from here, and the rest of the family is all within a couple of miles of there. This far south, you're not going to run into anything but cattle and cactus."

"Then look for a gate," he said. "Riley will expect us to get as far away from this area as possible, so he'll never think to look for us just down the road."

Surprised, Sydney turned from searching for a break in the fence that was nothing but a blur as they raced down the deserted road. "You think he'll come after us?"

"He was madder than hell," he said with a shrug. "If he decided he could hold us both for interfering with his investigation, there's no telling what he might do. Hold on. I think I see a gate up ahead."

Slowing down, he swung off the road and braked to a stop in front of a crude gate of cedar and barbed wire. It was held shut by a simple loop of wire draped around a fence post. Jumping out of the Jeep, Sydney quickly flipped the wire loop free and dragged the gate wide enough for Dillon to drive through. Seconds later, after hurriedly closing and latching the gate again, she was back in the Jeep and they were disappearing over a small rise. The only sign that they'd been there at all was the almost invisible tire tracks they left in the loose dirt near the gate.

On the other side of the rise, the Jeep headlights picked up nothing but cactus and brush and an occasional rocky ridge. The moon had yet to rise, and it was dark as pitch. And silent. Not even the breeze whispered in the night. Civilization could have been a million miles away.

Cocooned in the Jeep with Sydney, Dillon tried like hell to ignore the isolation of their surroundings, but he'd set himself an impossible task. Sydney only had to breathe for him to be aware of her. Then the situation turned abruptly dangerous when he helped her pitch the tent in the first level spot they came to and she insisted he share it with her.

Eyeing the small nylon structure doubtfully, he said, "I don't think so."

"But you can't sit up all night in the Jeep with your back the way it is."

"I'll be fine."

"This is ridiculous." When he only shrugged, she turned as stubborn as he. "Then we'll both sit up."

She'd do it, too, he thought irritably, just to prove that she could. And tomorrow, neither one of them would be worth a damn. "All right," he said grudgingly. "Have it your way. Just don't blame me if you don't get much sleep. That thing's not much bigger than a cracker box."

That proved to be an understatement when they both crawled inside and got situated. They could hardly move without brushing against each other in the dark. Hot, aroused, furious with himself for giving in to her in the first place, he had no choice but to stretch out beside her.

"Are you okay?"

So close that she couldn't breathe without him feeling it all the way to his toes, Dillon would have laughed if he could have managed to unclench his teeth. "Oh, yeah, I'm just peachy," he drawled. "How about you? Am I crowding you?"

"No, I'm fine. Really. Are you cold?"

"No!"

"Oh...well, I brought my sleeping bag just in case. I can open it up if we need it...."

They were as stiff as two strangers who suddenly found themselves pressed close in a crowded elevator, their conversation stilted and awkward. Lying flat on his back, staring blindly up at the tent only inches above his head, he tried to block out the feel of her hip just touching his and the innocent brush of her leg, but his nerve endings were screaming in awareness. Outside, the temperature was dropping, but sweat broke out on his brow. His hands clenched into fists, he fought the need to turn to her and shifted to give her more room instead . . . only to have her move at the same time.

Arms and legs rubbed against each other, and suddenly a soft feminine breast was crushed against his chest as she struggled to turn on her side. Stunned, they both froze in surprise. Then Dillon was jerking back, cursing, and Sydney couldn't seem to catch her breath.

He should have brought up Santiago then and reminded them both of their reason for being together in the first place, but his brain refused to cooperate. All his senses were focused on her—the scent of her, the feel, the remembered taste of her—making it impossible for him to string more than a few words together at a time. His jaw rigid, he said tightly, "You use it. I'm fine." Without another word, he turned on his side away from her and closed his eyes.

Back off! He didn't actually say the words, but Sydney had never been slow on the uptake and the message came through loud and clear in the darkness. *Don't get any ideas about me. Don't expect anything from me. It's not going to happen.*

Chilled, she lay perfectly still, staring at the unyielding line of his back, and tried to convince herself that the warning wasn't necessary. He might be able to make her forget her own name, but she'd learned the hard way not to read anything into kisses in the dark. She wouldn't be stupid enough to forget that at this late date. If her heart was still skipping beats at the remembered feel of his hard chest against her breast, it was just because he'd caught her off guard. That was all it was, just surprise.

"Yeah, and next year, you're going to the moon to cover the next shuttle landing," she muttered under her breath. Grabbing her sleeping bag from where she'd tossed it to the end of the tent at her feet, she unrolled it and crawled inside. Beside her, Dillon didn't move so much as a muscle, but she knew he wasn't asleep. Casting him an irritated look, she snuggled down into the enveloping warmth and slammed her eyes shut. She wouldn't sleep, she thought grimly, but she could pretend as well as he could.

Within minutes, she was out like a light.

Dillon knew the exact second she fell asleep. One second she was stiff as a board beside him, and the next she was breathing softly, the tension draining right out of her. His tight jaw gradually relaxing, he let out a slow breath, wishing he could doze as easily as she did. But the air that slipped through the zippered tent opening was already chilly. And with every drop in the temperature, he felt it in his back.

He lay there for as long as he could, trying to distract himself by thinking of a hundred different things, from the old '55 Ford he'd rebuilt from the ground up when he was sixteen to all the places in the county where Santiago could be lying in wait for him. But the pain in his back grew steadily worse, until it flared into a fire that burned hotter than the flames of hell and he couldn't stand it a second longer. Stifling a groan, he eased over onto his stomach, unzipped the entrance and stiffly crawled out of the tent.

The night breeze, cold and playful, whispered around him as he straightened and slowly began the exercises his doctor had recommended after he was shot. Stretching never completely relieved the pain, but it did help allay it some, and after only a few minutes, he felt the pressure start to fade to more bearable limits. His face lifted to the millions of stars decorating the night sky, he sighed tiredly, half tempted to spend the rest of the night walking around patrolling the area. But he was going after Santiago in the morning and only a fool did that with no sleep. Turning back to the tent, he silently eased inside.

Surprising himself, he slept after that, but only until his back tightened up again and he inadvertently moved the wrong way in his sleep. His defenses down, not even aware of what he was doing, he came awake with a groan of pain.

At his side, Sydney stirred, a frown working its way across her brow as she tried to figure out what had disturbed her. Then she heard it again, a low moan that jerked her to attention faster than a fire alarm. "Dillon?"

"Go back to sleep," he grated roughly. "It's just my back."

Cursing the sleeping bag that clung to her like a drowning victim, she yanked the zipper down and turned to him, already on her knees. "You should have woke me sooner. Maybe I can help."

He laughed at that, the strangled sound holding little humor. "Help? Don't you get it, lady? Nobody can help. That's the problem."

Ignoring him, her hands searched in the darkness...and encountered fingers that were as cold as ice. "My God, you're freezing! No wonder your back's killing you. Here, let me open up the sleeping bag...."

He tried to protest, but she was having none of it. Raising up so she could tug the sleeping bag out from underneath her, she unzipped it the rest of the way and unfolded it over both of them with a snap of her wrist. The chill in the air was sharp, and the sleeping bag alone wasn't enough to warm him. Hesitating, she studied the rigid line of his back as he lay on his side, facing away from her. Every breath he drew in was slow and measured, as if he couldn't manage anything more and still keep the pain bearable.

Just watching him broke her heart. It wasn't fair, she raged silently. For God knew how many years, he'd put his life on the line for a job that paid too little and asked more of him than it had a right to. And all he had to show for it was a pain that was better than the alternative—no feeling at all.

Wanting to help, needing to touch him, she threw caution to the wind and did what she'd been longing to do ever since they'd first crawled into the tent. She lay down beside him under the sleeping bag and boldly pressed up against his back.

Startled, he jumped like a scalded cat. "Dammit, Sydney, what do you think you're doing?"

"Trying to warm you up," she murmured, her heart thundering in her breast as she crowded closer, loving the feel of him against her. "It'll help your back."

Help? He almost choked on a strangled laugh. Didn't she realize she wasn't helping anything? That she just made him want things he couldn't have? Her. He wanted her. And he didn't even know how it had started. He could no longer remember what it was like not to have an ache lodged in his gut, a ball of need that urged him to toss his principles aside and forget that he had nothing to offer a woman, forget everything but her touch, her warmth, the passion that was such an inherent part of her and colored everything she did.

Without even trying, she could have tempted a saint—he didn't want to think about what she could do to him if she set her mind to it. Knowing that, he should have pushed her away immediately and made it clear he could no longer tolerate her closeness. But warmth was already seeping into him, slowly easing the constriction in his back. And she felt so damn good against him. Soft and giving, she wrapped herself around him like a fantasy come to life, heating him from the inside out. His eyes closing with a silent moan of pleasure, he promised himself he'd just lie here for a moment. After all, what could it hurt?

But a moment stretched into a minute, then a minute into a half hour. Somewhere in the back of his brain, the thought lodged that he could lose himself in her and delight in the loss, but tiredness was catching up with him and he didn't have the strength to care. Later, he promised himself as sleep overtook him. He'd deal with it later.

Morning was still a promise away when a lonely mockingbird started to warm up for its first song of the day. Sprawled on his back, Dillon heard nothing but the thunder of his own heartbeat as the woman in his dreams stirred against him, her breast rubbing against his chest as she settled into a more comfortable position, the soft warmth of her sigh a moist caress at his throat. Instinctively his arms tightened around her. Soft. She was so soft, so sweet, so damn hot. His fingers blindly searching, he filled his hands with the curve of her hips, the roundness of her bottom, a low groan vibrating up from the very heart of him as she sleepily moved against his arousal. Murmuring her name, he rolled to his side with her still in his arms, his mouth roughly seeking hers.

It wasn't the first time he'd dreamed of loving her. She always came to him at the darkest hour of the night, just before dawn when his defenses were down, stealing into his dreams with a slow, secretive smile that seduced and promised at one and the same time. She never spoke, never got in a hurry. Every move was for his pleasure, every knowing glide and caress of her hands and mouth guaranteed to drive him slowly out of his mind.

And for all of two minutes, this time was no different. Sleepily kissing him back, she melted into him, her mouth lazily opening to his with the sweetest of invitations. Seduced, he couldn't have resisted her even if he'd tried. Tangling his fingers in the silken fire of her hair, he slanted his mouth over hers and deepened the kiss.

At the first hot, wet, enticing taste of her, full consciousness returned with a dizzying rush. Stiffening, the thunder of his heart loud in his ears drowning out common sense, he jerked back, trying to clear his head enough to think straight. But she was boneless in his arms, nuzzling him, the slow kisses she dropped along his throat distracting the hell out of him.

He had to stop this, he thought in growing desperation. She was still half-asleep and not responsible for her actions. Still, one of them had to try to see reason. "Sydney, sweetheart, you don't know what you're doing—"

"Yes, I do," she murmured sleepily, nibbling at his ear. "I'm kissing you and it feels wonderful."

He groaned, wondering if she was going to regret this when she came to her senses. God, she was making this difficult! "Honey, I think we should talk."

Nipping at his earlobe, she smiled when she felt him stiffen, her blue eyes wide-awake and dark with wanting in the shadowy light as she drew back just far enough so she could look him in the eye. Lifting her hand to his beard-roughened jaw, she slowly rubbed her thumb across his bottom lip. "You don't really want to talk, do you?" she teased huskily. "Now?"

Yes! the voice of reason thundered in his head, but it was too late. The blood was already rushing through his veins, and the fire in his loins was a dozen times hotter than any pain that had ever burned in his back. She was too warm and giving in his arms, the hunger she touched off in him a living thing that clawed at his insides until he was raw with need. Cursing himself, he felt his control shatter and couldn't do anything but swoop down and take her mouth like a man possessed.

Gasping, Sydney clung to him, her head spinning, shaky laughter bubbling up in her. Yes! This was what she wanted, what she'd yearned for from the moment she'd first laid eyes on him—the wildness, the passion that was there in the depth of his gray eyes any time their gazes chanced to meet, every time they kissed. Oh, he hid it well, but it was there, nevertheless, carefully kept under lock and key, just waiting to be let free.

His hands rushing over her, fumbling at the buttons of her blouse, the snap of her jeans, he didn't give her time to do anything but murmur his name before he stripped her bare, then tore at his own clothes. And all the time, he never stopped kissing her. Slow and leisurely, hard and fast, he threw her off kilter with kisses that fired her blood and dazed her senses and left her reeling, not knowing if she was coming or going. And she loved it.

Mindless, restless, she was a puppet in his hands, lost to everything but the desire that swam in her blood. His clever fingers skimmed over her breasts, teasingly avoiding her sensitive nipples and the touch that she burned for. Then, just when she thought he'd never end the sweet torture, he crushed her close, holding her to him as he rubbed the soft, thick pelt of hair covering his chest against her breasts. Startled, she cried out in pleasure. And deep inside, the ache that lodged in the core of her femininity began to throb.

Feverish, she moved against him, but that only turned her blood hotter. Urgency driving her, her fingers anything but steady as they raced over him like a hot breeze, she learned the texture of his skin, the play of his muscles, how to make him groan with just a touch, how to destroy him. Her hand high on his thigh, she'd barely grazed his hardness when she suddenly found herself flat on her back, his steely gray eyes glittering down into her startled blue ones from only inches away, his fingers trapping her hand between their hot, naked bodies.

Time stopped; neither of them moved. Tension crackled in the air like a storm waiting for just the right conditions to break. Then his fingers moved on hers, teaching her how to please him, and the tempest broke over them with an intensity that left them both gasping.

Her name a hoarse groan that seemed to come from the depths of his being, he kissed her until her lungs were crying out for air, her body crying out for him. And then he was surging into her, coming home, claiming her, making her his as his heart hammered in time with hers. Nothing had ever felt so right. Tears welling in her throat and filling her eyes, she wrapped her arms and legs around him and held him as if she would never let him go.

Outside, the sun peaked over the horizon, and within seconds, the shadows that filled the tent vanished. Her eyes closed to hold in the light that seemed to glow from somewhere in the region of her heart, Sydney heard a mockingbird break into song and knew just how it felt. If she'd had the energy, she would have been humming.

So this was what all the hullabaloo was about, she thought dreamily, unable to stop smiling. How had she managed to miss out on it all these years? She and Adam had made love and she'd thought at the time it was nice enough, but even then she hadn't seen why poets had immortalized the act or songwriters crooned on about the wonder of it. Why hadn't somebody told her?

Too replete to move, content just to hold him, she could have lain there all day with Dillon's face buried in her hair, his breathing a ticklish caress against her neck. But as she lifted her hand to the thick hair at the nape of his neck, he rolled off of her and turned on his back, his movement stilted and jerky as he searched for and found his jeans. Not sparing her so much as a glance, he tugged them on, the sound of his zipper being jerked up loud in the suddenly cool silence.

He didn't say a word, but he didn't have to. His back was stiff with regret, his jaw—what she could see of it—locked tight on the words he wouldn't say. Hurt, feeling horribly exposed, Sydney grabbed the sleeping bag and dragged it to her breast, her heart hammering against her ribs as she scooted into a sitting position as far from him as the small tent would allow.

Another woman might have waited for him to say something—*anything*—but his silence was killing her at the same time that it closed her out, and she couldn't stand it. Refusing to huddle under the sleeping bag, she sat stiffly, her back ramrod straight as she clutched it to her, and said huskily, "Don't you think we should talk about this?"

With a vicious jerk, he pulled on his boots. "There's nothing to talk about," he said grimly. "I lost my head—end of story. If you're worried about it happening again, don't be. It won't."

"Why?"

"*Why?*" Stunned by the question and her attitude, he jerked around to stare at her as if she'd lost her mind. "Good God, woman, do you even have to ask? I would have thought it was perfectly obvious."

"Then I must be incredibly dense," she said simply. "Explain it to me."

"I have nothing to offer you—"

"I don't remember asking anything of you," she cut in, bristling.

"You didn't have to," he snapped. "I've been in your house." Cursing himself for the inane remark the second it was out of his mouth, he didn't blame her for looking confused. "You don't just live in a house, Sydney. It's a home. The kind that's crying out for a husband and kids and a swing set in the yard. Somewhere out there, there's a man who can give you that. I can't."

For a minute, he thought she was going to hotly claim that he'd read not only her, but her house, all wrong, but then the temper simmering in her eyes cooled. Cocking her head, she studied him as if he were a story that she couldn't quite figure out. "For the sake of argument, let's forget what I want and talk about you. Is there any medical reason why you can't be a husband and father?"

Bitterness twisting his mouth, he arched a mocking brow. "You mean other than the fact that it's only a matter of time before I end up in a wheelchair?"

"Your ability to move has nothing to do with whether or not you'd make a good husband and father," she pointed out quietly. "It's what's in your heart that counts."

"Tell that to an eight-year-old who wants to play touch football with his old man and has to tackle a chair. Or a wife who only wants to dance with her husband on their anniversary and he can't even stand up."

He flung the words at her accusingly, as though she were the one who had put the bullet in his back, and they stung like the sharp flicks of a whip. Her eyes hot with sudden tears, she snapped, "That eight-year-old might not give a damn about football—if he's into video games, he'd rather have a dad he can play Pac-Man with. And as for the wife, she might be so thankful she has her husband to hold her during the night that she'd rather have that any day of the week than a stupid old dance."

He gave her a withering look. "Spare me the fairy tales. If I want fiction, I'll go to the bookstore."

"Fine," she retorted. "And while you're at it, spare me the excuses. It's obvious this has nothing to do with your back. You're just not interested in a relationship. Why don't you say so and quit beating around the bush? I'm a big girl. I can take it."

"I'm not interested in a relationship," he repeated coldly. "There. I said it. Have I made myself clear?"

"Perfectly."

They glared at each other like strangers, the closeness they'd shared only moments before widening into a chasm that neither could cross. Because they hadn't made love, she told herself, blinking back tears she was determined not to let fall. They'd had sex. Nothing more. She'd wanted honesty and she'd got it in spades. He wanted nothing to do with a relationship. Or her.

Her heart battered and bruised, she would have given anything to make the same claim. But she couldn't. Because she already cared more than she should, and nothing, not even his lack of feelings for her, was going to change that.

And it was killing her.

But she'd be damned if he'd ever know it. Her chin lifted haughtily in spite of the fact that she was sitting naked under the sleeping bag, she said coolly, "That's settled then. If you'll wait outside, I'll get dressed and then help you take the tent down. If we're going to find Santiago before he finds us, we'd better get started."

Chapter 9

Later, Sydney didn't know how she did it. Dressed in jeans and a sweatshirt, she crawled out of the tent with as much dignity as she could muster and proceeded to dismantle the tent. She would have preferred to do it herself, but Dillon, as cool as she, insisted on helping, and she was in no shape for an argument. All business, she didn't so much as flinch as his hand accidentally grazed hers, but she felt his touch all the way to her core. And it hurt, dammit, more than it should have. Swallowing the hot lump of tears that lodged in her throat, she quietly shied away.

If he noticed, he didn't say anything, but his jaw was a block of granite and he didn't seem the least inclined to break the silence that grew colder by the second. Without a word, he started to repack the tent in its carrying case.

Her heart bruised and battered, she would have given anything to be just as aloof, but she just didn't have it in her. The silence ate at her until she couldn't stand it. "Tell me more about Santiago," she said, wincing at the edge of desperation that sharpened her voice. "What's his M.O.?"

For a moment, she didn't think he was going to answer her. His gray eyes shuttered in the morning light, he finished repacking the tent, then deposited it in the back of the Jeep, along with the sleeping bag. "He's a tricky son of a bitch who doesn't make many mistakes," he finally replied stiffly. "He's not the type to do things on the spur of the moment. He bides his time and works out all the kinks, then, when he's covered all his bases and is sure nothing can go wrong, he strikes."

"So you don't think his breaking out of prison was just a fluke? A mistake by a guard that he impulsively took advantage of?"

His mouth curled contemptuously. "If a mistake was made, he had some of the thugs on his payroll engineer it. He's too careful to leave anything to chance. By the time he broke out of that prison, he'd planned this whole scenario down to the smallest detail. Then he came looking for me."

Something in the way he said the last sentence—as if a final showdown with the man who had put a bullet in his back was a fated confrontation that was going to happen regardless of what they did to prevent it—chilled her to the bone. Fear clenching in her gut, she wanted to reach out to him, but he'd already made it painfully clear that he didn't want anything more from her than she'd already given.

Forcing back the hurt that threatened to choke her, she frowned. "But how did he find you so quickly? He had to have help—"

"Angelo," Dillon retorted, his mouth twisting as if the name left a bad taste in his mouth. "He and Santiago have been as thick as thieves for twenty years. He was his eyes and ears when he was locked up, and you can bet that Jeep of yours that he was right there waiting for him when he broke out. He'd do anything for him, including kill.''

"Wonderful," she drawled. "Now there are two of them to contend with. So where the devil are they? They didn't just drive into town and take a room out on motel row.''

His gaze narrowed on the distant horizon, he studied the endless miles of desert that surrounded them. "No, but they had digs when they got here. Locating a deserted, out-of-the-way ranch and renting it under an assumed name, complete with references, would have been a piece of cake for Angelo.''

"A deserted ranch, hmm?'' Chewing her bottom lip, Sydney scanned her brain for a likely place that met that description. "Last I heard, the Dawson spread was still empty. And the Crazy Rabbit has been on the market for years, ever since Cecil Jennings hung himself from the windmill when all his cattle died in a drought. The high school kids say its haunted.''

"Does it have an airstrip? Santiago wouldn't have chanced driving all the way from Florida, not when he knew the Feds were scouring the country for him," he added. "They set up roadblocks the second they realized he was loose, and he knew he had to get out of there fast. He's a licensed pilot and has his own plane. If Angelo met him somewhere with the Cessna, he could have been in the air before the DEA had even been notified of his escape.''

"Then we'd better check out the Dawson place first,'' Sydney replied. "I know it's got an airstrip, but I'm not so sure about the Crazy Rabbit. I was only out there once—to cover Cecil's death—and as far as I know, he didn't have a plane.''

Since she was more familiar with the area than Dillon, Sydney drove, taking little-used back roads as they headed for Frank Dawson's place, which was twenty miles away in

the southeast corner of the county. They didn't pass a single vehicle, but Dillon didn't relax his vigilance for a second. Seated tensely next to her in the passenger seat, he kept
an eagle eye out for Riley and the DEA agents who, if they
chose to, could arrest them for interfering in a government
investigation.

Her gaze lifting to her rearview mirror for the umpteenth
time, Sydney let out a sigh of relief. The road behind them
was still empty—she just prayed it stayed that way. "How
are we going to know the agents if we do stumble across
them? Do you know them?"

"No. Riley said they were rookies, but don't worry. I'll
know them when I see them."

"How? They're not going to be wearing a sign around
their necks with DEA stamped on it."

For the first time since they'd made love, the sternness
that hardened his features softened slightly. He didn't smile,
but there was a definite twitch to his lips. "They might as
well be. They've got a look to them you can't miss."

Now that he mentioned it, Sydney knew exactly what he
was talking about. She'd noticed it before but hadn't been
able to put a finger on what it was about him that reminded
her of Riley and vice versa. They were both tall and dark-
headed, but there the physical resemblance ended—except
for a self-confidence, a sureness, a quiet fearlessness that
stuck out all over both of them. And now she knew why. It
came from putting their lives on the line and facing the
worst that humanity had to offer, then living to tell about it.

The Dawson ranch came into view then, effectively ending the conversation. Her hands tightening on the steering
wheel as Dillon straightened in his seat, Sydney lifted her
foot from the accelerator and let the Jeep coast as she nodded toward the cattle guard a hundred yards in front of them
on the right. "That's the back entrance," she said quietly.

"If you stay on this road another mile, it intersects the highway that runs right in front of the main gate."

"Where's the main house and landing strip?"

"From this entrance? Maybe a couple of miles. I'm really not sure. They're much closer to the main entrance. In fact, you can just make out the house from the road."

It was a tempting thought, just driving by and checking the place out from the Jeep as they shot past, but Dillon knew Santiago too well. Wherever the bastard was, he'd have guards posted to watch every vehicle that came within a half a mile of the place. "We'd better play it safe and scope the place out from here. Let me check the drive first, though, and see if anyone's been through here recently."

Climbing out as soon as she braked to a stop in front of the cattle guard, he knelt down to examine the dusty dirt drive that led in and out of the ranch. If it had been used anytime in the past few weeks, there was no sign of it. Which didn't necessarily mean that Santiago wasn't using the place—he was clever enough not to leave tracks.

"Nothing there," he told Sydney as he rejoined her in the Jeep. "But let's not take any chances. Go slow so we won't kick up any dust, and stop the second you get a glimpse of the house."

Moving at what was little more than a crawl, they crossed the cattle guard and carefully made their way deeper into the interior of the ranch. It was a nerve-racking pace, and time dragged. His eyes narrowed on the road in front of them, Dillon leaned forward in his seat as they approached a blind curve around a pile of huge weathered boulders that looked as if it had just been dumped there by the hand of God.

"Let's stop here," he said suddenly, not liking the looks of things. He'd learned a long time ago not to go rushing around a corner without knowing what was on the other

side. "I'd rather walk around this than chance coming face-
to-face with something we're not ready for."

Her foot already on the brake, Sydney said agreeably,
"That sounds good to me. Lead the way."

Grabbing the binoculars from where she'd stowed them
behind the seat, she eased open her door and soundlessly
stepped out of the Jeep. It was still early yet, and cold, the
bite of the wind sharp as it swirled around them. It could
have been twenty below in the shade, however, and it still
wouldn't have been as chilly as Dillon's eyes as he joined
her. As cold and gray as an Arctic dawn, they spoke of a re-
solve that went soul deep.

Shivering, Sydney didn't want to think about the kind of
pain he must have endured to put that look in his eyes. It
must have been horrible, and the worst of it was, there was
nothing she or anyone else could do to change the past or
make his future any brighter, not when he walked around
with a bullet in his back. Her heart breaking for him, she
silently followed him around the curve.

What had once been the headquarters of the Dawson
ranch lay a quarter of a mile away, and even at first glance,
it was obvious the place was deserted. The airstrip was a
pothole-ridden accident waiting to happen, and the roof of
the house and barn were both in sad shape. Sydney counted
six broken windows just on one side of the old ranch house
and didn't see how anyone could stay there even one night
without being very uncomfortable.

Dillon, however, was taking no chances. He held the binoculars to his eyes, examining every inch of the place several times, searching for signs of life. But there were none.
Satisfied, he dropped the binoculars. "If Santiago's been
here, he's gotten a lot less particular than he used to be.
How far's the other place from here?"

"The Crazy Rabbit? About fifteen miles. It's farther north, back toward town."

"Can we reach it by avoiding the main roads?"

"It'll take some maneuvering, but it can be done. It'll just take longer."

"We've got all day," he drawled, and turned back toward the Jeep.

If they'd taken the most direct route, they could have been scoping out the Crazy Rabbit Ranch in a little under fifteen minutes. The more circuitous one, however, took time, and it was another twenty minutes before they turned onto a narrow road and Sydney announced, "The main entrance is on the left two miles ahead at the end of the road. As far as I know, there is no back one."

Dillon straightened, interest sparking in his eyes. "The end of the road, huh? It sounds like this place might have definite possibilities. It's private. Santiago wouldn't have to worry about being spotted by someone driving by—"

Her gaze directed straight ahead, Sydney said, "Uh-oh. Looks like someone's had trouble. I wonder what they're doing way out here."

Dillon took one look at the car a half mile ahead that appeared to be stranded on the side of the road with its hood up and he said sharply, "Pull over behind that cactus. If we're lucky they haven't seen us."

"Who?" Confused, Sydney instinctively did as he said, abruptly turning off the road behind a large ocotillo cactus. The spindly arms of the plant didn't offer much cover, but there was nothing else to hide behind. Turning to Dillon, who was already studying the scene up ahead with the binoculars, she said, "It's just a couple of guys who had car trouble. Why are we hiding?"

"Because those guys," he retorted, "have no more had car trouble than we have. They're DEA. Take a look."

"You're kidding!" Taking the binoculars from him, she adjusted them to her eyes and almost laughed at the sight of the two young men trying their best to look stranded. They weren't dressed in suits as she'd half expected, but they might as well have been. Their new jeans were starched, their Stetsons tilted at a comical angle and, judging from the gingerly way they walked around the car, they were having a tough time adjusting to new cowboy boots. Together, they gave a whole new meaning to the term *tenderfoot*.

Grinning, Sydney lowered the binoculars. "Surely they don't think they're fooling anyone? They look like a couple of extras out of a Gene Autry movie."

"Rookies," Dillon said in disgust. "It sticks out all over them. Look at the fools. They're parked right in front of the entrance to the damn ranch! Idiots! Don't they know there's no way Santiago's there? If he was, he'd have already killed them and taken off. C'mon, let's get the hell out of here."

Sydney didn't have to be told twice. Careful not to spin her wheels in the loose gravel on the side of the road, she swung the Jeep around in the opposite direction and beat a hasty retreat. Still muttering about the incompetency of young jackasses who didn't have the sense to know when they were in danger, Dillon swiveled around in his seat toward the back to make sure they hadn't been spotted.

Her own gaze lifted to the rearview mirror, Sydney asked worriedly, "Did they see us?"

"Hell, no. They're too busy adjusting the set of their cowboy hats. Boneheads! They're hardly old enough to shave, and they think they can catch Santiago."

Shaking his head over the incompetent bureaucrat who sent them there in the first place, he pulled his cellular phone from his pocket and quickly punched out the number of the sheriff's office. The minute the dispatcher came on the line, he growled, "Myrtle, this is Dillon. Patch me through to Riley."

"Dillon?" she echoed, shocked. "Land's sake, boy, where are you? Riley's been turning over every rock in the county looking for you."

At any other time, Dillon would have been amused by the old woman's blatant busybodyness, but not today. "It doesn't matter where I am, Myrtle. Get Riley on the line. *Now.*"

"Well, you don't have to get huffy about it," she retorted, stung. "Jeez, everybody's in a bear of a mood today. I don't know what's got your shorts in a twist, Dillon Cassidy, but next time you want to jump down somebody's throat, pick on somebody else!"

Struggling for patience, he sighed. "I'm not in a bear of a mood, Myrtle. I'm sorry if I was short with you. I just need to talk to Riley. It's important."

"Well, why didn't you say so?" she said, mollified. "Hang on and I'll patch you through."

Before Dillon could do more than grind his teeth on an oath, Riley was on the line. "It's about time you called in. I was beginning to get worried. Are you okay?"

Expecting him to rage at him the way he had the last time they'd talked, Dillon arched a brow in surprise. "I think I've got the wrong number. This can't be the same Sheriff Whitaker who ordered me to get my butt back to the safe house last night."

Chuckling, Riley drawled, "Cut the crap, Cassidy. I was hot that you didn't let me know what you were up to before you took off, that's all." His tone turning somber, he added, "And you were probably right to do it. Your place and Sydney's were trashed last night."

Dillon swore, but he wasn't surprised. Santiago was obviously through with his little game of cat and mouse and ready to close in for the kill. "Did anybody see anything?"

"No. The bastard's as slippery as a damn shadow. I had a man at each house and he still got past them without them even noticing him. Any idea yet where he might be holed up?"

"Not a one." He told him about the Dawson ranch, then the situation at the Crazy Rabbit. "Those two yo-yos better be thanking their lucky stars that Santiago wasn't there," he concluded irritably. "You should have seen them. They were parked right in front of the ranch entrance like a couple of homesteaders putting down roots. I couldn't believe it! These are the two wonder kids who are supposed to crack this case wide open?"

Riley swore long and hard in his ear. "If this is an example of the kind of help we can expect, we're in big trouble. I'll get on the horn and see if I can get them reassigned. In the meantime, you might as well know—we've got another problem."

"Worse than Fred and Barney trying to trap Santiago? This I gotta hear."

"Somebody's turning I-10 into a drug pipeline between Tucson and El Paso. The Feds have confiscated ten shipments in just the last two weeks alone. And guess, just guess where the Feds say it's all coming from."

His gut twisting, Dillon didn't have to guess. He knew. "Here. Santiago's flying it in from South America."

"Got it in one," he said approvingly. "You've got to give the jerk credit—he hasn't wasted any time. He's already got a major distribution center up and running, and it's barely been a month since he escaped. I don't know how the hell he's done it. You can't do something like that from just anywhere. You've got to have a runway, trucks—the whole nine yards."

"And that right there limits his choice of hideouts. From what Sydney tells me, there aren't that many places around here that are vacant, let alone equipped with an airfield."

"And the few that are available are going to be the first place we look."

Dillon agreed. "He knows that. Which means we need to concentrate on less likely places. Any suggestions?"

"As a matter of fact, I do." He rattled off a list of a dozen places that normally wouldn't appeal to a man who had, through his drug sales, become accustomed to a more affluent life-style. But for anyone trying to keep a low profile, they were perfect. "I don't see any other way to do this but to divide the list up between us and check them out separately. That's going to leave you and Sydney on your own if you stumble across Santiago, but I can't give you any protection without tipping the bastard off as to your whereabouts."

"He'll be watching you, that's for sure," Dillon agreed. "If for no other reason than to make sure you aren't closing in on him." Glancing over at Sydney, who had her ears blatantly cocked to the conversation and her eyes on the road, he said, "Don't worry about us. We'll stick to the back roads and keep our eyes peeled. If we see anything, you'll be the first to hear."

He went over the list with him then, deciding which properties they would each check out. As soon as he hung up, Sydney said, "Santiago's up to more dirty tricks, isn't he? He's flying in drugs."

"And shipping it up and down the interstate between Tucson and El Paso like candy. The Feds can't stop it."

Her hands tightening on the steering wheel, Sydney felt sick at the thought of what could happen if Santiago de-

cided to lace crack with the same *aspirin* that killed Lawrence Osborn at the Crossroads. "We've got to stop him
before we've got a real disaster on our hands. What's the
first ranch on the list?"

"The Dry Gulch," he retorted. "It sounds like a place
where snakes hang out."

"Then Santiago ought to feel right at home." Chuckling, she turned left at the next intersection and headed for
the southwest corner of the county. "From what I know of
the place, there's nothing there but dust and rocks."

The Dry Gulch did, indeed, turn out to be a bust. Run-
down and deserted, the old windmill near the deserted house
creaking eerily in the wind, it had the look and feel of an old
ghost town and gave Sydney the creeps. Suppressing a
shiver, she couldn't get away from the place fast enough.
Glancing over at Dillon, she asked, "Where to next?"

"The High Chaparral. You know it? Riley said the Rios
family owns it."

Sydney nodded. "Actually, there's nobody left but a sister, and she moved to town years ago. Said she couldn't
stand the loneliness of the place. It's pretty remote."

They headed farther south, racing against the clock and
the catastrophe they both knew Santiago could set into motion whenever the mood struck him. Unwilling to waste time
by stopping to eat, they ate on the run, snacking on the dried
fruits and granola Sydney had raided from her kitchen.
Rabbit food, Dillon called it with a grimace, but it was better than nothing and allowed them to keep moving.

Unfortunately, the Rios place was as deserted as the Dry
Gulch. This time, when they stopped to check it out, however, Dillon took the time to stretch his back. Then they
were moving on.

They drove out two tanks of gas and checked out more than half of the properties that Riley had suggested, ignoring the tiredness that pulled at them as the day lengthened. But then, before either of them was ready to call it a day, the sun set, enclosing them in shadows that seemed to come out of nowhere to wrap them in intimacy. Just that quickly, the awareness that had been a silent passenger in the Jeep all day was there between them, a living, throbbing, physical thing that would no longer be ignored.

Staring straight ahead into the darkness, his expression harsh in the glow of the dash lights, Dillon said gruffly, "We might as well find a place for the night. We've done all we can do for today."

Her heart thumping just at the thought of crawling back into her tent with him, Sydney knew she couldn't do it. She couldn't lay beside him all night long, so close she could feel every breath he took. Not after the loving they'd shared this morning. Not without going quietly out of her mind. Up until the moment she'd gone into his arms and given herself to him, she'd foolishly thought she had some control over the feelings he stirred in her so effortlessly. Now she knew better, and it scared her witless.

"There's a canyon about ten miles from here," she said stiffly. "It forms the western edge of the Double R and runs for miles. It's pretty rough territory, but there's a creek that flows all year and a line cabin that's kept stocked with food. Harley told me about it. The Rawlingses keep it up for their hands, in case they get caught in a storm or hurt or something and can't make it back to the bunkhouse. I don't think they'd care if we pitched the tent there and one of us used the cabin for the night."

She couldn't have been any clearer if she'd posted a sign. Dillon didn't have to worry about her losing her head—not to mention her heart—again because it just wasn't going to happen. As far as she was concerned, the time she spent in his arms this morning never happened. And even if it did, it wouldn't be repeated; she'd make sure of it.

Glancing at him from the corner of her eye, she expected to see relief written all over his face, but his expression was shuttered, his thoughts carefully concealed from her. "Fine," he said shortly. "One place is as good as another."

Without a word, she turned onto the rocky path that led to the canyon.

The night sky was thick with stars by the time they reached the cabin, but their faint glow hardly penetrated the inky blackness that shrouded the canyon. Stepping from the Jeep, Sydney glanced around in wonder as her pupils adjusted to the darkness, unable to believe her eyes. If she hadn't known better, she would have sworn the desert was a thousand miles away instead of just beyond the rocks that marked the entrance to the canyon.

Except for an occasional mesquite, trees were scarce in the desert, but here they were thick as thieves—juniper, pine and aspen that caught the whisper of the wind in their branches and softly murmured in reply. Their intoxicating scent filling her lungs, Sydney stood transfixed while somewhere off to the right and out of her sight, the creek bubbled merrily.

Delighted, she couldn't believe she'd lived in Lordsburg for years without even suspecting such a wilderness was nearby. Huge boulders, like dark, hulking shadows, seemed to loom in the darkness, while high above the canyon floor, sheer rock cliffs rose toward the sky, dark, silent sentinels that stood guard in the night. Untouched by man except for the rough cabin that blended in with the trees, it must have looked much the same when the first pioneers stumbled across it while looking for the California gold fields.

"This place is something else," Dillon said softly, his husky voice pitched low so that it hardly caused a ripple in the stillness that surrounded them. "And you say the Rawlings family owns this?"

She nodded. "Every inch."

"Then why aren't they living here instead of in the desert, for God's sake?"

"Kat does," she said, referring to the only sister among three brothers. "After she married Lucas Valentine, they built a place at the other end of the canyon. But you can't run many cows through these trees. The ranch headquarters was built by a cowboy looking to get rich after the Civil War, and evidently he knew what he was doing. The family's been in the cattle business ever since."

"Well, they can have the rest of the place—I'll take this."

Sydney had to agree. The canyon had a serenity to it that called to her soul, and had circumstances been different, she would have claimed a spot on the porch of the rough-hewn cabin and just listened to the soothing murmur of the creek for hours. But she wasn't on vacation, and Dillon wasn't with her by choice. They still had the night to get through, and although separate sleeping quarters would definitely help, bedtime was still hours away.

Dragging in a bracing breath of pine, she forced a bright smile. "Well, we might as well get the tent out and set up, then see about supper," she said cheerfully as she turned to the back of the Jeep and opened the tailgate. "It's been hours since the granola bars ran out, and my stomach's starting to think my throat's been cut."

Before she could pull out the bright orange nylon bag that held the tent, however, Dillon was there before her, taking it from her. "I'll do this," he said firmly. "You've been driving all day and you're probably tired. Why don't you go take a bath in the creek? By the time you're finished, I'll

have a campfire going, and then we can scrounge around in
the cabin for something to eat."

"Oh, but I couldn't. You have to be tired, too—"

"I'll take my turn while you're cooking supper. Go on,"
he urged, pressing her bag of clothes into her arms. "It
doesn't take the two of us to put the tent up."

He had a point, she reflected ruefully. And she really did
need some time to herself. "All right," she said, giving in.
"I'll be back as soon as I can."

"Take your time," he said, already turning away to find
a flat, rock-free stretch of ground where he could pitch the
tent. "We've got all night, and it's only going to take a few
minutes to open a can of stew and heat it."

We've got all night.

His words dodging her every step as she struck off
through the trees toward the creek, she tried to focus her
thoughts on Santiago and the search they would once again
pick up tomorrow, but the solitude of her surroundings
made that impossible. With every whisper of the wind, she
was reminded that they were alone... again. In the majes-
tic quiet of the canyon, she could call out and only he would
hear. Only he would answer. And later, when one of them
was in the cabin and the other in the tent, only he and the
memory of the heaven she'd found in his arms would fill her
dreams.

Just thinking about it made her heart lurch in her breast.

"Stop it!" she ordered sternly as she finally reached the
creek. "You're acting like a lovesick teenager. You're on the
trail of one of the biggest stories of your life and all you can
think about is a man who doesn't want you in his life. Accept it and get over it, for God's sake!"

Muttering curses, she tossed her makeshift duffel bag to
the ground and sat down on a nearby boulder to tug off her
shoes. Beside her, the creek gurgled and danced, and be-

fore she quite realized how it happened, she found herself grinning. She could have a broken heart later. Right now she was going skinny-dipping for the first time in her life and she intended to enjoy it!

She had, thankfully, brought everything she would need for a few nights away from home, including her favorite Opium-scented soap, and within seconds she had everything laid out on the grassy bank of the creek. Her fingers lifted to the buttons of her blouse, she glanced around, feeling naughty, exposed and daring at one and the same time. But there were no Peeping Toms in the darkness for her to worry about, only Dillon struggling with the tent a hundred yards away. Through the trees, she just caught a glimpse of him, the campfire he'd already built providing enough light for him to see what he was doing. Reassured, she quickly shed her clothes and sank into the water.

"Oh!"

The water was like ice, straight out of the Arctic. Gasping, she instinctively lurched to her feet, shivering, only to discover that the wind that played tag in the tops of the trees was colder than she'd first thought. Teasing and taunting her, it snaked around her bare body, dragging goose bumps in its wake, chilling her to the bone. A strangled laugh of frustration catching in her throat, she quickly plopped back down in the water and reached hurriedly for the soap.

As far as baths went, it was the fastest—and coldest— she'd ever taken in her life, but she'd never felt so refreshed. Ten minutes after she'd stumbled from the creek and snatched up her shirt to dry herself, her heart was still thundering and her skin tingling. Knowing now why people joined polar bear clubs and went swimming in the Atlantic in the dead of winter, she couldn't seem to stop smiling as she pulled on her clothes and shoes, then made a beeline through the trees to the campfire.

His back to her as he added more wood to the fire, Dillon heard her long before she stepped into the small clearing near the cabin where he'd pitched the tent and built the fire. She'd been gone hardly any time at all, which didn't surprise him. If he remembered his geography, just about all of the rivers and streams in this part of the state had their headwaters in the mountains to the north. At this time of the year, the water would be frigid.

A slow grin starting to curl one corner of his mouth, he added a last log to the fire and turned to face her. "That was quick," he began, intending to tease her about the water. But the words died on his tongue at the first sight of her. Lord, she was gorgeous! The chilly water had put roses in her cheeks and a sparkle in her eyes, but it was the smile on her lips that was unconsciously provocative. As seductive as a siren's, yet still somehow as fresh as a young girl's, it reached out and clutched his heart, instantly captivating him in spite of the alarm bells clanging in his head.

"The water was freezing," she said, laughing as she moved to the fire and held her hands out to the dancing flames. Closing her eyes, she sighed dreamily. "Oh, that feels good!"

Unable to drag his eyes away from her, Dillon watched the firelight turn her creamy skin golden and her strawberry-blond hair to fire. All too easily, his blood heated and his body hardened. Dressed in faded jeans and a white long-sleeved tailored cotton shirt that fell halfway down her thighs, there was nothing the least bit tantalizing about her clothes, but all he could think of was stripping her down to bare skin and laying her down in the pine needles. If he could find a way to hang on to his self-control, he could make love to her until they were both too weak to move and the fire was nothing but ashes.

And then what? the caustic voice in his head drawled. *Are you going to push the lady away again when you finally come to your senses? Is that when you're finally going to remember that damn bullet in your back?*

Stiffening, he said tightly, "While you were at the creek, I checked out the canned goods in the cabin. We've got two choices for supper—canned stew or canned stew."

Sydney chuckled. "Then I guess we're having canned stew."

"Right." The clean clothes and toilet articles he'd retrieved from the Jeep earlier were lying on a nearby rock. Grabbing them, he brushed past her. "While you're heating it up, I'll be at the creek." Cooling off.

He was gone before she could say another word, his long legs quickly carrying him away from her and into the night. Her smile abruptly vanishing, Sydney stared after him, chilled again in spite of the nearness of the fire. It was, she realized somberly, going to be another long night.

Chapter 10

Supper was a silent affair.

Hardly touching the food in her bowl, Sydney sat across the fire from Dillon, her back propped against a convenient log, her eyes drawn like a magnet to his brooding figure. No man had a right to look so good by firelight, she thought resentfully, swallowing a tasteless bite of stew. He'd shaved, then donned jeans and a red plaid flannel shirt that she vaguely remembered Riley wearing. But she'd never noticed them fitting Riley half so well. Softened by countless washings, the faded material stretched across his wide shoulders, emphasizing their breadth, and all too clearly she remembered the feel of his muscles under her hands and the way his bare skin heated at her touch.

Suddenly flushed, she set her bowl down with a clatter on the ground next to her. "I've had all I want," she said huskily. "I think I'll work some."

Desperate for the distraction, she jumped to her feet and quickly retrieved her laptop from the Jeep. But even as she settled back by the fire to record her notes and impressions about the search for Santiago, Dillon was pushing to his feet and gathering up the dirty dishes.

"I'll rinse these at the creek, then I'm turning in," he said coolly. "I left your sleeping bag in the cabin for you. I'll take the tent."

"But you should be taking the sleeping bag since you're sleeping outside."

"I found some old wool army blankets in the cabin. They're scratchy as hell, but they're warm. So don't lay awake all night worrying about me freezing to death. I'll probably be warmer than you."

Reminding her to put out the fire before she went to bed, he strode off toward the creek, and Sydney found herself struggling with the perverse need to call him back. Let the man go, she sternly ordered herself. While you still can.

It was good advice, but that didn't make it any easier to turn back to her computer. All her senses attuned to his whereabouts, she knew the exact moment he returned from the creek. Staring blankly at the screen, she heard him crawl into the tent, but even then, she couldn't concentrate. The silence that surrounded her was too thick, the thunder of her heartbeat in her ears too loud, the need to go to him almost more than she could bear. She tried to remind herself of the lessons she'd learned from Adam, the heartbreak she'd suffered from trusting the wrong man too much. She didn't need anyone in her life—she enjoyed her independence. But at that moment in time, with the darkness pressing in on her and a future without Dillon the only one she could see stretching out before her, she'd never felt so lonely in her life.

Lost in thought, she sat there until her computer beeped a warning that her battery was getting low. Shocked to discover that she'd been brooding for more than an hour, she quickly saved the little bit that she had managed to write, then hit the power switch. "You're getting too old for this, Syd," she mumbled to herself. "Go to bed!"

Pushing stiffly to her feet, she quietly returned her computer to the Jeep and retrieved her flashlight from behind the driver's seat, then kicked some dirt over what was left of the fire. The night turned abruptly darker and colder. Hugging herself, she lingered only long enough to make sure that every ember was dead, then hurried to the cabin, stepping around the darkened tent without a sound, the soft glow of the flashlight lighting her way.

The cabin was little more than a one-room shack, and the only bed was a bunk built into the side of one wall. Long enough for the tallest cowboy, it had a thin mattress that looked only marginally softer than the wood floor, but for a ranch hand caught too far from the bunkhouse at the end of the day, it was probably more comfortable than a king-size bed.

Knowing she was lucky to have it, she laid the flashlight on a crudely made wooden table that sat next to the bed, then tugged off her shoes and jeans. She hadn't noticed it until then, but there was a draft somewhere—the cold night air brushed against her bare legs, sending goose bumps racing across her skin. Snatching up her sleeping bag, which Dillon had tossed onto the bed, she quickly scrambled into it, sighing in relief when its warmth closed around her. Seconds ago she would have sworn she'd never be able to sleep, not when her thoughts kept drifting outside to the tent and Dillon, but as soon as she switched off the flashlight, she couldn't seem to stop yawning. Closing her eyes, she settled more comfortably into the sleeping bag.

Dillon was almost asleep when he heard her scream. His heart stopping in midbeat, he jerked up, throwing off the

army blankets and grabbing his gun in one smooth motion.
Within three seconds flat, he was running for the cabin,
bursting through the door like a commando on a rescue
mission, his .38 gripped securely in his two hands, his sharp
eyes already searching for the enemy.

The cabin was empty, however, except for Sydney.
Dressed in her blouse and little else, she was standing next
to the bed, muttering curses as she pounded the mattress
with a flashlight. "What the devil are you doing?" Dillon
demanded, lowering his pistol. "You scared the life out of
me!"

"Out of you? What about me? There was a scorpion in
my bed!"

"Did he sting you?"

"No, I just felt him on my leg." Giving the mattress another fierce wallop, she gingerly lifted up one corner and
directed the beam of the flashlight to the darkness underneath.

Watching her, Dillon almost laughed. He couldn't believe this. She'd gone after some of the most notorious
criminals in Chicago, interviewing thieves and pushers and
murderers just to get a story, but it took nothing more than
a bug on her leg to make her scream in the night.

"Sydney..." Smothering a grin, he set his gun on the
bedside table and reached over to take the light from her.
"Are you sure it was a scorpion? Did you see it?"

"No, but—"

"Maybe it was just an ant or something." Dragging the
mattress completely off the bed, he inspected the wood
frame of the bunk, as well as every inch of the floor, but the
place was surprisingly clean. There weren't even any cob-
webs in the corners, and the mattress was just as bug-free.
Checking both sides, he flipped it back onto the bunk, then

picked up the sleeping bag from the floor. When he found nothing on the outside, he quickly turned it inside out.

There weren't any scorpions, but there was a string that had come unraveled from a side seam. Arching a brow at her, he started to grin. "Could this be your scorpion?"

"No, of course not. At least I don't think so." Suddenly not so sure, she frowned, trying to remember what exactly had sent her scrambling out of her sleeping bag like a woman possessed. Now that she took the time to think about it, she had been half-asleep. She'd turned over to get more comfortable...and something slid across her calf.

"Oh, God." Heat stinging her cheeks, she couldn't help but laugh. "I don't suppose it would do much good to mention now that I usually don't have a problem with bugs, would it?"

"Not a bit."

"It's just scorpions," she assured him. "They're just so wicked looking."

"Everybody's got their hang-ups," he agreed dryly, his gray eyes glinting.

Cocking her head, she smiled up at him. "That's true. What's yours?"

You. The admission hovered on his tongue, unspoken. Staring down at her, caught in the warmth of her teasing smile, Dillon knew she didn't have a clue how tempting she looked dressed in nothing but a long-tailed shirt that ended at midthigh, but he'd had a hard time taking his eyes off her legs from the second he'd crashed through the door.

"I need to get out of here."

The words were half mumbled to himself, a warning that a smart man would have heeded immediately. But the thought had hardly registered when he saw her eyes flare and she realized just what her state of undress was doing to him.

A delicate blush slowly spilled into her cheeks, but she didn't glance away.

"That probably would be for the best," she said faintly. "It's late."

She nodded, but made no move to show him the door. "We're both tired."

She couldn't have been more agreeable if she'd been a saint. Or more desirable if she'd stood before him stark naked. His throat as dry as dust, the spicy scent of the perfumed soap she'd used earlier teasing him, seducing him, he told himself one last time to get the hell out of there. But when he moved it wasn't toward the door.

"Nothing's changed," he warned her in a low growl that was sandpaper rough. Taking the single step that eliminated all but an inch of space between them, he stood so close that he could almost feel her breasts rise against his chest as she dragged in a small, quick breath in reaction. But still he didn't touch her, not until they reached an understanding. "I have nothing to offer you."

"Just tonight," she whispered. "No strings attached."

Her words held a promise, something he couldn't give her. Guilt twisted in his gut, but it was too late. He wanted her more than he could remember ever wanting a woman in his life, and right or wrong, there was no walking away from her. Not now. Taking her hands, he carried them to the buttons of his shirt. When she slipped the first one free, he dropped his head and took her mouth in a kiss that he only just then realized he'd been starving for all day.

Bemused, the taste of her going to his head like a straight shot of vodka, he couldn't for the life of him figure out what she did to him. Granted, she was beautiful, but he wasn't a green kid. He'd kissed his share of pretty women, but none of them had ever knocked his feet out from under him the way Sydney did. He didn't like it, couldn't explain it, but every time he really let himself look at her, his heart jerked in his chest like a teenager's. He didn't have a clue how it had happened, but she was everything he'd ever wanted in a woman. And he couldn't have her.

Just tonight. No strings attached.

Her promise echoing in his ears, haunting him, offering him what he himself claimed he wanted, he closed his arms around her, his mouth heated and tender on hers. They had all night. Somewhere in the back of his head the thought registered, reminding him that he could take his time with her and make every moment last. But already the minutes were slipping through his fingers with a speed that shook him to the core. Urgency tearing at him, he fumbled for the buttons to her blouse with fingers that were suddenly anything but steady.

Her heart jumping at the first blind touch of his fingers at her breast, Sydney felt the hunger, the incessant need that coiled through his body like liquid steel. Breathless, her heart pounding out a driving rhythm, she wanted to tell him that there was no hurry—neither one of them was going anywhere tonight—but he ripped her shirt from her then and his hands cupped her breasts. His fingers teased and treasured her nipples, sending a rush of dizzy heat straight to the core of her. Moaning, she clung to him, her knees buckling. "Dillon!"

"I'm here, sweetheart," he rasped, nipping at her mouth, the lobe of her ear, the pulse beating wildly at the base of her throat as he pulled her hard against him. "Let's go to bed."

The bunk was only a step away and though it wasn't intended for two, she was more than willing to squeeze into it with him . . . if she could have found the strength to move. But all her concentration was focused on him—on the way his breath shuddered through his lungs when she ripped his shirt open and flicked her tongue against his small, flat nipples, on the way he tensed as she reached for the snap of his jeans.

Given the choice, she would have undressed him with painstaking slowness and delighted in the fire she lit in his blood, but the second her fingers closed around the tab of his zipper, his hand gripped hers, stilling her. In the soft glow of the flashlight, which had fallen to the floor without her noticing, his face was etched in tight lines, his gray eyes dark and turbulent as they met hers.

"Let me," she whispered huskily in the sudden silence.

He wanted to—he loved the feel of her hands on him— but he was too hot, his control ready to shatter at her slightest touch. "Next time," he promised in a rough growl, only to recall too late that this was all there would ever be for the two of them. And it wasn't enough, dammit!

Suddenly furious at the Fates, at Santiago, at the doctors who had, in their wisdom, decided that it was better for him to live with a bullet in his back rather than chance the operation, he wanted to rage, to throw something, to hit somebody square in the gut. But the only one there was Sydney, with her sweetness and fire, her passion for life, not to mention truth and justice. He didn't want the ugliness of his past to touch her in any way. Not tonight, not ever. The fury suddenly draining out of him, his hand tightened on hers, but only to help her tug the zipper down.

The rasping sound was like the unexpected blast of a gun in the silence. His smile crooked, he leaned down to give her a slow, lingering kiss. "You're asking for trouble, honey," he warned roughly when he finally lifted his head. "I don't know if you've noticed, but you've got me hotter than a firecracker."

He watched her blue eyes darken to sapphire with the unexpected admission, the sensuous smile she made no attempt to hold back slowly slide across her mouth. Oh, she

knew all right—he could see the knowledge in her eyes. And
it delighted her. Tenderness curled in him, sweet and strong
and oh, so right, and just that quickly, he knew he would
have given her his heart if he'd had one to give.

The thought shook him to the core, but before he could
figure out when she had come to mean so much to him, her
hands glided slowly up his chest to push his shirt off his
shoulders, each little brush of her fingers setting off small
sparks under his skin. Swallowing a soundless groan, he
closed his eyes to better savor every nuance of her touch, the
furrowed lines that weathered his brow etched with intense
pleasure.

His head thrown back as if he were in pain, he fought the
need to tumble her onto the mattress and take her like a wild
man. But the burning deep in his gut told him he was fighting a losing battle. Her name a hoarse whisper on his lips,
he felt her start to tug his jeans down, and the friction of the
denim against his arousal was slow torture.

"Enough!" he said thickly, and pushed his jeans the rest
of the way off with a savage motion. Kicking them out of
the way, he swept her up in his arms, startling a laugh from
her, and bore her down to the bunk. "You're driving me
crazy, woman."

"Good," she purred. "Because that's what you do to me,
too."

The admission was as close to a declaration as either of
them was willing to get. Then her arms were twining around
his neck, his hips settling against her and neither of them
could think straight. His head lowered, her mouth lifted
sweetly to his and there was no more time for conversation.

He kissed her as if there was no tomorrow, as if the world
began and ended with just this: a sharing of breath, the
heated press of mouth against mouth, the hot rush of blood
through their veins. Her head spinning, Sydney would have

sworn she knew what making love was all about, but every time he touched her, kissed her, rubbed his body against hers in a carnal caress that left her breathless and aching for more, she was struck again and again by how little she knew about the needs and wants of her own body. With the slow glide of his finger, he could make her tremble, while the hot flick of his tongue could push her over the edge into mindlessness. And when he entered her by slow, gradual degrees, taking care with her to make sure she was with him every step of the way, he filled her with a yearning that brought the sting of tears to her eyes.

She would remember this, she promised herself with a sob as her mind began to blur and her body to tighten with anticipation. Every touch, every brush of his mouth, every groan she drew from him with flattering ease. When she was old and gray and he was just a memory that no longer had the power to hurt her, she would remember it all and try not to cry for all the years she had missed out on loving him.

But for now he was hers, just hers, if only for one night. Holding him as if she would never let him go, she moved with him, her hips lifting to his as they both caught a rhythm that was older than time. Her heart slamming against her ribs, her lungs straining, she rushed with him to the edge of white-hot rapture, where she hovered, wanting to savor the moment. But the need was too great, his instinctive knowledge of her body too profound. Murmuring her name like a cadence, he moved over her, in her, driving deeper, taking her higher. Helpless, she shattered.

Long after their bodies cooled, long after she fell asleep in his arms, Dillon lay awake, unable to stop touching her, holding her, his thoughts in turmoil. He loved her. Stunned, torn between the need to shout with triumph and curse the Fates at one and the same time, his arms tightened around her, drawing her closer, even as his stomach knotted with tension. Nothing had changed. He still couldn't have her.

Grimly staring at the darkened ceiling, he had no choice but to accept the inevitable. He wouldn't saddle her with half a man. He loved her too much to do that to her just because he didn't want to live without her. A lot of women might be able to handle that kind of thing, but not Sydney. She was too passionate about life, too active, too physical. She went at everything full speed ahead and she needed a man who could keep up with her. For now he could, but tomorrow that could all change.

He had to leave before that happened. Before he found himself stuck in a wheelchair. Before the need he saw in her eyes changed to pity. Before they both began to hate what he was destined to become.

There's no time like the present. Cassidy. What are you waiting for?

Stiffening at the thought, he instinctively tried to reject it—he wasn't ready to give her up yet, dammit! But there was no denying that conditions couldn't have been more perfect if he'd arranged them himself. Yesterday, they'd eliminated all but a few places where Santiago could be hiding. There were closing in on him, tightening the noose, and there was a good chance that between the two of them, he and Riley would have him in custody within twenty-four hours. It wasn't going to happen, though, without a fight, and he didn't want Sydney anywhere near the bastard when they cornered him. If he left her here at the line cabin, he could continue the search without having to worry about her.

She would be safe—from both him and Santiago—but she wouldn't thank him for abandoning her in the middle of nowhere. She would, in fact, never forgive him for coming between her and a story.

Regret left a bitter taste in his mouth. Given his choice, he would have preferred to part as friends, but that was a pipe dream and he knew it. There was too much emotion between them, too much fire, for either one of them to ever settle for anything as tepid as friendship. They could be lovers or enemies but nothing in between.

Which meant he had to leave. Now. While she was warm and soft and naked in his arms, as trusting as if they'd slept together for years. She would be safe here, and he would have Riley send one of his deputies for her first thing in the morning.

Later, he never knew how he did it. Needing to love her one more time more than he needed his next breath, he had to force himself to release her. His jaw rigid, he froze as she murmured in her sleep. If she so much as opened her eyes, he knew he'd never be able to walk away, but she only shifted against him, searching for a more comfortable position, then lay still again. Slowly, silently, Dillon let out the breath he'd been holding and eased the rest of the way out of the bunk.

Deprived of her body heat and the warmth of her sleeping bag, he swallowed a curse as the cold night air hit him. Naked as the day he was born, he tried to remember where the hell he'd dropped his clothes, but Sydney's hands had been driving him wild at the time and he had only a vague recollection of tearing everything off and reaching for her. Swearing under his breath, he dropped soundlessly to his knees and blindly searched the floor with his hands. Expecting Sydney to raise up any moment and ask him what he was doing, he sighed in relief when he finally found his jeans and shirt half-hidden under the bunk.

He was almost to the door when he remembered that his gun was still on the bedside table, where he'd laid it once he'd realized that the only bogeyman after Sydney was an imaginary bug. Stopping in his tracks, he reluctantly turned back toward the bunk, all the while listening for any change in Sydney's breathing. But she didn't so much as stir a muscle, not even when he searched the tabletop for the gun in the dark and made enough racket to wake the dead. His fingers closing over the pistol just seconds before he almost sent it clattering to the floor, he grabbed it and hurried to the door.

Seconds later, he was dressed and stomping into his boots, which he'd left in the tent without a thought when he heard Sydney scream earlier. A quick search of the Jeep revealed that her keys were still in the ignition—he wouldn't have to hot-wire it. So all he had to do was leave her a note, unload her computer, then get the hell out of there.

It should have been simple, writing her a quick explanation of why he had to leave her, but his mind was a blank slate. Seated in the front seat of the Jeep, the dome light shining on the blank notepad he'd found in the glove compartment, he stared down at it in frustration, conscious of every tick of the clock on the dash. Finally, disgusted, he wrote a few curt lines that didn't come close to what he wanted to say, then scrawled his name across the bottom.

He left the note on the cabin steps, where she wouldn't miss it, weighted down by her computer. It was, he told himself as he started her Jeep and drove away, the right thing to do. But being right didn't stop him from feeling lower than dirt.

The morning was overcast, the sun nothing but a fuzzy disk in the sky that did little to take the damp chill from the air. Warm as toast under her sleeping bag in the cabin, Sydney stretched languidly, coming awake slowly, images from the night drifting in and out of her consciousness. Dillon, searching the cabin for bugs like a dragon slayer of old. Dillon, warning her that nothing had changed, then loving her with a gentleness that had brought tears to her eyes. A sleepy smile curling the corners of her mouth, she reached for him, needing to recapture the magic of the night one more time.

But the bed was empty beside her, the mattress cold. Her eyes flying open in surprise, she bolted up, shivering as the morning air caressed her bare shoulders. The cabin was empty—the silence fairly shouted in her ears—the only sign that Dillon had been there at all was the shirt he'd stripped from her last night and dropped to the floor. Dropping back down to the mattress, she laughed shakily. She hadn't dreamed it.

He was probably at the creek, she decided, grinning as she pictured him washing the sleep from his eyes in the cold water. Talk about a wake-up call! He'd probably be back any second. Then they'd talk—about last night...and this need they had for each other that could no longer be ignored. He might claim there was no place for her in his life, but every time he touched her, kissed her, his body told a different story. Pretending otherwise wasn't going to make it go away. They had to deal with it.

It was going to be all right, she assured herself. It had to be. Nothing else was acceptable. But when she glanced at her watch twenty minutes later and he still hadn't put in an appearance, she started to get concerned. Where was he? It didn't take that long to wash up at the creek. Unless something had happened to him.

Her heart stopped at the thought. Dear God, could Santiago have found them, after all? Panic racing like wildfire through her blood, she threw off the sleeping bag and struggled into her clothes, cursing her stiff, unsteady fingers as they fumbled with the buttons of her shirt. She was still struggling with them when she jerked open the cabin door.

She saw her computer first, sitting on the top step like an orphan who didn't have anywhere else to go. It was enclosed in its carrying case, the one she kept in the car in case she was caught in an unexpected rainstorm without an umbrella, but she hardly noticed. Instead, all her attention was focused on the single sheet of paper that had been placed underneath the laptop. Obviously torn from a small spiral notebook, the ruffled edges at one end fluttered in the strong morning breeze that raced unchecked through the canyon.

> I had to leave. You know why. You'll be safe here. One of Riley's men will come for you first thing this morning.

He'd signed it simply *Dillon,* nothing more, then took off in her Jeep. Staring down at his bold signature, she felt the hurt first, so strong and fierce it stole her breath and stung her eyes. He'd left her, just walked away as if last night had meant nothing. As if *she* had meant nothing. Stunned, she couldn't even manage a sob. She loved him, dammit! She hadn't realized just how much until last night when he'd rushed into the cabin with his gun drawn, ready to shoot a scorpion.

From the tender way he'd made love to her, she'd thought he felt the same way.

She'd obviously been wrong.

It was then that the anger hit, a red-hot wave of fury that swept over her in a rush and practically set her hair on fire. Not only had he left her, he expected her to sit here twiddling her thumbs like a good little girl until one of Riley's deputies could find the time to come for her. And all the while he would be out searching for Santiago.

Like hell!

Crumbling his note in her clenched fist, she would have burned it if the campfire had still been lit, but the only right thing she'd done last night was put out the fire. Well, one of them, anyway, she fumed, whirling to toss the note into a corner. God, how could she have been so stupid? While she'd been lying in bed, dreaming of happily-ever-afters and undying declarations of love, he'd already run off in *her* car, not only leaving her stranded, but cheating her out of the biggest story to hit town in years!

She'd kill him. No, she thought furiously, killing was too good for him. When she caught up with the rat, she was going to string him up by his thumbs and leave him to twist in the wind. And then she'd have Riley arrest him for stealing her car. Then she'd get serious about revenge.

But first, before she did anything, she was going to tell him exactly what she thought of him. And to do that, she had to find a phone.

Too mad to care that she might have to walk twenty miles or more before she reached the nearest ranch house, she scrambled through her bag of clothes and pulled out the first pair of jeans and sweatshirt she came to. The jeans were too baggy and the sweatshirt was her favorite color—red—and clashed horribly with her hair, but she wasn't out to impress anyone. Especially a tall, good-looking former DEA agent who had a real talent for driving her right up the wall. She could tell him off just as easily dressed as a bag lady as she could in silk. And boy, was he going to get an earful!

Already anticipating what she would say, she hurriedly dressed, then hid her computer in the far back corner of the bunk. Normally, she wouldn't have even considered leaving it behind, but she had a long walk ahead of her. And while it didn't weigh all that much, a couple of pounds could get awfully heavy when it had to be carted all over the countryside.

Closing the door behind her, she struck off down the dirt road that led to the highway. Kat Rawlings's place was farther north through the canyon, but she had no idea how far it was or how rough the terrain was along the way, and her flats weren't exactly made for hiking over rocky ground. So she stuck to the main road when she reached it, heading north.

For the first mile, her anger alone set the pace and it was a clipped one. But she couldn't sustain it. A stitch in her side pulled painfully every time she took a step, and she was forced to slow down. Furious with Dillon all over again, she took great delight in picturing his face when he discovered she hadn't stayed at the cabin.

Caught up in the image, she didn't hear the car approaching from the north until it was almost upon her. Suddenly realizing a potential ride was about to pass her by, she waved frantically, trying to flag the driver down. "Hey, stop! I need a lift...." she shouted.

But it was too late. The brown sedan was already past her and showed no signs of slowing down, which was surprising. People around Lordsburg were usually pretty quick to stop and offer assistance when they came across someone in trouble—it was one of the things she especially appreciated about living in a small town. You could usually depend on someone to offer a helping hand when it was needed. And anyone looking at her could see that she was in definite need of some help. She'd hadn't walked forty miles from town just to get some exercise!

"Thanks for nothing!" she yelled after the retreating vehicle. Turning north again, she was still muttering curses when she heard another vehicle approaching, this time from the south. Relieved, she sighed, "Finally!" and quickly stuck her thumb out.

Expecting her rescuer to be a local rancher or cowboy in a beat-up pickup, she was surprised to see the same brown Ford that had passed her only moments before pull up beside her. The driver, a nondescript man with one of those faces that just seemed to blend into a crowd, quickly leaned over and rolled down the passenger window, a friendly grin tilting his mouth. "Hey, aren't you Sydney O'Keefe?"

It wasn't a question that normally would have set alarm bells ringing in her ears, but she hadn't forgotten that it was only a couple of days ago that Santiago had sat next to her at the Crossroads and offered her a deadly drug. He'd been disguised at the time, but there was no question that this man wasn't him—he was too big and his coloring was all wrong. The swarthy skin of his beefy forearms, revealed by the rolled-back cuffs of his shirt, was a very natural-looking bronze, his hair dark, not blond. Unless he'd gained forty pounds in the last two days and had a Hollywood makeup artist dye his hair and skin, he couldn't possibly be the drug lord.

But he was a stranger, and Sydney had no intention of taking any chances. Standing well back from the car, she nodded. "Yeah. How'd you know?"

"A waitress at the diner in town pointed you out to me one day last week. I'm new in town, just moved here from Chicago. She said that's where you were from originally, too."

It was a plausible explanation, one that Sydney normally would have accepted without a second thought. But it did nothing to quiet the alarm bells still clanging in her head, and that worried her. Her instincts didn't usually steer her wrong. And right now, they were telling her that something wasn't quite right here, especially this man's accent. If he was from Chicago, she was a Gypsy fortune teller.

Her heart starting to pound out a panicky rhythm in her chest, she cast a surreptitious look up and down the road, but there wasn't another vehicle in sight. Forcing a smile, she said, "No, kidding? What part of Chicago?"

"The South side. How about you?"

"The same." She laughed, then wished she hadn't when it caught in her throat. "Well, it's been nice talking to you. Maybe I'll see you around town."

Not waiting for a response, she quickly resumed walking, but he easily kept up with her just by lifting his foot from the brake and coasting along beside her. When she shot him a narrow-eyed look, he merely smiled and said, "Can I offer you a ride somewhere? What are you doing out here, anyway? I thought you lived north of town."

As far as Sydney was concerned, he knew far too much about her for a man who had supposedly only recently moved there. Where she lived was no secret—her address was in the phone book—but she couldn't think of a single innocent reason why this man would look it up. "No, thanks," she said, declining the ride without offering an explanation for her presence there or verification of where she lived. "It's a good morning to get some exercise."

"But you shouldn't be all alone out here," he insisted. "If your car broke down, I'd be happy to give you a ride into town."

He was, Sydney almost retorted, a regular prince. The only problem was he hadn't been willing to stop, let alone come to her assistance, until he recognized her. And that was really starting to worry her. Who the devil was he? And what did he want?

Afraid she'd made a drastic mistake in leaving the canyon, she instinctively knew she couldn't let this man see her fear. Stopping in her tracks, she decided it was time to get tough. "Look, I appreciate the offer—I really do. But the truth is I'm out here by myself because I want to be alone. I don't want a ride. I don't want anything except for you to go away and leave me alone."

She couldn't have been clearer if she'd carved it in stone, but when she turned and started walking again, the brown sedan was right beside her, trailing her, stalking her. Her eyes trained straight ahead, she swallowed as sick dread spilled into her stomach.

Don't panic, she told herself. You can handle this jackass. All you have to do is use your head, don't go anywhere near his car and keep him talking until someone comes along. You're not on the far side of the moon even though it might look like it. The deputy Dillon's sending for you is bound to come by any second, and between the two of you, you can send this jerk packing.

It was a good plan, one that might have worked if her companion hadn't run out of patience. Suddenly swerving over to the shoulder of the road without warning, he braked to a screeching halt directly in front of her. Startled, she gasped and found herself looking at the business end of a .38.

"Get in," he growled, leaning across the bench seat to shove open the passenger door. "You and I are going for a little ride."

For all of two seconds, Sydney seriously considered running for it. But something about the glint in his black eyes told her that he would take great delight in shooting her, then leaving her body out here in the desert for the buzzards to pick clean.

"Who are you?" she demanded hoarsely.

"Angelo. Now are you going to get in the car or do I get to pull this here little trigger? Either way is okay by me."

Angelo, she thought shakily, the last of the blood draining from her face. The man who did Santiago's dirty work. Unable to manage a word of protest, she got in the car.

Chapter 11

By eight o'clock in the morning, Dillon had checked the rest of the places on Riley's list. Too uptight to even think about finding a place where he could bunk down for the rest of the night after he'd left Sydney in the canyon, he'd called Riley on his cellular phone to tell him about the change in plans and arrange a ride for Sydney in the morning. He then spent the rest of the night driving over back roads, looking for Santiago under every rock and crevice that was disguised as a ranch. But the man was as elusive as the devil himself and nowhere to be found. The last place on the list was as deserted as the first, leaving Dillon no choice but to call Riley again and give him the bad news.

"Well, I'm finished," he said in disgust as soon as his friend came on the line. "I checked every place you suggested, but I didn't find a damn thing."

Riley swore. "I was almost positive he was holed up at the Tripper place. You didn't see anything?"

"Nothing. In fact, I pretty much had the roads to myself most of the night. I didn't even see another vehicle until a damn trucker pulling a trailer full of cattle almost hit me pulling out of the Lazy Susan out on Highway 70 around dawn. If I hadn't swerved off the road, the damn jackass would have flattened me."

"I don't know how some of these idiots got their commercial license," Riley retorted. "Well, what now, buddy? I haven't had any better luck than you have and we've just about run out of places to look. You know the bastard better than I do. Where the hell do you think he is?"

Dillon rubbed his scratchy eyes tiredly. "Damned if I know. I know he's here. I can smell him—"

"Wait a minute," Riley cut in suddenly. "Back up. You said you saw a cattle truck pulling out of the Lazy Susan? Are you sure it was carrying cattle?"

"Of course. The sun was already coming up, and the damn trailer almost sideswiped me. It was loaded with white-faced Herefords. Why?"

"There aren't any cattle on the Lazy Susan, Dillon. Tom and Susan Anderson bailed out of the cattle business months ago and sold their entire herd. The last I heard, they were on an extended trip to Texas to buy quarter horses and aren't expected home for another three weeks."

"Does it have a landing strip?"

"One of the best in the county."

Dillon swore, wanting to throw something. He'd been right there and hadn't had a clue! "Dammit to hell. That's it, then. Somehow Santiago found out the owners were gone and just moved in and no one even noticed."

"It's the perfect setup," Riley agreed. "The bastard's been flying in drugs from Mexico, then concealing it in cattle trucks and hauling it to Tucson and El Paso right under our noses. Son of a bitch!"

"I'm only ten miles from there," Dillon said grimly, already swinging the Jeep around to head back in the opposite direction. "I'm going after him."

"Dammit, Dillon, this isn't the time for you to play the goddamn Lone Ranger! Wait for backup. You hear me? Twenty minutes, that's all I'm asking. Give me and the rest of the men time to get there. You've waited this long. Another few minutes isn't going to kill you."

The speedometer climbing toward eighty, Dillon would have liked nothing better than to rush in with his gun drawn and take on Santiago face-to-face. He'd been waiting for this for a long time, and by God, nobody was going to stop him. But he wasn't a fool. Revenge was one thing, stupidity another. "Twenty minutes," he agreed curtly. "Is there a back entrance?"

Riley told him where it was and promised to get there as fast as he could round up his men. He also had to put in a call to the DEA. Dillon didn't care if he called in the National Guard, just as long as he got Santiago. Agreeing to meet him there, he hung up and turned right at the next ranch road he came to.

The Lazy Susan was a two-thousand-acre spread in the western part of the county. Rockier than most of the other places Dillon had investigated, it had a back entrance that wound through a series of jagged outcroppings that gave a commanding view of the ranch headquarters a half a mile away. Parking well out of sight behind the rocks, Dillon checked to make sure his gun was loaded, tucked into the waistband of his jeans, then grabbed the binoculars.

Sending up a silent prayer of thanks that Sydney was waiting patiently for a ride at the line cabin on the Double R, he climbed the highest rock promontory and stretched out on his belly with the field glasses focused on the compound. He didn't have to wait long to get an eyeful.

He'd hardly settled into position when a cattle truck roared through the front entrance of the ranch and braked to a stop at the large barn near Tom and Susan Anderson's house. A dozen men rushed out. Within minutes, the cattle in the truck were unloaded into the nearby corral and the floorboards of the trailer were popped up with crowbars. Anger seething in him, Dillon watched Santiago's men conceal under the floorboards hundreds of thousands of dollars' worth of what looked like heroin, then reload the cattle. The entire operation took less than fifteen minutes.

Cursing himself for not bringing a camera, Dillon had to admit that this time Santiago had outdone himself. No wonder the Feds hadn't been able to pinpoint how the drugs were being transported up and down the interstate. No one would think to look under manure for the heroin, and the smell would throw off the dogs at state border crossings.

Pulling back as the truck drove out of the compound, he just barely resisted the urge to charge down from his observation point and stop it. Dammit, where the hell was Riley? He should have been here by now.

Without warning, his cellular phone rang like an alarm in the silence. "Damn!" Muttering a curse, he hurriedly snatched it out of his pocket and answered it before it could give away his hiding place. "Where the hell are you?" he demanded in a terse whisper, expecting the caller to be Riley. "A truck just pulled out—"

"Dillon?"

At the familiar sound of Sydney's sexy voice, he frowned. How the devil had she managed to call him? There was no phone at the cabin. "Sydney? Dammit, where are you? Riley said Joe couldn't get out to the canyon till ten."

"I wasn't thinking straight—"

That was all she had a chance to say. Then a smooth, oily voice straight out of one of Dillon's worst nightmares mockingly taunted, "I've got her, Mr. Cassidy. And if you want her back, you're going to have to talk to me face-to-face...when I say and where I say. Got it?"

Every drop of blood in Dillon's body turned to ice. "Damn you, Santiago. If you hurt her, you're going to answer to me, you son of a bitch! You hear me? If you so much as lay a finger on her, I'll make you wish you'd never been born."

"Now, now, Mr. Cassidy, is that any way to talk to the man who holds the lady's life in his hands? I wouldn't push me if I were you. If I chose to, I could make sure she was never seen or heard from again. And you know I can do it. Is that what you want?"

If he could have got his hands on him then, Dillon would have choked the life from him without a qualm. Forget the legal system. The bastard was evil incarnate and deserved to die. And he had Sydney. Just thinking about her in that lowlife's hands sickened Dillon. Santiago would hurt her—and laugh while he did it.

God, he had to get her back! And the only way to do that was to pretend to cooperate. Rage burning like an inferno in his gut, he said coldly, "All right, we'll talk...anywhere you want. You set the time. After you let Sydney go."

Amused, the drug lord laughed. "Surely you don't think I'm that stupid, Agent Cassidy."

"Just plain old Mr. Cassidy will do," Dillon retorted coldly. "I'm no longer with the agency."

"Oh, yes," the other man purred smugly. "It seems I did hear that I was responsible for ending your government career. And the Feds wanted me to think you were dead. Wouldn't it be tragic if Miss O'Keefe ended up that way instead of you? You'd have to live the rest of your life knowing it was your fault.''

It was a threat, pure and simple, one Santiago wouldn't bat an eye at carrying out. His hands curling into fists, Dillon snarled, "Damn you, you scumball, don't even think about trying it—"

Not the least impressed with his fury, Santiago laughed, delighted that he could push his buttons so easily. "Or what? You'll come after me and squash me like a bug? I don't think so. I've been here for weeks and you didn't even know it. So don't threaten me, Cassidy. I have your woman. And if you want her back in one piece, you'll meet me when I tell you to. I'll call you back with the time and place. I suggest you be ready."

Dillon was still swearing when Riley and his men arrived a few minutes later and climbed up to join him at the observation point. "He's here," he told Riley curtly. "I just watched his hired thugs concealing heroin in a cattle truck— it's under the floorboards. But that's not the worst of it. He's got Sydney."

"What? How the hell did that happen? I thought you left her at the line cabin at the canyon."

"I did. But either she hiked out on foot or Santiago knew we were there all along and grabbed her the second I left." Guilt twisted his insides. Repeating the rest of his conversation with the drug lord, he stared at the Lazy Susan headquarters in the distance, searching for some sign of Sydney. There was none, of course, but he knew she was there. He could almost feel her standing at one of the windows of the clapboard ranch house, staring back at him. "This is all my fault," he said harshly, half to himself. "I should have waited until Joe got there before I left, but I thought she'd be safe."

"There's no way you could have anticipated this," Riley assured him. "The bastard's as tricky as they come, but that doesn't mean he's won yet. Quinn's flying in some of his best men from Tucson—they should be here within the hour. And don't forget—Santiago doesn't know that we know where he is. He won't meet you at the Lazy Susan and give away his hiding place. He'll set up a trap for you and probably take most of his men with him to make sure you don't try to pull a fast one. While you and the DEA go after him, I'll take my men in after Sydney."

It was the only logical thing they could do. "I want her safe," Dillon said. "Do what you have to do."

"I'll treat her just like I would Becca," Riley replied. "In the meantime, I'm more worried about you. You know Santiago's not meeting with you to shoot the breeze. He's going to kill you if he gets the chance."

"Then I'll have to make sure he doesn't get the chance."

After that, there was nothing more they could do but wait. And Santiago didn't drag that out. An hour later, he called. "I'll meet you at dawn at the line cabin," he told Dillon the second he came on the line. "Don't be late," he warned, then hung up.

The wheels in his head already turning as he repeated the message to Riley and his deputies, Dillon guessed immediately what Santiago had in mind for him. With the cabin surrounded by the high cliffs of the canyon, he could move his men into place in the rocks long before dawn, then blow Dillon away the second he stepped out of the Jeep.

Echoing his thoughts, Riley said, "It's a perfect place for an ambush. With his men hidden in the cliffs, waiting to pick you off, you'd never stand a chance."

"If we let him get as far as the canyon," Dillon said. "I'm going to make sure that doesn't happen. When Quinn's men get here, we'll set up our own trap between here and the

canyon. Once Santiago leaves the ranch—and Sydney—
we'll have him. He'll never know what hit him until it's too
late.''

As far as plans went, it was a good one—simple, uncom-
plicated, with the odds of anything going wrong slim. But
no one knew better than Dillon just how wrong the most
perfect plan could go when it came to second-guessing
criminals. If Santiago did the expected, the slime was as
good as back in prison. If he didn't... Dillon didn't even
want to think about it, not when the bastard had Sydney.

Standing at the window of the large bedroom she had
been given at the Lazy Susan, Sydney watched as the last
faint gleam of twilight faded from the western sky and the
stars appeared one by one. She'd lost track of the hours
she'd stood there, waiting for the night...and escape. God,
she had to get out of here! Now, while there was still time to
possibly get to Dillon. She had to warn him, stop him.

He was going to walk into a trap because of her.

The thought had eaten at her like a cancer ever since
Santiago had forced the number of Dillon's cellular phone
from her, then made her stand there and listen as he called
him to set up the meeting with him. Afterward, he'd glee-
fully plotted Dillon's death with his men, not the least bit
concerned that she was openly listening. The moment she'd
been dragged before him by Angelo, she'd been warned that
there was no way out. With a smugness that had nauseated
her, he'd pointed out the guards posted around the compound, guards who had been ordered to shoot to kill if she
so much as stepped foot outside without him by her side.

Too late, she now understood how Dillon could hate the
man. He was totally without conscience. He'd talked of
killing Dillon, of killing her, as if they were nothing more
than bugs who got in his way and had to be stepped on. Re-

pelled, unable to comprehend how anyone could be so amoral, she'd questioned him about the drugs and the innocent kids whose lives would be ruined by it, about the murders he'd committed just to taunt Dillon with his presence in Lordsburg, and he'd only shrugged and explained that he was a businessman who did what he had to do to ensure that that business flourished.

Sickened, she'd wanted to rage at him, to fly at him and literally scratch his eyes out, but she'd forced herself to play the helpless female instead, to tearfully plead with him to reconsider. She would have gladly got down on her knees and begged him for Dillon's life, but he didn't give her the chance. As cold as stone, he laughed at her efforts and told her she was wasting her time. Because of Dillon, he'd spent nearly a year of his life penned up like an animal in prison, and no man did that to him and got away with it. Just as judgment had been passed on him, he had passed it on Dillon. He would die at dawn.

Determined to do whatever she had to to warn Dillon, she'd retreated to her room then to wait for the night, intending to slip out under the cover of darkness. But as she now searched the deepening shadows outside for signs of the guards, security lights sprang on, lighting every inch of the compound until it was as bright as day. "Oh, no!" she cried. Now what was she supposed to do?

Panic seizing her, she could feel time slipping through her fingers in a terrifying rush. It was hours yet before Santiago and his men would leave to set up the ambush at the canyon, but she couldn't wait until they were gone to escape. She was miles from the line cabin and she'd never reach Dillon in time if she didn't leave soon.

Turning from the window, she stared at the comfortable furnishings of her surroundings, her mind working furiously. She wasn't a prisoner in her room—Santiago was too confident of the shooting skills of his guards to resort to locking her up. Every door in the house was unlocked; if she wanted to try to escape, all she had to do was make a run for it ... through a hail of bullets.

There had to be another way, she thought in growing desperation. Within a couple of hours, Santiago and the men he would take with him to the canyon would go to bed and be up again at three so they would have plenty of time to reach the canyon and get into position before Dillon arrived. The house would be quiet and dark, the halls deserted, the guards outside hopefully relaxed. If she was going to make a move, she would have to do it then.

The idea, when it came to her, was so simple she couldn't believe she hadn't thought of it sooner. A distraction. She needed a distraction, one that would draw even the guards from their posts, one that would cause such chaos that no one would notice when she slipped outside and escaped into the desert. And nothing did that like fire. Once everyone was asleep, she could start it, then make a break for it while they were trying to put it out. By the time Santiago thought to check on her, she would be long gone.

Smiling for the first time since she'd been captured, she returned to the window to study her escape route.

From his position atop the rocky promontory a half a mile away, Dillon watched the last light wink off in the house. It was barely nine o'clock and not, he knew from the times he'd set up surveillance on him in the past, Santiago's usual bedtime. The man never slept before two or three in the morning ... unless he meant to make a move in the middle of the night.

His smile grim with anticipation in the darkness, Dillon couldn't wait for the bastard to do just that. This time he was ready for him. Glancing to where the three agents Quinn sent talked quietly with Riley's men, he freely admitted that he'd had his reservations about letting the Feds in on his plan. They might have been handpicked by Quinn, but they were still government agents with their own agenda, which might interfere with his. They had rules to follow—he didn't, not when the bastard had Sydney—and he wasn't letting them or anyone else get in his way.

When they'd arrived a little over an hour ago, however, they'd been quick to assure him that they were there to help, not take over. They just wanted Santiago back in custody. If Dillon was able to get revenge by helping them capture him, that was all right by them.

Already anticipating the satisfaction he would feel when he slapped handcuffs back on his old enemy, it was several moments before Dillon caught on the breeze the first faint scent of something burning. Straightening suddenly, he frowned, wondering what could possibly be burning out in the middle of the desert. Grass fires were a real danger during the long, dry summer, especially during lightning storms, but that was still months away.

Then he saw the ghostlike smoke rising from the left wing of the ranch house. Before he saw the flames, a second spiral of smoke curled lazily in the night sky, this one rising from the opposite end of the old wood frame house, near the garage.

Tensing, Dillon didn't wait to see more. Grabbing the rifle Riley had loaned him when he'd arrived, he said harshly, "The plans have changed, guys. Sydney's not waiting to be rescued—she's set the house on fire and all hell's about to break loose down there. Let's go!"

The smoke in the study was so thick, Sydney could hardly breathe. Choking, hot tears streaming from her burning eyes, she blindly made her way toward the room's only window as chaos erupted all around her. She'd set the fires carefully, knowing that anyone waking from a sound sleep would instinctively try to make their way to the front or back door before they realized they could escape through any ground floor window. So she'd locked the doors, then set fires at the entrance to the living room and kitchen, as well as at each end of the hall where the bedrooms were located. Then all she had to do was sit back and wait. It hadn't taken long to wake the household.

The guards outside had noticed the flames first and had come running, only to be brought up short by the locked doors. Shouting and banging, they woke up the others, but by then the house was full of smoke. In their confusion, the occupants of the other bedrooms did just as she expected and stumbled through the smoke to the front and back doors, where they coughed and shouted for help.

Quickly raising the window, Sydney unhooked the screen, and slipped outside. The floodlights illuminating the compound were still lit, but smoke hung thick and heavy in the night air, providing the only cover she was likely to get. Her heart hammering, she glanced around, but she was out of sight of both the front and back doors, which was why she had chosen the study to escape from.

Knowing this was her only chance, she dragged in a bracing breath and started running toward the darkness that waited just beyond the reach of the compound security lights.

Her blood roaring in her ears, she never heard the man behind her. Then he grabbed her by her hair, nearly yanking it out by the roots. She screamed, clutching at her head as she was jerked back against a hard male body.

"Not so fast, sweetheart," Santiago growled icily in her ear as he wound his fingers deeper into her hair and jerked her head back. "Your little trick might have fooled the others, but I knew what you were up to the minute I smelled the smoke. I ought to kill you for this right now and be done with it.''

Grimacing in pain, Sydney could do nothing to stem the tears streaming from her eyes. She'd been so close. ''No! Please...''

She would have begged then, promised him anything, just to buy some time until she could figure out a way to escape and get to Dillon, but before she could manage another word, the sound of several rifles being cocked was like an explosion in the night. Behind her, Santiago stiffened just as Riley stepped out of the darkness.

''Riley...thank God!'' Her knees going weak at the sight of him and his deputies, their rifles loaded and ready, Sydney was never so glad to see anyone in her life. If Riley was here, then Dillon had to be also. Her heart starting to pound in her breast, she searched the darkness for him, but nothing moved but Riley's deputies as they fanned out behind him.

''You're not killing anyone ever again, Santiago,'' Riley said coldly. ''Let her go. We've got you surrounded.''

''You haven't got jack squat, Sheriff,'' the other man retorted, and quick as lightning, he whipped an arm around Sydney's throat to pin her against him as a shield, the .38 he held to her head as black as sin and very businesslike. ''One move and she dies right here,'' he said sharply when Riley swore and automatically took a step forward. ''I mean it. You so much as blink, and she's history.''

Standing well back in the darkness, Dillon instinctively jerked up his rifle and took aim the instant Santiago touched Sydney. Rage flared red-hot in his eyes at the thought of that piece of slime laying so much as a finger on her, but as much as he wanted to pull the trigger, he couldn't do it, not when the bastard held Sydney so close. If his aim was off the slightest bit...

Swallowing a curse, he lowered the rifle, every nerve in his body tight with fury. This wasn't supposed to happen, dammit! He and the agents Quinn had sent had kept out of sight in the shadows just in case backup—and an element of surprise—was needed. Knowing just how slippery and evasive Santiago could be when he was cornered, Dillon would have sworn he was on guard, ready for anything. But nothing could have prepared him for the sight of Sydney held in front of Santiago like a human shield. If he could have got his hands on the man then, he would have torn him limb from limb, to hell with the consequences.

But as much as he wanted to launch himself at the drug lord, he didn't dare make the mistake of letting him know he was there. From the moment he'd escaped from prison and made his way to New Mexico, Santiago's every move had been calculated to taunt and mock him. He'd killed twice before without batting an eye. He'd take great delight in killing Sydney right in front of his eyes just to show him that he could. Sick with frustration, he had no choice but to stand there, helpless, as the bastard took a step backward, toward the barn, dragging Sydney with him.

Just then, Santiago's men came running around the corner of the burning house, only to stop short at the sight of Riley and his deputies spread out before them at the edge of the light, their rifles aimed right at them. "You even think about going for your guns and you're dead men," Riley warned.

Caught off guard, they hesitated, glancing to their boss for guidance. Santiago, however, wasn't worried about anyone's neck but his own. His eyes locked on Riley, the gun he held to Sydney's temple never wavering, he forced her to take another step back with him, his smile triumphant in the glare of the fire that was quickly consuming the ranch house. "It looks like we've got us a little standoff," he taunted. "Whoever blinks first loses. What do you want to bet it's going to be you, Sheriff? Huh?"

Quietly circling around behind Riley, shadowing the drug lord's every move, Dillon could practically see the tension crawling up his friend's back. There was nothing Riley hated more than a cocky bastard who thought he could outsmart the law, but you'd have never known it. His rifle trained with deadly accuracy on the other man, he said in a voice that was remarkably cool and steady, "I don't think either one of us wants a running gun battle here, so why don't you tell me what it is you *do* want? Maybe between the two of us, we can come up with a solution we can both live with."

"A free ride out of here," Santiago retorted coldly. "I've got my plane at the landing strip behind the barn. The lady lives to see the next sunrise if you let me fly out of here without interference."

"Alone?" Riley clarified. "You'll leave the girl behind?"

"Of course. I won't need her once I reach the plane."

No! Dillon almost shouted, outraged. The bastard was lying. He would say anything, do anything, to get out of a tight spot. There was no way he was going to give up a hostage until he was sure he was safely away from there. And once he had no use for her, there would no longer be a reason to keep her alive.

Riley had to know that, Dillon silently assured himself. He'd told him everything there was to know about the scumbag—he killed just for the hell of it; it was that easy for him. He wouldn't know a scruple if he tripped over it, and no one in their right mind made a deal with him when he was holding a gun to Sydney's head. Any second now, Riley was going to tell him to stuff it.

But Riley was caught between a rock and a hard place. Even though Dillon was still well behind him in the shadows, he could feel Dillon's silent anger, the fury his friend didn't dare voice—not if he wanted to keep Sydney alive—and he didn't blame him for wanting to commit murder. If it had been Becca in Santiago's clutches, he would have felt the same way. Just thinking about giving in to the dirtbag's demands turned his stomach, but he had them both over a barrel. Unless they wanted to watch Sydney die right before their eyes, he had to agree to whatever he wanted.

"You hurt a hair on that girl's head and I'll personally hunt you down like a rabid dog," Riley said coldly. "You understand, Santiago? You hurt her and you're dead, no questions asked."

"No!" Sydney croaked, her fingers biting into the arm that pressed against her windpipe. "Dammit, Riley, you can't let him do this!"

Alone in the dark, Sydney's strangled cry stabbing him right in the heart, Dillon almost lost it then. Rage blinding him, he suddenly found himself at the edge of the light and had no memory of how he'd gotten there. All his thoughts centered on getting his hands around Santiago's bony throat, he barely heard Riley say pointedly, "Go with him to the plane. It'll be all right. I promise you."

Go to the plane.

The message couldn't have been plainer if Riley had hit him right between the eyes with it. Dillon's brain, clouded with anger, abruptly cleared. God, how could he have been so dense? he wondered, swallowing a curse. Go to the plane. . . . Of course! As far as Santiago knew, there was no one else there but Riley and his deputies. Sensing freedom at his back, he'd never expect anyone to be waiting for him at the plane.

Signaling his intentions to the nearest DEA agent, who was fifty yards away to his right in the dark, Dillon silently headed for the airfield by clinging to the shadows and cutting a wide circle around Santiago. Not sure what to expect, he darted around the back side of the barn, out of sight of the others, only to stop in consternation. Like the rest of the ranch, the landing strip was lit up like a Christmas tree, with Santiago's Cessna sitting right in the middle of a stark white circle of light. Not even God himself could have snuck up on it without being seen.

Swearing under his breath, Dillon hesitated. The second he left the protection of the barn, anyone who cared to look in the direction of the airstrip would see him. But with Santiago and his men watching Riley and his deputies like hawks, expecting some kind of a trick, that wasn't likely. Setting the rifle against the barn wall, he pulled his gun from his shoulder holster and took a quick look around the corner of the barn.

The tense scene had changed little since he'd darted behind the barn. Santiago was still slowly backing toward the barn with Sydney captive before him in a choke hold, his .38 gouging her in the temple. Riley and his deputies hadn't moved, but they hadn't dropped their rifles, either. Across the compound, Dillon's eyes met his friend's. Riley didn't move so much as an eyelash but there was no question that he'd seen him. The glint in his eyes told Dillon the next move was his. Giving him a silent nod, he pulled back behind the barn, tugged off his boots and silently ran to the Cessna in his stocking feet.

They were going to let him take her. Cold with fear, Sydney wildly looked around for Dillon, but there was no sign of him. Riley and his deputies were the only hope she had of being rescued, and they weren't doing a damn thing to help her. Hurt, more scared than she'd ever been in her life, she was suddenly furious. Damn them, what was wrong with them? This was the man that had put a bullet in Dillon's back! They all knew he couldn't be trusted as far as he could spit, yet they were just standing there, letting the lying snake carry her off. Didn't they know he was going to kill her?

"Let go of me!" she choked out fiercely, struggling against the suffocating hold across her throat. "Just shoot me here and be done with it. Do you hear me? I don't care what you do to me, but I'm not getting on that plane with you!"

"You'll do as you're told," he said through his teeth, jerking her more firmly against him as they reached the tarmac of the landing strip. "Or I'll put a bullet through that tin-star friend of yours before he can even think about squeezing the trigger of that rifle of his. You don't believe me, just keep struggling, lady."

She knew he would do it. He was that arrogant, that ruthless. He'd shoot an innocent man right between the eyes without a second thought just to prove he was the one calling the shots. Her stomach knotting with frustration, she blinked back furious tears, knowing when she was beaten. Without a word, she went still in his hold.

He laughed softly in her ear, the wicked sound raising goose bumps up and down her arms. "Thata girl. I knew you had a brain under all that red hair. Easy now, the plane's right here. Don't even think about trying anything."

The gun still pressed to her temple, he released her to fumble behind him for the door latch, his gaze still trained on the sheriff and his men, who tensely watched his every move. When the door finally swung open, Sydney's heart stopped.

"Get in."

The harsh order was meant to be obeyed without question, but even when she had a gun pressed to her head, Sydney found she hadn't lost her spunk. "The hell I will. You said—"

Snarling a curse, he grabbed her and shoved her into the dark interior of the plane. Before she could push herself up off the floor, he was jumping in after her and slamming the door shut. "Get in the passenger seat and shut your trap," he snapped, jerking her up and planting her where he wanted her before he slipped into the pilot's seat. A split second later, the motor roared to life.

Long past panic, Sydney glanced frantically around for a way out, but the gun was lying in his lap and the man was lightning quick. "You can't do this!" she cried. "It isn't going to solve anything. Dillon will come after you—"

"Dillon Cassidy's nothing but a joke, a has-been," he said, laughing, as he reached the end of the runway and swung the small plane around to prepare for takeoff. "The man's practically in a wheelchair," he boasted. Revving the motor, he hardly gave her time to snatch her seat belt across her lap before he was racing the plane down the tarmac and lifting into the air with a quick movement that had her stomach falling to her feet. "Even when he knew I was in his own backyard, he couldn't catch me. What makes you think that's going to change?"

Sydney opened her mouth to tell him that Dillon would come after her even if he had to crawl, but she never got the chance. Suddenly the silence was broken by the sound of a gun being cocked directly behind Santiago's seat. "Oh, I caught you, all right," Dillon drawled. "You just didn't know it."

Chapter 12

"Dillon! Thank God!" Tears stinging her eyes, she brushed them away impatiently and tried to swivel around in her seat to face him, but her seat belt held her captive. Cursing it, she fumbled for the catch. "How did you know where I was?"

Not taking his eyes off his captive for so much as a second, Dillon said roughly, "Riley and I were watching the ranch all afternoon, sweetheart, just waiting for this jackass to make a mistake. Did he hurt you?"

There was a hardness in his tone, a suppressed violence that warned her he'd taken just about all he was going to take from this man. He'd been pushed to the edge by a piece of trash he had every reason to hate and he was just itching for an excuse to pull the trigger on the gun he held tightly pressed to the back of Santiago's head. Alarmed, she said quickly, "No! I'm fine. Really."

"If he touched you—"

"I didn't lay a hand on her," Santiago said icily, spitting the words at him like a cornered cat. "But the night's not over yet." And with no more warning than that, he jerked the controls of the plane and sent it reeling sharply to the right.

Caught off guard, Dillon lost his balance and slammed into the side of the fuselage, the force of the impact knocking his gun from his hand. Swearing, he dove for it just as Santiago whirled in his seat with his .38 firmly clasped in his hand.

"No!" Horrified, Sydney finally released her seat belt, only to be flung half out of her seat as Santiago jerked the controls in the opposite direction. Sobbing, she caught herself before she could be thrown to the floor and kicked out wildly, surprising both her captor and herself when she caught the gun with her heel and sent it clattering toward the back of the plane.

"Bitch!" he screamed, backhanding her. "I should have killed you when I had the chance!"

Her head snapping back from the blow, Sydney hardly heard Dillon's bellow of outrage for the ringing of her ears. Then Santiago surged up out of his seat and both men were scrambling for their guns in the dark, hitting and clawing at each other like animals. Her face stinging, a bruise already forming on her cheek, Sydney heard someone crying and didn't realize it was herself. Dillon. She had to help Dillon.

But just as she pushed to her feet, Santiago found his gun. Staggering, he fired wildly, the bullet missing Dillon by a hairsbreadth before slamming into the plane's control panel. Sparks flew, and just as Dillon found his own gun, the Cessna took a dive. Losing his balance, Dillon fell against the pilot's seat and hit his elbow against the dash, the blow causing his fingers to automatically tighten on the gun in his hand.

Santiago never knew what hit him. The bullet struck him in the chest, knocking him backward. His hand clutched to the bloody wound, he fell to the floor with a groan.

Her heart stopping, Sydney wouldn't have let a dog bleed to death before her eyes without trying to help, but in the sudden silence, it was obvious from the man's labored gasps that there was nothing anyone could do for him. In a matter of seconds, he was dead.

Stunned, Sydney just stood there, unable to believe that the nightmare was finally over. Then the floor shifted under her feet, and only a quick grab at the copilot's seat saved her from an ugly spill across Santiago's body. Glancing over her shoulder out the front windshield, she paled as the dark ground seemed to be rushing up to meet them. "Dillon! The plane—"

"Hell!" Quickly stepping over Santiago's slumped body, he urged her into her seat, then slipped into the pilot's seat. "Buckle up, honey. This could get a little bumpy."

Wide-eyed, she watched him take charge of the controls and tried to take comfort from the fact that he seemed to know what he was doing. But they were still diving toward the ground with frightening speed, and nothing he did seemed to slow them down. "Bumpy I can handle," she said hoarsely, clinging to her seat. "Right now I'm more concerned about whether or not you have a license to fly this thing. You do know what you're doing, don't you?"

His smile grim in the darkness, he said, "The operative word here is *fly*. I've got a license to do that. Crash landings fall into a different category."

She paled. "Oh God! You don't mean—"

"I'm afraid so. Some of the controls were damaged by that bullet Santiago fired into the dash." His fingers curled tightly around the throttle, he pulled back on it, trying to slow them down, but it was a lost cause. "The best I can do is try to find a smooth place to bring her down and hope we don't go nose first into the dirt. Take a look outside your window and see if you can see a good spot."

Forcing back the lump in her throat that threatened to choke her, she did as he asked. What classified as a good spot to die? she thought wildly, fighting hysteria. The land was as flat as a washboard, but this far west of Lordsburg, there were occasional outcroppings of rock that rose up from the arid landscape like dark giants waiting to flatten them. One miscalculation, and there would be nothing left of them to bury.

"There!" she cried, suddenly pointing to a smooth, pale, uninterrupted stretch of desert sand off to her right in the distance. "Can we make it?"

Glancing back and forth between the altimeter and the expanse of sand that gleamed like a beacon in the night nearly a half mile away, he nodded stiffly. "It's going to be by the skin of our teeth, though. We're dropping fast." Reaching over suddenly, he grabbed her by the back of the neck and squeezed softly. "I love you, honey. Now put your face in your lap and your arms over your head. We're going in."

Not giving her time to say a word, he pushed her head down and braced himself for impact. But nothing he could have done could have prepared either of them for that jarring first thud with the ground. Screaming and groaning in protest, the plane sounded as if it were tearing apart as it bounced and skidded over the rough terrain, out of control. Cursing, every bone in his body rattling, Dillon hit the brakes and struggled to regain control, but the desert continued to whiz by at what seemed like the speed of sound.

The unconstructed sand quickly gave way to arroyos and cactus. Then suddenly, from out of nowhere, a red boulder as large as a two-story building rose up before them. There was no time to think, no time to do anything but jerk the wheel sharply to the right. Shuddering, the Cessna made a wild, forty-five-degree turn…only to fishtail into the rock.

Caught on the boulder's jagged edges, the metal covering of the fuselage ripped, the high keening sound echoing in the night like the cries of a woman in labor. A curse trapped between his clenched teeth, Dillon felt the seat belt cut into his hips and thanked God for it. A split second later, the force of the impact threw him against the side of the plane and slammed his head against the metal framework. Pain, radiating down his spine like a white-hot bolt of lightning, burned all the way to his toes. Then everything went black.

Long after the plane had finally staggered to a stop, Sydney sat bent over in her seat, her face pressed painfully to her knees, her fingers clutched in her hair. Silence engulfed her, cold and clammy, the pounding of her heart frenzied in her ears.

They were safe.

The thought came to her slowly, pushing past the fear shrouding her brain. Holding her breath, she slowly unclenched her jaw, half expecting that slight movement to set the plane in motion again. But nothing moved. Laughing suddenly, she straightened. *They were safe!*

"Dillon! My God, you did it! I don't know how, but we're still in one piece."

Reaching over to touch him, she froze when she saw him slumped against the side of the plane, his face ashen in the darkness. "Dillon? *Dillon!*"

Whimpering, she clawed at her seat belt and never remembered unlatching it. Suddenly she was free and on her knees at his side, her fingers trembling as she felt for the pulse at his throat. When she finally found it, tears of relief flooded her eyes. It was strong and steady.

"Dillon? Honey, can you hear me? C'mon, wake up. We're safe."

The pain in his head throbbing in time with the beat of his heart, Dillon heard Sydney calling him from a long way off, but his eyelids were so heavy, he couldn't force them open. Frowning, he groaned.

"Oh, thank God!" Sydney exclaimed, cradling her palm against his cheek. "Are you okay? What happened?"

"I was hoping you could tell me," he murmured, a twinge of a smile working its way across his mouth as he finally managed to open his eyes. "The last thing I remember was a big rock."

Glancing at the huge boulder that had sheered off one of the wings before stopping the plane in its tracks, she grinned. "A rock is something you trip over when you're hiking. That thing could give Gibraltar a run for its money. Did you hit your head?"

Still not totally alert, his eyes started to drift shut again. "I must have...can't remember. Everything's numb."

Needing to touch him, she started to brush the hair from his forehead, only to freeze. "Numb? Where?"

"My legs..." Rousing, his eyes flew open. "I can't feel my legs."

The nightmare that followed was straight out of hell. Sydney, stubbornly refusing to believe the paralysis was anything more than a temporary condition caused by the crash, chattered like a magpie, afraid that if she stopped, she would start to cry. In direct contrast to her nervous yammering, Dillon's silence was chilling. His thoughts and expression closed to her, he didn't say a word. Not when she got on the radio and frantically called for help. Not when

Riley and an ambulance finally arrived thirty minutes later. Not once during the long drive to the hospital in Silver City did he even look at her, let alone speak.

Her heart breaking for him, for them, Sydney refused to leave his side until she was forced to as he was wheeled into the emergency room. Stopping the nurses before they could take him away from her, she leaned down to hug him and tried not to cry when he made no attempt to return the embrace. "This doesn't change anything," she whispered fiercely. "You told me you loved me, and I'm holding you to it. Because in case you hadn't noticed, Dillon Cassidy, I'm crazy about you. You got that? I don't care if your skin turns green, your hair falls out and you can't do anything but crook your little finger. I love you. Nothing's ever going to change that."

For a minute, she thought she actually got through to him. Something flickered in his eyes, a small spark of emotion that, even if it was negative, was better than total indifference. Then Riley was there, leaning over her to gently pull her back.

"There's a waiting room down the hall on the left," he said gruffly. "C'mon. I'll buy you a cup of coffee."

She didn't want coffee. She didn't want anything but Dillon. He was gone, however, whisked away behind swinging double doors she wasn't permitted to enter. "He's going to be all right," she said tightly, her flashing blue eyes just daring Riley to disagree with her. "The crash probably dislodged the bullet, but as soon as the doctors remove it, he'll be fine. You'll see."

A wise man, Riley didn't disagree.

Three hours later, the doctor that came looking for them in the waiting room couldn't be nearly as optimistic. An older man who performed everything from appendectomies to heart surgery at the small hospital, Dr. Leirue had done the best that he could, but he was no expert on spinal injuries and didn't claim to be.

"At this point, all we can do is wait," he said tiredly. "If the nerves were just bruised, they should heal pretty quickly now that the bullet's been removed. Paralysis could last anywhere from a couple of days to a week or two. If the damage is more extensive . . ." His shrug, the regret in his faded blue eyes, said it all. "We just don't know."

Her heart squeezing with pain, Sydney hugged herself, her chin thrown up at a belligerent angle. "He'll walk out of this hospital, Doctor," she said coolly, refusing to accept any other prognosis. "It may take him a while, but before it's over with, he'll walk out of here on his own two legs. He has to." Because if he didn't, she'd lose him without ever really having him.

The doctor, not the least put off by her barely suppressed hostility, smiled and patted her on the shoulder. "I like a fighter. With injuries like this, sometimes attitude is the only thing that makes a difference between winning and losing. So you hang in there. He's going to need you in the next couple of days. For tonight, though, there's nothing anyone can do but let him rest." Looking past her to Riley, he suggested, "Why don't you both go home and get some sleep? Things'll look better in the morning."

Sydney didn't want to go, but Riley was insistent. "You're not going to do him any good by wearing yourself out pacing the halls till dawn. You've had a rough night yourself, Syd. Not many people go down in a plane and live to tell about it. Let me take you home and I'll come back with you first thing in the morning."

She knew he was right, but her house was nearly thirty miles away from the hospital and everything inside her protested at the thought of being that far away from Dillon. If something happened during the night, she'd never be able

to get to him in time. "All right, I'll leave. But I'm not going home. I'll stay at a hotel until I'm sure he's going to be
okay."

They both knew that under the best conditions that could
be awhile, but Riley only thanked the surgeon for everything he'd done, then got her out of there while she was
willing to go. The nearest hotel was within walking distance
of the hospital, but Sydney didn't have so much as a penny
with her to book a room. She'd had to leave her purse behind when she crawled out of the study window at the Lazy
Susan, and the place had burned to the ground.

"You can pay me back later," Riley told her after he put
the room on a credit card and gave her what cash he had on
him. "I'll get your things from the cabin and have someone drive up your Jeep tomorrow so you won't be afoot. If
you think of anything else you need between now and then,
just call. Okay?"

Her smile shaky, her eyes bright with the sting of tears,
she went up on tiptoe to give him a fierce hug. "I will," she
said thickly. "Thanks for being here. I don't know what I
would have done without you."

"He's my friend, too, honey," he said gruffly. "He's going to be all right. You just keep believing that."

Sydney clung to her optimism like a lifeline, but it wasn't
easy. The following morning, Dillon was awake and alert . . .
and still paralyzed from the waist down. His face carved in
stone, he listened as the doctor told him there was every
reason to be hopeful that he would regain feeling in his legs
sometime soon, then dismissed him simply by turning his
face to the wall. When she tried to talk to him, she got the
same response—nothing but silence.

Twelve ... twenty-four ... thirty-six hours after the operation nothing had changed, and you only had to look at his somber face to know that he was convinced it never would.

She was losing him. Frantic with worry, Sydney could feel it in her bones, but nothing she said got through to him. He didn't want her there—he couldn't have made it clearer if he'd shouted it from the rooftop. Hurt, constantly battling tears, she haunted the hospital hallways like a ghost that didn't know where it belonged, until Riley, watching it all, finally had had enough.

"Here," he said, shoving her laptop into her arms when he arrived the second evening following Dillon's operation. "In case you've forgotten, girl, you've got a helluva story to write. Harry and Marge have covered for you over the last couple of days, reporting the basic facts of the story itself. Everyone knows by now that Santiago is dead and his men were captured at the Lazy Susan, but the real news is what happened in that plane before it went down. The Perkinses want your firsthand account. Don't you think you owe them that?"

His words stung, stirring a nagging guilt. He was right. When she'd come to Lordsburg four years ago with a less-than-stellar reputation, Harry and Marge Perkins had reserved judgment about the fiasco in Chicago until they'd heard her side of the story. Needing nothing more than her word, they'd believed her and not only hired her, but brought her into their fold like a long-lost daughter. For that alone, she owed them. They gave her complete freedom to go after whatever story she thought was newsworthy, and the least she could do was give them their money's worth.

Clutching her laptop to her breast, she nodded. "I'll be in the cafeteria. Call me if Dillon needs me or there's any change in his condition."

They both knew that neither of those things was likely to happen, but he only turned her toward the cafeteria and gave her a gentle shove. "Don't worry, you'll be the first person I come looking for. Now go."

She went, convinced she wouldn't be able to write a word. But the second she sat down and hit the computer's power switch, the emotions she hadn't allowed herself to feel since Dillon realized he was paralyzed came surging forward. Rage, resentment, contempt of a drug dealer who was less than human, helplessness in the face of an injury she couldn't make better with a little TLC. Her eyes trained unseeingly on the backlit screen, she wrote like a woman who was possessed, driven, her fingers flying over the keys. When she was finished, she didn't have to read the piece over to know that it was the best thing she'd ever written.

And the response when it came out in the paper was flatteringly positive. Calls came into the *Gazette* from all over the county and state. Harry and Marge Perkins were ecstatic, especially when the story was picked up by the wire services.

Sydney knew she should have been elated—it wasn't every day that her work was read across the country. She even got a job offer from a paper in L.A. that she would have jumped at a lifetime ago. But she didn't want another job. She loved her adopted family at the *Gazette*—even Blake Nickels when he was being his most irritating—and couldn't imagine living anywhere else.

Without Dillon, however, she was stunned to discover, nothing meant anything. Once that would have terrified her. She'd always prided herself on her independence. Even when she thought she was desperately in love with Adam, she'd always known, deep down inside, that she could get by without him. But she didn't want to even think about living without Dillon. She loved him more than she'd ever thought it was possible to love anyone.

And he felt the same way about her. Oh, he'd only said the words once—and only when he thought they were about to die—but she read him like a book. He wouldn't be trying nearly so hard to push her out of his life if he wasn't nuts about her. Why, she wondered in growing frustration, out of all the men in the world, did she have to fall for one with an overdeveloped sense of honor? Any other man would have been thankful to have her at his side at such a horrible time, but not Dillon. Oh, no. He was the one going through hell, and all he seemed to be worried about was not saddling her with a paraplegic.

And he wasn't going to get away with it, dammit! she fumed as she returned to the hospital after spending the morning at the paper. They were made for each other and it was high time he admitted it.

Her eyes sparking fire, she marched into his private room and found him doing the same thing he'd been doing every time she visited him for the past three days—staring out the window like a man who didn't have a thing to live for. Before, her heart had contracted with pain at the sight of him, but not this time. Oh, no, she thought grimly. He had more than enough pity for himself; he didn't need any more from her or anyone else.

Her hands planted on her hips, she stood at the end of the bed and glared at him. "You're letting him win, you know. I hope you realize that."

She saw in an instant that she'd caught him off guard. He wanted to ignore her, but he couldn't. A frown creasing his brow, he dragged his gaze from the boring scene out the window and looked at her for what seemed like the first time in days. That was all the encouragement she needed.

"Santiago," she clarified flatly, ignoring the fact that he hadn't asked for an explanation. "You're lying here feeling sorry for yourself when he's the one who's lying cold in his grave. Dammit, you ought to be celebrating. Not because he's dead but because he'll never hurt anyone ever again."

"Oh, yeah," he drawled, his mouth twisting bitterly. "I've got a lot to celebrate. Shall I jump in a wheelchair and dance a jig for you? You see, I've got this small problem. My legs don't work."

He threw the words at her like darts and had no idea how each one made her want to sing. He was talking to her. Finally! Gripping the metal footboard of the bed, she retorted, "Maybe now they don't, but what about your head? Your heart? Are those still working?"

"Of course," he snapped, scowling. "Isn't that obvious?"

"I don't know—you tell me," she challenged. "Three nights ago, when there was a good chance we were both going to die in a plane crash, you told me you loved me. Do you remember?"

To his credit, he didn't glance away, but there was a flush in his cheeks that said louder than words that that was something he wasn't ready to talk about. "I'm not likely to forget it," he muttered. "What about it?"

"Did you mean it?"

"Of course I meant it!" he growled, insulted. "Do you think I go around telling women I love them just for the hell of it? What kind of man do you think I am?"

"The kind I love," she said softly, the sheen of tears stinging her eyes. Daring to reach out to him, she clasped his bare feet through the sheet that covered them and began a gentle massage. "I love you and you love me," she said huskily. "Can't you see that nothing else matters?"

Caught in the warmth of his heated gaze, she thought for a moment that she'd finally gotten through to him. No man in her life had ever looked at her with such longing. The barriers he'd erected over the past three days to keep her at a distance were stripped away, his heart and soul there for her to see. If he'd just held out his hand to her, she would have gone into his arms in a heartbeat.

But then he glanced away, his expression once again stony. "What matters is I can't ask you to tie yourself to a man who can't even walk you down the aisle," he said coldly. "You'd end up hating me, and I can't say I'd blame you."

"Dammit, there's more to you than your legs—"

"That's easy for you to say. I don't see you having any problem standing on yours."

Frustrated, she unconsciously tightened her grip on his feet, wanting to shake him. "Don't you understand? I don't care about your legs! It isn't individual parts that make you what you are. I love *you*—Dillon Cassidy, former DEA agent, lone ranger, the man who would kill a scorpion with a gun for me, the man who makes me laugh and cry and ache so badly that most days, I can't think of anything but you. I love you on your feet, in bed, any way I can get you, it doesn't matter. I'll always love you. Always."

Caught up in the moment, in her need to make him finally see how she felt about him, she didn't realize how tightly she was gripping his feet. Then the toes on his left foot moved under her hand suddenly, tickling her palm. Stunned, her gaze flew to his. "Dillon?"

He was as tense was a newly strung barbed-wire fence, his eyes, dark with intensity, narrowed on where her fingers covered his toes. "It could have been a spasm...."

He was afraid to hope, she realized, her heart breaking for him. After three days of trying to come to grips with the very real possibility that he would never walk again, he wasn't going to take any chance that someone up there was playing a little trick on him. Blinking back tears, she squeezed his toes, the smile that bubbled up inside her refusing to be contained. "Do you really think it was a spasm?" she asked softly.

Staring at his feet, his heart slamming against his ribs, Dillon didn't know what to think. He could have sworn he felt the caress of her hand against his toes through the sheet. But he'd discovered over the past few days that he had a damn fine imagination. Every morning when he woke up, he was so sure he'd moved his legs in his sleep that he actually checked, but they were always in the same position.

A muscle clenching in his jaw, he couldn't find the words to tell her how much he wanted to believe that if she trailed her hand up from his toes to his thighs that he could feel every hot, sweet brush of her fingers. If this was just another cruel case of wishful thinking, he didn't think he could stand the disillusionment. "Maybe you'd better get the doctor," he said huskily. "Just in case."

A single tear spilling over her lashes, she nodded. "I'll be right back."

Fifteen minutes later, after a quick but thorough exam, a beaming Dr. Leirue gave Dillon the good news. "Well, young man, it looks like you're definitely on the mend. You'll need therapy—I can't say how much at this point— but the damage doesn't seem to be nearly as extensive as I first feared. In fact, if you continue to improve the way I think you will, I see no reason why you won't be back on your feet within a matter of weeks."

His hand tightly wrapped around Sydney's, who he'd insisted stay by his bedside during the examination, Dillon couldn't seem to stop smiling. "A matter of weeks, huh? Good. I'm planning on having a hot date that night. You see, there's a certain lady I'm going to walk down the aisle if she can throw a wedding together that fast, and it's important that I be able to move under my own steam.''

His faded blue eyes bouncing from Dillon to Sydney and back again, the doctor laughed and headed for the door. "I know an exit line when I hear one. Congratulations, you two. Make sure you send me an invitation."

For several long tense moments after the door swished shut behind him, the silence was so loud that Dillon could have sworn it echoed. His hand still wrapped around Sydney's, he felt her fingers tremble and was suddenly afraid he'd just blown it. Just because she claimed she loved him didn't mean that she was ready for marriage. She'd almost made the plunge once before only to discover she was about to tie herself to a man who not only didn't put any stock in her word, but wouldn't stand by her in the biggest professional crisis of her life. After that, who could blame her for avoiding anything that even hinted of commitment?

"Did I make a mistake?" he asked quietly. "If you're not ready for marriage, I won't push you, honey. We can take this as slow as you want—"

"No! I..." She laughed shakily, her fingers tightening around his. "You just caught me off guard. Everything's changed now. I wasn't sure you would want to still hang around here."

"Hang around?" he repeated, frowning. "What are you talking about? What's changed?"

"You," she said simply. "That bullet in your back was the only reason you retired from the DEA. Now that it's been removed and you'll be on your feet soon, I'm sure your old boss would be thrilled to have you back."

He didn't deny it—he couldn't. They both knew his physical condition had forced him into early retirement. "I'm sure he would, but I was thinking about retiring long before Santiago shot me, honey. If you don't believe me, ask Riley. Two years ago, I was out here for a short visit and told him I was thinking about getting out of the business. I was tired of putting my life on the line day in and day out and not ever seeming to get anywhere. I wanted more.''

Tugging on her hand, he pulled her down until she perched on the side of the bed beside him, her hip snug against his. ''When I first moved out here, I just wanted to hole up somewhere and lick my wounds. With my government retirement, I didn't need to work, but I had thought that one day I would try my hand at writing a book about some of my experiences with the DEA. But I didn't even want to think about that at first. I was in such a foul mood, I probably would have snapped at a rattler if it'd looked at me wrong. Then I met you.''

His voice dropping to a low rumble, he cradled her fingers in his and slowly, absently, ran his thumb back and forth across the soft skin of her hand, unable to get enough of touching her. ''I took one look at you and never knew what hit me. Even when I kept telling myself that there was no place in my life for any woman, I knew it was too late. I already loved you.''

There were tears in her eyes when he finished, tears she made no attempt to hide. A crooked grin tilting up one corner of his mouth, he slipped an arm around her shoulders. ''Those better be tears of joy, sweetheart, or I'm in trouble. Are you going to marry me or not? Give it to me straight—I can take it.''

''Yes.'' Promising herself to him with nothing more than that, she gave him a quick kiss, pulled back with a grin and slipped off the bed.

''Hey, where're you going?'' he protested, grabbing for her and missing. ''Come back here, woman. We just got engaged!''

"Later," she promised, her blue eyes laughing as she blew him a kiss. "I've only got two weeks to put a wedding together. I've got to get busy!"

She was gone before he could stop her, her wave jaunty as she slipped out the door. Listening to the brisk clicking of her heels as she hurried down the hall, he couldn't help but grin. Lord, she was something. And in a few weeks she would be his. Forever. He couldn't wait.

* * * * *

COMING NEXT MONTH

#679 HIDE IN PLAIN SIGHT—Sara Orwig
Heartbreakers
Safeguarding single mom Rebecca Bolen and her two cuddly kids from a crazed killer was tying Detective Jake Delancy into some serious knots. He'd had worse assignments, more crafty adversaries, but he'd *never* before taken his work to heart—or fallen in love....

#680 FIVE KIDS, ONE CHRISTMAS—Terese Ramin
They'd married for the sake of the children, but Helen wanted more. She *needed* Nat Crockett as surely as any love-struck bride. Only problem was, Nat didn't seem to share her newlywed notions. But with mistletoe and five darling matchmakers, Helen vowed to change his mind.

#681 A MAN TO DIE FOR—Suzanne Brockmann
One minute her life was normal, the next Carrie Brooks was on the run with a man she hardly knew. Felipe Salazar *was* dangerous, but he'd somehow captured her trust. And while she knew in her heart to stand by him, only the face of death revealed the extent of her devotion.

#682 TOGETHER AGAIN—Laura Parker
Rogues' Gallery
How dare he? Meryl Wallis knew James Brant for the power-hungry tycoon he was. She'd loved him once, only to be betrayed. Now she *needed* her to save his reputation. Well, she had control this time around—of everything but herself....

#683 THE MOM WHO CAME TO STAY—Nancy Morse
Native American Trace McCall had done his best, but there were some things he simply couldn't teach his preteen daughter. So when Jenna Ward took an interest in his parenting dilemma, he figured there was no harm in letting her "play" a maternal role. Then he found he wanted her—for real.

#684 THE LAST REAL COWBOY—Becky Barker
Jillian Brandt knew there was no place safer than Trey Langden's remote ranchland—and rugged embrace. Her enemies were getting closer, and her life depended on staying out of sight. But hiding away with her former love posed problems of a very different sort....

MILLION DOLLAR SWEEPSTAKES (III)

No purchase necessary. To enter, follow the directions published. Method of entry may vary. For eligibility, entries must be received no later than March 31, 1996. No liability is assumed for printing errors, lost, late or misdirected entries. Odds of winning are determined by the number of eligible entries distributed and received. Prizewinners will be determined no later than June 30, 1996.

Sweepstakes open to residents of the U.S. (except Puerto Rico), Canada, Europe and Taiwan who are 18 years of age or older. All applicable laws and regulations apply. Sweepstakes offer void wherever prohibited by law. Values of all prizes are in U.S. currency. This sweepstakes is presented by Torstar Corp., its subsidiaries and affiliates, in conjunction with book, merchandise and/or product offerings. For a copy of the Official Rules send a self-addressed, stamped envelope (WA residents need not affix return postage) to: MILLION DOLLAR SWEEPSTAKES (III) Rules, P.O. Box 4573, Blair, NE 68009, USA.

EXTRA BONUS PRIZE DRAWING

No purchase necessary. The Extra Bonus Prize will be awarded in a random drawing to be conducted no later than 5/30/96 from among all entries received. To qualify, entries must be received by 3/31/96 and comply with published directions. Drawing open to residents of the U.S. (except Puerto Rico), Canada, Europe and Taiwan who are 18 years of age or older. All applicable laws and regulations apply; offer void wherever prohibited by law. Odds of winning are dependent upon number of eligibile entries received. Prize is valued in U.S. currency. The offer is presented by Torstar Corp., its subsidiaries and affiliates in conjunction with book, merchandise and/or product offering. For a copy of the Official Rules governing this sweepstakes, send a self-addressed, stamped envelope (WA residents need not affix return postage) to: Extra Bonus Prize Drawing Rules, P.O. Box 4590, Blair, NE 68009, USA.

SWP-S1195

Who needs mistletoe when Santa's Little Helpers are around?

Santa's Little Helpers

brought to you by:

Janet Dailey

Jennifer Greene

Patricia Gardner Evans

This holiday collection has three contemporary stories celebrating the joy of love during Christmas. Featuring a BRAND-NEW story from *New York Times* bestselling author Janet Dailey, this special anthology makes the perfect holiday gift for you or a loved one!

FREE GIFT
with purchase
see inside

You can receive a beautiful 18" goldtone rope necklace—absolutely FREE—with the purchase of *Santa's Little Helpers*. See inside the book for details.

Santa's Little Helpers—a holiday gift you will want to open again and again!

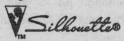

Silhouette®

SLH95

It's our 1000th Special Edition and we're celebrating!

Join us these coming months for some wonderful stories in a special celebration of our 1000th book with some of your favorite authors!

Diana Palmer   **Nora Roberts**
Debbie Macomber   **Christine Flynn**
Phyllis Halldorson   **Lisa Jackson**

Plus miniseries by:

Lindsay McKenna, Marie Ferrarella, Sherryl Woods and Gina Ferris Wilkins.

And many more books by special writers!

And as a special bonus, all Silhouette Special Edition titles published during Celebration 1000! will have **_double_** Pages & Privileges proofs of purchase!

Silhouette Special Edition...heartwarming stories packed with emotion, just for you! You'll fall in love with our next 1000 special stories!

1000BK-R

You're About to Become a

Privileged Woman

Reap the rewards of fabulous free gifts and benefits with proofs-of-purchase from Silhouette and Harlequin books

Pages & Privileges™

It's our way of thanking you for buying our books at your favorite retail stores.

```
PROOF OF PURCHASE
SIM-PP78
Offer expires October 31, 1996
```

Harlequin and Silhouette— the most privileged readers in the world!

For more information about Harlequin and Silhouette's PAGES & PRIVILEGES program call the Pages & Privileges Benefits Desk: 1-503-794-2499

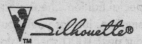

Silhouette®

SIM-PP78